"What a joy it is to read Marta Perry's novels! . . . Everything a reader could want—strong, well-defined characters; beautiful, realistic settings; and a thought-provoking plot. Readers of Amish fiction will surely be waiting anxiously for her next book."

—*New York Times* bestselling author
Shelley Shepard Gray

"A born storyteller, Marta Perry skillfully weaves the past and present in a heart-stirring tale of love and forgiveness."
—Susan Meissner, bestselling author of
The Nature of Fragile Things

"Sure to appeal to fans of Beverly Lewis."
—*Library Journal*

"Perry carefully balances the traditional life of the Amish with the contemporary world in an accessible, intriguing fashion." —*Publishers Weekly* (starred review)

"Perry crafts characters with compassion, yet with insecurities that make them relatable." —RT Book Reviews

"[Perry] has once again captured my heart with the gentle wisdom and heartfelt faith of the Amish community."
—Fresh Fiction

A
HARVEST OF
LOVE

MARTA PERRY

JOVE
New York

A JOVE BOOK
Published by Berkley
An imprint of Penguin Random House LLC
penguinrandomhouse.com

Copyright © 2021 by Martha Johnson
Excerpt from *A Christmas Home* by Marta Perry copyright © 2019 by Martha Johnson
Penguin Random House supports copyright. Copyright fuels creativity, encourages
diverse voices, promotes free speech, and creates a vibrant culture. Thank you for buying
an authorized edition of this book and for complying with copyright laws by not
reproducing, scanning, or distributing any part of it in any form without permission.
You are supporting writers and allowing Penguin Random House to continue to
publish books for every reader.

A JOVE BOOK, BERKLEY, and the BERKLEY & B colophon
are registered trademarks of Penguin Random House LLC.

ISBN: 9781984803238

First Edition: October 2021

Printed in the United States of America
1   3   5   7   9   10   8   6   4   2

This book is dedicated to my dear husband,
Brian, with all my heart.

CHAPTER ONE

Dinah Hershberger came to the end of the early-morning rush at her bakery and coffee shop and let out a breath. She'd hoped to keep the shop going after her husband's death, needing the sense of purpose it gave her. But if the bakery continued to be this busy, she would need some help.

Adding three tables and coffee service seemed to have made the difference. Most of the small community of Promise Glen seemed to stop by for morning coffee and one of her baked treats. Maybe her younger sister, Lovina, would be willing to work a few hours a week. The thought made her smile. Lovina would liven up the mornings—that was certain sure.

Brushing off the white apron that protected the black dress she'd worn during the two years since Aaron's death, she headed for the pantry at the rear of the shop. She'd need a few more muffin tins if she were to use up the abundance of zucchini from the garden in zucchini-nut muffins. They were popular even with customers who'd never touch a zucchini any other way.

The pans she wanted proved to be on a high shelf. Standing on tiptoe to reach them, she managed to lose her grip and send the whole stack clattering to the floor, and her breath caught. Not because of the noise—because of the memory that sprang out at her, clawing at her heart.

She pressed her hand against her ribs, trying to ease her breathing back to normal. The memory of the grief and anger on Aaron's face chilled her. He'd dashed a rack full of pans to the floor, letting the anger come to the surface. If only . . .

No. She wouldn't let her mind travel back to that pain. But if they could have grieved together instead of parting in anger that day . . .

Dinah stopped herself again. Gathering up the pans, she hurried back to the kitchen. Look at the time—she hadn't yet taken Jacob Miller his morning coffee. Her landlord's harness shop was only a swinging door away. Maybe this would be the morning when he'd stop trying to press money on her for the coffee and jelly doughnut that he claimed got him through the time until lunch. She owed Jacob so much more than her rent and the morning coffee. Without him, she'd never have been able to continue the business after Aaron's death.

It took just a moment to pour the coffee and take a jelly doughnut from the glass-fronted cabinet. She preferred crullers herself, but Jacob certain sure had a sweet tooth. With the thick mug in one hand and a small plate with the doughnut in the other, she pushed through the swinging door.

The harness shop was fairly quiet, as it usually was this time of day. She inhaled the scents of leather and neat's-foot oil. With a blindfold on she'd still know which shop she was in. She'd come here with her father when she was small, and it smelled and looked the same today, except that Jacob's father had sat at the heavy sewing machine where Jacob was now.

Dinah walked toward him, thinking he hadn't heard her. But before she reached him, some sense must have alerted him. He slowed the needle, and the heavy belt that extended below the floor stopped. Jacob turned to her with the wide grin that was so friendly that folks couldn't help returning it.

"Ach, I thought I smelled a jelly doughnut coming." He reached the counter in a couple of long strides and relieved her of cup and plate.

"I'm not so sure jelly doughnuts have a smell once they're cool," she said. "Don't you think it's the coffee?"

He shook his head and then bit into the doughnut, raspberry jelly spurting out onto his chin. He wiped it away, smiling with satisfaction. "If I ever marry and grow a beard, I'll have to be more careful of where the filling goes, ain't so?"

"I'm sure you'll manage." The community had been wondering for years when Jacob would take the plunge into marriage. It certain sure wasn't that the women weren't attracted. Every girl in her rumspringa group had had a crush on Jacob, with his light brown hair, lively smile, and broad shoulders.

It seemed odd, when she thought about it, that she'd never succumbed to his attraction, but that was probably because the two families had lived next to each other for generations. Jacob had been more like an extra brother to her than anything else.

He wasn't the boy he'd been, of course. His shoulders were even broader now, probably from wrestling with the heavy harnesses all day long. And if his bright blue eyes sometimes had a tinge of sorrow and there were more lines around his firm mouth than there once were, that was normal enough, given the loss of both his parents within such a short time.

Jacob had had to take over the harness shop much

earlier than anyone had expected, but no one denied he was doing as fine a job as his father had done.

The last bite of the doughnut disappeared, and Jacob gave a sigh of satisfaction before diving into his coffee. She shook her head, smiling.

"I never saw anyone consume a doughnut faster than you. Another one?"

Jacob shook his head. "With the fall festival coming at us and four or five weddings as well, I'd best save myself or I'll regret it." He slapped his flat stomach.

"I don't think you need to worry about your figure. You don't look an ounce heavier than when you were side-sitter at our wedding."

As Aaron's close friend, Jacob had been seated next to Aaron on that day, along with Aaron's brother. She'd had her dear friends Sarah and Dorcas sitting next to her. They were all so young and so happy then, with no experience of the sorrow life could bring.

"Ach, I must be a few pounds heavier by now," Jacob said, always careful about mentioning Aaron around her. "Even if there's no one to cook for me."

That reference to his empty house surprised Dinah. He seldom let anyone see that side of his life. Rallying, she shook her head.

"Don't tell me your cousin Sarah and all the relatives don't keep you supplied with home cooking, because I won't believe it. Besides, my mamm is feeding you half the time anyway."

Sarah, Jacob's cousin, was one of Dinah's closest friends. Sarah had been married in the spring to the man she loved, becoming the devoted mother of twin boys. And now Dorcas Beiler, the third of their circle of rum-springa friends, would marry her Thomas in one of the flurry of fall weddings coming up.

Jacob smiled again at the reference to his cousin

Sarah. "Actually, Sarah sent Noah over with two shoofly pies first thing this morning. Just in case I didn't have enough for breakfast."

"That doesn't surprise—"

The sound of the telephone from her shop interrupted her. A good thing, because he was just reaching into his cash box. Shaking her head at the money in his outstretched hand, she rushed back through the swinging door and snatched up the phone, catching her breath.

"Hershberger's Bakery. How may I help you?"

"Dinah? Is that you?"

The voice sounded familiar, but who . . . and then she realized, and it was like a roll of thunder on a sunny day. "Anna? Anna Miller?" She gasped. "Where are you?"

"Never mind that. I want—"

"You want your bruder." Excitement coursed through her. "I'll run and get him."

"No!" Anna's shout froze her in place. "Just listen, Dinah. I need your help."

"Your brother . . . ," she tried again. Two years ago Jacob's younger sister, Anna, had disappeared into the Englisch world, leaving Jacob with no one. If she was coming home to him . . .

"Not Jacob. Just you. Please." Anna's voice wavered on the last word, and Dinah's heart melted.

"I'll do anything to help you, Anna. You know that."

"Gut. I want you to get the bus to Williamsport this afternoon. You still close the shop on Tuesday afternoons, don't you?"

"Yah, but . . . Williamsport?" The city was a fairly long bus ride, and one she'd made only a few times in her life. "Why Williamsport?"

"I'll explain when I see you." Anna sounded rushed. "Just come, Dinah. I'll meet you at the bus station. Today. Don't let me down."

She wanted to argue, wanted to say that Jacob would be better able to help than she would. But she feared that Anna's mind was made up and any mention of her brother would ruin this first contact with home.

"Yah, all right. I'll be there." But first, she'd speak with Jacob. Jacob would know what to do for his sister.

"Denke. I knew I could count on you." She paused slightly and then went on. "Just one thing—don't tell Jacob."

"But, Anna—"

"Don't tell him! Not now, anyway. Afterward you can tell him whatever you want, but I have to see you first."

"Anna, listen to me."

"Promise me. Promise me, or none of you will ever hear from me again." Her voice was demanding and shrill, and Dinah gripped the receiver tightly, her stomach churning.

She didn't want to keep anything from Jacob, but it seemed she had no choice. She knew Jacob's headstrong little sister about as well as he did. She knew Anna meant it.

"All right. I'll do as you say. I promise."

"Gut." Anna sounded relieved. "I'll meet you at the bus station."

Before Dinah could say a word, Anna had hung up. Dinah stood there, staring blindly at the buzzing receiver. She ought to tell Jacob, all her instincts told her that, but how could she? If she didn't, he'd be angry, and he'd have the right to be.

It had been two long years since Jacob had seen Anna's empty bedroom and found a note telling him not to look for her.

He did try, of course, but Anna had managed to lose herself completely. Finally he'd come back home, settled into his work, and most of the time looked like a man content with his place in life. Most of the time, anyway, except to those who saw the pain beneath the surface, like Dinah.

Her heart ached to tell him. But she'd promised Anna, because if she hadn't, she would have lost Anna completely. Jacob would have to understand. He would know, as surely as she did, that she had to help his lost sister, even if it meant keeping a secret from him.

JACOB CONTINUED TO stare at the door even after Dinah had gone through. She looked better now—he was sure of it. For a long time after Aaron's death she had been a shadow of the girl he'd known. He'd understood, that was certain sure, but even so, it was a relief to see a little of her old self in the laughter in her face and the lift of her head.

For a moment he seemed to see Aaron and Dinah on their wedding day. As one of Aaron's oldest friends, he'd been a side-sitter that day, so he'd had a good view as they sat at worship. They'd looked so happy, but seemed barely old enough to get married. Still, they'd been sure.

Aaron had bubbled with enthusiasm and a sort of triumph at having been the first of his group to marry, hardly able to keep solemn enough to suit the bishop and ministers. As for Dinah . . . well, Dinah's sweet face had glowed with the warmth of an inner fire, so much so that he'd seemed to feel its heat even two seats away. Too bad that things hadn't stayed that way.

The bell on the shop door jingled, and he brought his mind back from the past. Noah Raber, husband of his cousin Sarah, came in. He raised his hand with a smile of greeting.

"Wilkom, Noah. What's happening? You don't often have need for the harness shop."

That was a running joke between them. Noah's furniture workshop was well-known and thriving, so aside from the family horse and buggy, Noah didn't have much use for Jacob's services. He claimed the last harness Jacob's daad had made for him would last a lifetime.

Noah grinned. "Everybody ends up here sooner or later, yah?" He dropped a leather headstall on the counter between them. "I noticed the buckle pulling loose when we got back from worship last Sunday. I figure it's best to get it fixed before it pulls clean off."

"A stitch in time," Jacob said, running the headstall between his fingers. "I wish everybody paid that kind of attention to their gear. I'd certain sure rather do a little fix more often than a big fix that takes me a couple of days."

"Careful, that's me. After all, I'm a family man, not like some people." He shot Jacob a meaningful look.

"Don't tell me you and Sarah have joined the line of relatives who think it's time I was married. Did she tell you to nudge me?"

Noah chuckled. "Well, she might have mentioned it a time or two. When you're happy, you want everybody else to be happy, too, ain't so?"

"You tell her I'm happy enough as I am." He turned the subject off with a laugh, as he always did when someone urged marriage on him. "How are the boys? And how is Sarah? Thriving, I hope."

Everyone in the community knew that Noah and Sarah were soon to add to their family, but as was the custom, a man didn't comment on it until the new arrival was safe in his or her cradle.

He couldn't vouch for what went on in a group of women. They probably talked the subject to death while they were busy quilting crib blankets and knitting little booties and hats.

"You know Sarah. She won't slow down. But she insists she's fine. Even the twins have been rushing around trying to help her." His face warmed at the mention of his twin boys, seven now and devoted to their stepmother.

"Gut for them." He gestured toward the buckle with his coffee mug. "I'll repair while you wait if you have time. It won't take a minute."

"Sure thing. Finish your coffee first." Noah nodded to the mug. "And you might want to wipe the red jelly off your cheek before any more customers come in."

"You don't think it adds to my image as a craftsman?"

"Maybe not. But I see Dinah is taking gut care of you. It's a gut thing, working right next to a bakery." Noah sniffed. "Smells wonderful gut. I might have to stop by."

Jacob grabbed a tissue and mopped his cheek. "Dinah insists my daily coffee and doughnut are part of her rent. Who am I to argue?"

Noah glanced in the direction of the bakery. "I hope she's not giving baked goods away to everyone. She's determined to earn a living, Sarah says, even though her family is standing in line to provide for her." He sobered. "It's a shame about Aaron. It's hard to understand God's will sometimes when we see young people gone so early."

He seemed to be looking at something far away for a moment, making Jacob wonder if he was thinking of his young wife, gone all these years. But Noah had his Sarah now, and they were certain sure a happy family with the two boys and now a new baby on the way.

Noah came abruptly back to the present. "Most likely Dinah is as excited as Sarah is about Dorcas and Thomas getting married next month. Sarah's determined to be there, but I don't know if she ought to try."

"My cousin Sarah's a sensible woman," Jacob pointed out. "She'll do the right thing."

"I hope so." Noah still sounded concerned. "And with Dorcas married, it must be about time Dinah was marrying again, ain't so? Those women will be working on that next."

"I guess so." He tried to sound happy about it. Noah was right. There were plenty of men who'd be attracted by the youthful gravity in Dinah's green eyes and her sweet smile.

They wouldn't know what put that gravity there. No one did, and it would stay that way. He was the only one but Dinah who knew about the pain behind that outwardly happy marriage.

His mind flickered to the things he'd inadvertently overheard. Given her problems with Aaron, would Dinah even want to remarry? He wouldn't think so, but who was he to guess?

He was suddenly disgusted with himself for even speculating about Dinah's happiness. He had no right to judge what others did or didn't do when it came to marriage. Not him. He hadn't even been able to take care of a sister, let alone taking on a wife and family.

DINAH GAZED FROM the window as the bus neared the city, feeling a mix of excitement and apprehension that set butterflies dancing in her stomach. If Anna's call meant that she was coming home, how happy everyone would be. The whole community would celebrate that the lost sheep was found, and Jacob most of all.

She'd seen how shattered Jacob was when his little sister had disappeared into the outside world. He'd been desperate to find her, probably carrying a load of guilt because he felt he should have taken better care of her after the death of their parents.

If only Anna had written or called or something to let him know she was all right.

But maybe she wasn't all right. The thought froze Dinah for a moment. Maybe that was the whole point of calling her instead of calling Jacob. If something was wrong, what could it be? What would she think Dinah could help her with better than Jacob?

No one was immune to the evils of the world. Even in the Amish communities there was the occasional teenager who succumbed to drugs or drink or otherwise went wrong. Was Anna hoping Dinah would intercede for her with her brother?

A sense of her own helplessness rushed over Dinah. How could she? She wasn't old enough or smart enough or wise enough to advise anyone else. On the contrary, there'd been plenty of moments when she could have used some wise advice herself.

Maybe it was fortunate that the bus pulled up at the bus stop just then. At least it cut off that line of thought and pushed Dinah into action. She couldn't sit here and imagine any longer. She had to move forward to meet the problem.

In the jumble of people getting off, the driver unloading packages, and other passengers struggling to get bags down from overhead, Dinah didn't have a chance to look around for Anna. She was too busy worrying about getting herself off the bus before the driver started up again.

Finally the aisle was clear, and she scurried off. The crowd of people on the sidewalk set about their own business, leaving Dinah standing and staring around her. She shook herself. She wasn't a country bumpkin who'd never ridden the bus before. It might not be an everyday event, but she'd done it before. Just not alone. Now it was time to find Anna, ready or not.

But Anna wasn't there—not outside, and when she went to look, not inside the small station, either. She even checked the restroom, to no avail. Anna had said she'd be here, but she wasn't.

The only thing to do was wait. Surely she wouldn't bring Dinah all this way and then change her mind. Deciding that she'd stand a better chance of spotting her outside, Dinah found a convenient bench on the sidewalk, against the wall and in full view of anyone coming down the street.

Her normal instinct when alone in a strange place was to hide—to slip back where she wouldn't be noticed. But she had to be where Anna would see her. She couldn't risk losing her after coming all this way.

Minutes passed. From where she sat, Dinah could see a large clock on the front of a jewelry store across the busy street. How long should she wait?

Well, that was silly. She'd wait as long as she had to, but she certain sure hoped Anna would appear before the bus that returned to Promise Glen pulled up. She couldn't risk being stranded in Williamsport, and—

A car pulled suddenly to the curb, and a young woman in jeans and a sweater that looked too warm for the sunny September day climbed out of the passenger seat. Her long blond hair fell forward, hiding her face, as she reached back into the car for something. Then she straightened, turned, and headed straight for Dinah. It was Anna.

Not the Anna she had known, that was sure. This girl was as far as she could be from the sweet, shy teenager with the soft voice and the intense curiosity that Dinah had known.

As Dinah started to get up, Anna was upon her. "Anna, what—" Before she could get the question out, Anna had plopped her burden in Dinah's lap. *Not a burden*, she corrected herself numbly. *A baby.*

A boy, she guessed, given the little blue romper with a teddy bear embroidered on the front. He looked her over with huge blue eyes and smiled, exposing a rosy mouth and dimples in both cheeks. Dimples just like Anna's, she realized, still numb with shock. A chubby little hand reached for her face, patting her and trying to catch the string of her kapp.

She sucked in a deep breath and tried again. "Anna—"

"Yes, he's mine." Anna's voice was defiant. "His name is Isaac, after Grossdaadi."

Dinah had a vague memory of an elderly man with twinkling blue eyes and a white beard sitting in the back of the harness shop and watching Jacob's daad at work. Supervising, she supposed.

Questions whirled in her mind, and she didn't know what to ask first. "Why didn't you ever tell anyone?" she blurted, scolding herself for starting with something that was hardly the most important point. "Are you . . ."

"Married?" Anna sounded scornful. "No, and I don't want to be." She stared at Dinah, averting her eyes from the baby in her lap. "And I don't want a baby, either."

Dinah almost pointed out that it was too late for that, but managed to stifle the words. "He's a beautiful boy," she said gently, patting him. "How old is he?"

"Six months." Anna slid a sidelong glance toward him with a touch of pride. "He's big for his age, ain't so?" The Pennsylvania Dutch expression slipped out, making her seem a little more like the girl Dinah had known.

"Anyway, that doesn't matter." Anna rushed on, "The point is that I don't want to keep him. I can't take care of a baby. So you have to take him to Jacob."

"Me? Take him to Jacob?" She could only stammer.

"Who else?" Anna jumped from the bench as if she couldn't sit there any longer. "He's my brother. He always wanted to take care of me, even when I didn't need it or want it. Well, now he can use all that caring on Isaac. He should be glad to have someone to boss around."

The bitterness in her tone caught Dinah by surprise. "Anna, you don't mean that. You know your brother just wanted to keep you safe and well after your daad and mammi passed on."

Anna shrugged, face sulky, making her look like a teenager again. "Maybe. But I didn't need him then and I don't need him now. And tell him he shouldn't bother trying to find me. By the time you get back to Promise Glen and tell him about this, I'll be long gone."

Dinah reached out impulsively and grasped her wrist. "No, Anna, no. You can't run away like that. Not when you have a baby relying on you. We'll all help take care of him. Come home. Come back where you belong."

For an instant, something that might have been longing dawned on Anna's face. Just as quickly it disappeared. Anna jerked her arm free.

"No way. I'm done with all that." With her foot, she shoved a bag she'd put on the ground toward Dinah. A diaper bag, Dinah realized belatedly.

"There's all of his stuff. Take it to Jacob, too. Taking care of Isaac is up to him now."

"Wait!" She reached again, but her hand caught only empty air. Anna was already racing toward the waiting car. "Stop, Anna. Can't you—isn't there something you want to tell Jacob, at least?"

Anna paused, the car door open, arrested in the act of sliding in. She seemed to consider it. Then she shrugged. "Tell him thanks. And thank you, Dinah."

The man in the car leaned across the seat, seeming to say something. Anna nodded. She raised her hand as if to dismiss both Dinah and the baby. Then she slid inside and slammed the door, and the car pulled back into the line of traffic.

Dinah bolted to her feet, taking a step toward the street, and then stopped. What was she going to do—race after a moving car while holding a baby? She looked down, and Isaac's rosy cheeks dimpled as he smiled at her. She couldn't help smiling back as she sank down on the bench.

What could she do? She couldn't turn him in at the nearest police station as if he were a lost umbrella. Anna had left her with no choices. She'd have to do as Anna wanted and take little Isaac to Promise Glen and his uncle.

Onkel Jacob, she thought, trying out the words. What would Jacob say? What would everyone else say, for that matter, when Dinah got off the bus carrying a baby? It would keep the blabbermauls busy for a week, that was certain sure.

And who was to take care of the baby? Jacob had no immediate family. Isaac squirmed, whimpering a bit, and Dinah bounced him in her arms. The movement soothed him. It seemed to soothe her as well.

She didn't know the answer to any of that. She could only do what was right in front of her.

Let the present trouble be enough for now, she told herself. *Trust the good Lord for the rest.*

CHAPTER TWO

Abus trip alone with a small baby wasn't something Dinah had ever experienced until today. She just hoped she wouldn't experience it again very soon. Isaac started to fuss within minutes of her sitting down in the bus seat, and she couldn't miss the expressions of the people who carefully avoided sitting next to her.

A middle-aged Englisch woman across the aisle from her smiled. "Don't worry. Your little one will probably settle down as soon as we start moving. My children always did. I gave them a bottle and they slept the whole trip."

"Denke. Thank you." She didn't feel up to explaining that the baby wasn't hers. Or maybe she didn't want to. Wasn't it all right to imagine, for the space of a bus ride, that he was her own longed-for baby?

"Such a sweet little boy." She leaned across for a closer look. "How old is he?"

"Just six months." She relaxed, knowing this was just the sort of casual interest any woman, Amish or Englisch, would have in a baby.

Of course the woman was right about what Isaac needed. Dinah pulled the diaper bag to the seat beside her and burrowed into it. Sure enough, Anna had vided two filled bottles in an insulated bag . . . probab. enough to get them home.

The instant a bottle appeared in front of him, Isaac grabbed for it, his eyes nearly crossing in his attempt to focus on it. Almost immediately, silence reigned. She cradled him close, loving the feel and scent of a baby. He certainly looked happy and well cared for. How did that fit in with Anna's insistence that she couldn't take care of him? Could something as simple as a bad sleepless night have motivated that stressed call?

The woman had been right about another thing . . . as the bus rolled along, Isaac relaxed, feeling somehow heavier as he snuggled against her, his eyes drifting closed.

Despite the fact that she was now caring for a baby, the trip didn't seem nearly as long going back. Maybe she had used up all her anxiety going, wondering what Anna wanted. At least now she knew what she had to face.

That was bad enough.

How could she begin to explain all of this to Jacob? He'd be shocked, that was certain sure. He'd at once come up with all the things she should have done differently, beginning with calling him to the phone. He'd probably be angry with her, but that didn't matter. Right now, what mattered was the baby.

Dinah didn't have any doubts about that part of it. Once Jacob understood who this was, he'd welcome his little nephew with open arms. Whether he'd understand her actions was the hard part. Yes, he'd undoubtedly think that he could have done it better.

The friendly Englisch woman got off the bus the stop before hers, with a final wave and smile.

And then the bus pulled up to the stop in Promise

Glen . . . almost too soon for comfort. Holding the sleeping baby, who definitely felt heavier, she struggled with the diaper bag. The driver moved quickly to help her. She climbed down, holding Isaac against her, and then took the bag. They were back, and it was time to face Jacob with a story that would both dismay and delight him.

The harness shop was only a half block away from the bus stop. Dinah forced her legs to move more quickly than they wanted to. She felt as if eyes were upon her, even though the few people she passed this late in the afternoon didn't seem to take any notice.

Rethinking her intention to head into the harness shop, she unlocked the bakery door and hurried inside, locking it again behind her. She didn't want any customers now, and she was relieved that the window shades were down as always when she was closed. Dropping the diaper bag on the nearest chair, she headed for the swinging door, where she stopped.

Isaac stirred in her arms, blinking his eyes, and looked up at her with his wide blue gaze. Once again, her heart melted. She brushed her lips against his soft cheek and then held him up against her shoulder. Seeming pleased, he reared back to gaze at the strange surroundings.

Now, she thought, it was time to act before she lost her nerve. She pushed the door open far enough to look inside.

The shop was quiet except for the hum of the leather-stitching machine. Good, no one was there but Jacob.

"Jacob?" she called. "Will you come in here please?" Better he should come here, where the window shades were down. Besides, she felt more in control in her own place.

The machine stopped, and she heard Jacob's footsteps, and then his voice as the door opened. "I didn't know you were coming back today. What's happening?"

He stepped inside, looked at her, and then blinked. For a second he was obviously startled, but then he smiled and came to touch one of Isaac's chubby hands.

"Who is this little person? Are you babysitting for one of your cousins?"

Dinah's chest was too tight to speak, but she had to. She forced the words out. "No. This is Anna's baby."

He didn't respond, seeming not to understand, maybe riffling through her cousins to come up with someone named Anna.

"Your sister, Anna," she said. "This is Isaac, your nephew."

His face darkened as his realization of what she'd said grew. "If that's a joke—"

"Ach, Jacob, you know me better than that. Anna . . . she called me earlier today. She wanted—"

"Here? Anna called here, at the shop? Why didn't you tell me? You should have said something to me at once." If anything, he looked worse.

"Please, Jacob, just listen." She kept her voice soft, hoping to encourage him to do the same. "I wanted to run and get you, but she said she'd hang up if I did that."

He didn't seem to take in that part of it. "You should have called me. Told me. She's my sister."

"Listen," she said again. "That's what Anna said. She just wanted me to listen, not to say anything to anyone. I had to agree. I couldn't risk losing contact with her. You see that, don't you?"

He nodded—reluctantly, she thought. Isaac was staring, entranced by this new face, but Jacob didn't look back. It was almost as if he was afraid to see the baby too closely.

"She didn't tell me about the baby then. She just said

she'd meet me in Williamsport when the afternoon bus got there, but that if you were there, she'd just keep going."

He started to speak, and she rushed on, feeling Isaac moving restlessly in her arms.

"She made me promise, and I couldn't break my word. She said after I met her I could tell you everything. I thought . . . I hoped . . . that she would come home."

Jacob's face tightened. "She didn't want to? Even with . . ." He gestured toward the baby.

"No. She said she didn't want to be a mother." The words hurt her to say, and she held Isaac so close he wiggled in protest. "She didn't want to come back. She just wanted you to take the baby so she could be free."

His expression didn't change, but it seemed to her that something crumbled inside him. This was about as far from her Amish life as Anna could have gone.

"I tried to convince her. Really I did." Dinah's voice shook. "But she wouldn't listen. She plopped Isaac into my arms and ran out to a car that was waiting. It was gone before I could do a thing."

"What kind of a car? What color?"

Dinah shook her head helplessly. "I don't know kinds of cars. It was dark . . . dark blue or black. I didn't even get a good look at the driver. Just . . . it was a man."

He turned away for an instant, maybe trying to control himself. Then he took a step toward the door. "I'll lock up my store. We can't talk when someone might walk in at any moment."

They both knew that he was unlikely to have more customers this late, but she suspected he needed the moment it would take. Isaac wiggled again, arching backward as if in protest at being held for so long.

"Ach, I know, little one," she said softly. "Soon. I'll make you more comfortable soon." He undoubtedly needed a diaper change and probably another bottle by this time, but she couldn't do anything until she'd dealt with Jacob.

He came back at that moment, his face tightening as he pushed through the swinging door. "You should have told me. No matter what Anna made you promise, you had no right to keep it to yourself. If I'd known, I could have—"

"What?" Exhaustion put a snap in her voice. "Yelled at her? What do you think you'd have accomplished by that? If she'd even have stopped long enough to listen to you."

"I'd have made her," he said stubbornly.

Her patience ran out, and she knew suddenly what to do. Anna had had it right. "Sit down," she snapped.

"What?" He'd never heard that tone in her voice, she knew.

"I said, sit down." She gestured to the nearby chair. "Now."

His temper flared. "Why?"

"Because I'm going to hand you this baby, and unless you know more about babies than I think you do, you'll want to sit down."

For once she'd made him speechless. He pulled out the chair, and before he could argue any further, she thrust little Isaac toward him. "You'd best take him, because my arm feels like it's breaking, and I'm about to drop."

He collapsed into the chair. He took a breath, probably preparing to argue. She plopped Isaac onto his lap, and his arms automatically curved to accept him. Then she spun and raced for the restroom in the back of the shop.

JACOB LOOKED AFTER Dinah for just a moment, still surprised by her unexpected assumption that she was in charge. Or, at least, that he'd do as she said. Well, she had been right about that. He could hardly help it when she'd thrust the baby at him.

Reluctantly, Jacob transferred his gaze to the child. Huge blue eyes stared back at him, seeming to weigh and judge him. Then a smile formed on the tiny lips. What could he do but smile back?

There was something familiar about the smile . . . something about the round face, the rosy cheeks, the dimples, and the little fluff of blond hair on his head. Jacob stared at him, bemused. He knew now what it was. He remembered. He'd seen that face before, when he'd been staring into a basket at his baby sister. Anna.

He blew out a breath. This was Anna's son, all right. He was the image of her—of the little sister whose first steps he'd guided, the child he'd comforted when she scraped her knee. The little sister he'd tried so hard to protect and keep safe.

Isaac. He hadn't even registered the name when Dinah said it. A family name, it was. Had Anna thought of that?

"Isaac." He said the name, smiling, and then chuckling when Isaac smiled back. "You look just like your mammi. Do you know that?"

The baby didn't answer, but he stretched, reaching up toward Jacob's face with one small hand. The fingers patted his lips first and then felt for his nose.

He caught the hand before it could poke him in the eye. Then it seemed natural to give it a kiss. "You're a silly one, ain't so?"

Isaac seemed to find that funny. He gave a little gurgle of laughter, and Jacob found himself slipping deeper under the spell of this tiny creature.

Movement distracted him, and he turned to see Dinah coming from the back of the shop. She looked tired, he realized. This had been a strain on her. But when she studied him holding the baby, her expression began to relax.

"He's quite a boy," she said. "Big for six months, Anna said."

The mention of her name was like a knife twisting in his heart. "She should be here. With her baby. With her family."

"I know." Dinah had regained her soft speech. "She should be, but she doesn't think so."

He expected her to take the baby from his inexperienced grasp, but instead she busied herself spreading a folded quilt on the table, then a couple of clean tea towels over the top.

"What are you doing? He can't sleep there."

Her eyes crinkled, laughing at him. "No, he can't. But after coming all the way back on the bus, he certain sure needs a diaper change." She glanced at him. "You can put him down here while I get things out of the diaper bag."

He obeyed, his mind busy with her words. "Anna gave you the diaper bag? Is there anything in it that would give me a clue to where she's been living? Or where she's going now?"

Dinah pulled out a diaper and a plastic bottle of something that was probably lotion. Jacob kept his hand on the baby, not sure whether Isaac could roll off or not.

She set things on the table, and Isaac promptly grabbed for them. She put the lotion bottle in his hands, and he turned it over and over.

"I haven't had time to search it for anything except what I needed on the way," she said. "You can check it out when you have time. Right now, you'd best pay attention. You'll need to learn how to take care of your little nephew. You're an onkel now."

Nephew. He repeated the word in his mind. He was

still in shock, he expected. Still not sure who this uncle she referred to was.

He started to say so, but she was preoccupied, so he just watched while she deftly unsnapped the little blue outfit the baby wore. With a spare diaper in her hand, she began to remove the soggy one. Jacob wrinkled his nose, but neither of the others seemed bothered by the smell.

The instant Isaac felt air on his skin, it seemed he decided it was time to relieve himself. Now Jacob understood why she held the extra diaper handy. She popped it over him.

"Smart. How did you get to know so much about babies?"

Her hands froze for just an instant, and he felt like hitting himself in the face. He of all people knew how her childlessness grieved her, let alone Aaron's—

He stopped, thinking of the things he shouldn't know. "Sorry," he muttered. "That was ¯. . ."

"No matter," she said. "Anyway, you forget that I have about seventeen cousins the last time I counted. There was always a boppli around."

"I guess so. A lot more than I have, anyway. We weren't a very prolific family in this generation."

He watched, holding the lotion when she thrust it into his hand. She fastened tabs, smoothed out the diaper, and pulled the little knit outfit down where it belonged, patting the teddy bear on the front of it.

"There." She leaned over the baby. "That feels better, doesn't it?" The string of her kapp dangled, and he tried unsuccessfully to grab it. *Isaac*, he thought again.

"Did Anna say why she gave him that name?" he asked abruptly, the thought of his sister like a pain in his chest.

"For your grossdaadi. That's what she said. I'd forgotten his name, if I ever heard it."

He nodded. That's what he'd thought. Grossdaadi had doted on Anna. It would have broken his heart to know what had happened to her.

Dinah didn't give him time to think about it. She turned briskly. "You watch him while I get something for him to sleep in."

Isaac's blue eyes blinked when Dinah disappeared from his view. Then he looked around and focused on Jacob's face, smiling as if he knew who Jacob was. *Onkel Jacob*, he thought.

She was back in a few minutes with a wicker laundry basket. Putting it on the table, she folded the quilt again and put it in the bottom of the oval basket, then spread fresh linen towels over that. In another moment, Isaac was settled in a bed of his own that fit him just right.

"Clever," he said. "I'd never have thought of that."

He was still for another minute, trying to think this through. But each time he tried to arrange it in some sort of order, it eluded him.

"Why me?" He shot the words at Dinah, feeling as if someone should have an answer, even though he didn't. "Tell me, Dinah. Why would she send her baby to me? She must know I don't have anyone to look after a baby. She has to know that."

"Why not you? You're her own brother." Dinah sounded convincing, but she didn't meet his eyes, and he knew at once that there was more.

"What did she say? You may as well tell me. I'll keep after you until you do. She said something to make you look that way."

"She . . ." Dinah stopped, then started again. "Anna told me to bring the baby to you. She said you'd always wanted to take care of her." She shrugged, as if she'd finished, but he could tell there was more. Dinah was too honest to tell a half-truth.

"And what else?"

Her face clouded. "She said you'd always tried to take care of her, even when she didn't need it or want it." She hurried on. "Little sisters and bruders always say things like that. Mine do."

He shook his head. "Yah, I know. But Anna means it." The words were as heavy as his heart. He waited, struggling to get out the rest of it. "What does she expect me to do? I can't run a business and take care of a baby at the same time."

Dinah studied his face for a long moment. "If you're determined to give him away, there are others who will take him." She started putting things back in the diaper bag. "I'll take him home with me until you make up your mind. Mamm and Daad will be thrilled to have a baby in our house again."

He'd known people to be disappointed in him before, but no one had ever sounded quite like Dinah did. For an instant he wanted to rage at her. But he couldn't, because what she was thinking was probably right.

"I'll go along with you," he said abruptly, and got a surprised look in return. "Well, I can't ask you to come with me and the baby to my house, can I?"

A flush came up in Dinah's cheeks. "I guess that's right. Well, you'll be welcome. You and Isaac both."

He nodded. "I'll go and hitch up both buggies, then help you carry things out." With the decision made, he moved quickly. He might not know what to do, but he did know one thing: He couldn't walk away from Anna's baby, no matter what.

ONE THING WAS certain sure, Dinah realized once they were safely in the farmhouse kitchen with her family around them and some supper leftovers warming on the stove. Isaac was a success here. Everyone vied to hold the baby. Even the twins, David and Daniel, were captivated by little Isaac, and at thirteen, there wasn't much that captivated them.

"Come on, Dinah." Teenage Lovina hung on her shoulder. "You've had him all day. Let me hold him. Please," she wheedled.

"All right, but you sit down first." Dinah had to admit that her arm was aching, but it was a good ache.

"I'm used to babies," Lovina protested, but she did sit down. Dinah put the baby in her lap, and Lovina's usual pert expression softened as she looked at him. "He's smiling at me. See?"

"He's a gut baby." Grossmammi leaned across ten-year-old Will, squishing him, to pat little Isaac. "Sweet and happy even after the day he's had."

"It's Dinah who looks tired out," Mammi said, setting a mug of coffee in front of her and another in front of Jacob. "You were right to bring him here." She put her hand on Jacob's shoulder. "We are happy to have him as long as needed, Jacob. You know that."

Jacob nodded, relief wiping the lines of strain from his face. "Denke. I know my cousin Sarah would want to help, but this would be a bad time for her. I couldn't ask her, not now."

Dinah suspected that he'd been running through his relatives, trying to think who would be most able to help with Anna's baby.

"Since you're willing to help, it'll give me some time to think it over," he went on. "I don't even know . . ."

He let that die away after glancing around at the kids. Daadi nodded approvingly. This wasn't the moment to talk about who the father might be.

Dinah thought about the man in the car—the one who'd looked eager to get going. Was he the father?

Probably not, Dinah thought. He hadn't seemed to show much interest in what was happening. But how could she know what a man might think in a situation like that?

Daadi cleared his throat, looking at the boys. "Seems to me you boys still have chores to do. You can see the boppli again later."

"That's right," Mammi added, her glance cutting off any grumbling from them. Daniel, the older twin, nudged his brother and got up.

"You come, too, Will. You need to shut the chickens up for the night."

"Chickens," he muttered, following the twins. "Silliest birds ever created."

"That's what happens when you're the youngest," Daniel told him. "You get the jobs nobody wants. But if you hurry up, you can bring the buggy horses in from the field."

Cheering up, Will trotted along after them.

"Maybe I should have told him what it's like to be the only boy," Jacob said. He was getting over the shock now, she thought. He glanced at Dinah and smiled as if he knew what she was thinking.

"It wouldn't hurt the boys to hear that," Daadi said, but he was smiling. "Is there anything else we can do to help you, Jacob? Will you be trying to find Anna?"

"I guess I'd better." He sounded discouraged. "It's hard to know where to start, but I'll have to go to Williamsport."

"While you're talking about it, we'd best get little Isaac settled for the night." Mamm took a bottle from the pan where it had been warming. "Lovina, let your sister carry him up the stairs. You can help with him again tomorrow."

Lovina pouted, but did what she was told. She

dropped a kiss on the top of Isaac's head as she handed him to Dinah. "See you tomorrow, sweet boy."

Mammi led the way up the stairs, with Dinah following. They'd set up the basket in Dinah's room near her bed, and the three-drawer chest had been converted to a changing table.

"Tomorrow I'll have the boys bring the crib down from the attic," Mamm said, obviously planning to hold on to Isaac for as long as possible. She was already longing for someone to supply her with grandchildren. After all, Micah was courting.

She was yet another person to be disappointed that Dinah hadn't had children, although she'd never hinted at such a thing. Unlike Dinah's mother-in-law, who had been quite open about her disappointment . . . to say nothing of making it clear whom she thought was to blame.

Dinah pushed those memories away to focus on the present. For now, she'd keep her mind on Anna's baby—the baby Anna had insisted she didn't want.

Dinah paused in the process of snapping up the soft onesie she'd found in the diaper bag. "Do you think it's possible that Anna will come back? I mean, once she realizes what she's done?"

"I wish I knew." Mammi moved next to Dinah, looking down at Isaac, who was trying to hold the lotion bottle in his chubby little hands. Mammi smiled at him, but a tear sparkled in her eye. "It's hard to imagine her leaving him, ain't so?"

"Yah." She held up her hand, letting Isaac grab at her fingers. "I would give anything . . ."

Mammi hugged her. "I know," she murmured. "But you must be careful."

"Careful?" She looked at her mother, a question in her eyes.

"It would be so easy to get attached to him." Mammi

stroked the soft fuzz of blond on Isaac's head. "I can feel it myself, and it's worse for you."

"Because I could not have children of my own." She tried to keep bitterness out of her voice.

"Ach, Dinah, you don't know that for sure. The doctor said there was nothing wrong with you. If only Aaron had been willing to go and have some tests . . ."

"I know," she said quickly, not wanting to hear it, because she still couldn't forgive herself. If she had handled it better, if she had been a better wife, their story might have had a happier ending.

"I know." Mammi patted her shoulder. "That's why I don't want you to get too close to this little one."

"Ach, what are you saying?" They both looked back to find that Grossmammi had come into the room. "How could anyone help but love the boppli?"

"I just don't want Dinah to be hurt, that's all." Mammi held out her hand to her mother-in-law.

Grossmammi took her hand, but she was shaking her head. "Hurting is the cost of loving," she said. "But loving is always better." She kissed Dinah's cheek and then Mammi's. "Good night, my dear girls."

One more hug, and then Grossmammi went off to bed.

"It's all right," Dinah said quickly, not sure she could talk about this any longer.

She picked up Isaac and held him close as she moved toward the rocking chair. "It's time this little man had his bottle and went to sleep." She managed a smile. "Let's hope he'll stay that way for a bit."

Mammi nodded, seeming to accept the change of subject. "Just call me if you need me. It would be fun to be up with a baby in the night again."

"That's not what you said when Will got you up every night for his first year," she said, teasing.

"Ach, I know. But you'll see what I mean if he wakes you up." She tidied the makeshift changing table and went softly out, closing the door.

Dinah picked up the bottle, laughing a little when Isaac grabbed for it. He knew what he wanted, that was certain sure.

And what about his uncle? Did Jacob know what he wanted in this situation?

Talk about being hurt . . . Jacob was so vulnerable that her heart hurt for him. He'd do what he thought was right, she had no doubts about that. Most likely he'd scour Williamsport for a sign of his sister. And when he didn't find her, he'd be hurt again. And if by some chance he did find her, she would probably tell him what she had told Dinah.

Maybe the only thing to do was to enjoy this little one and do the best they could for him.

As for Jacob, well, she'd have to do the best she could to be sure he didn't make a decision he'd regret all his life.

CHAPTER THREE

When Dinah got back downstairs, the kitchen had cleared out. Voices from the living room told her that Lovina and the boys were playing a board game—part of a long-running game that she didn't think anyone was ever going to win. Mamm was probably in there as well, sitting in the rocker with the never-ending stack of mending.

Daad and Jacob still sat at the kitchen table, cradling coffee mugs in their hands while they talked. Daad looked up when she came in.

"Come, Dinah. You should be in on this. Jacob wants to go and look for his sister."

She nodded, sitting down with them reluctantly. She'd been sure that was the first thing Jacob would do. No doubt he felt that if only he were the one dealing with Anna, she'd be home where she belonged.

"I'll go to Williamsport first thing tomorrow. Maybe I'd best try to get a driver so I don't have to depend on the bus schedule." He focused on Dinah. "Have you thought of anything else about Anna? About the car or the man?"

"No. I'm sorry." She added, "But I've told you everything that happened." She hesitated, thinking back through the words Anna had spoken and coming up with nothing. "It happened so fast. It was all over in a few minutes."

She suspected he was holding back, but she knew what he was thinking.

"It would have made no difference if you had been there, Jacob. Really. She jumped in the car, and they sped away. And nobody can chase a car on foot while holding a baby."

He almost managed to smile. "I guess not. I never checked the diaper bag. Did you have a chance to look through it?"

"Yah. There was nothing that would help except maybe this." She handed him a slip of paper with a small safety pin in it. "This was down in the bottom of the bag."

Frowning at the paper, Jacob shook his head. "It looks like a price sticker, but there's no store name on it."

"Written by hand," she pointed out. "You see that in thrift stores and charity shops. She probably got some baby things there, seeing how fast a child that age out-grows his clothes. Lots of people do that."

"Denke." His fingers closed around the paper. "At least it's a place to look."

Daad cleared his throat, his lean face wrinkled in thought. "Seems to me she might go to places like food banks, ain't so? And maybe the different charities for help. There are a lot of things she'd need for a baby, and if she didn't have money coming in . . ."

Daad let that trail off. They were probably all think-ing the same—that perhaps the father of the baby had been helping her. Or the man driving the car, if it was someone different. Dinah didn't want to think that, but Anna had made it clear she wasn't married and didn't want to be.

"You're right. At least it's a place to start." Jacob seemed encouraged to have a plan, at least. "The thrift stores and secondhand stores, and any local charities." He counted them up.

"When . . . when you looked for her before," she said hesitantly, knowing it would bring up thoughts of failure for Jacob, "I wondered if you went to Williamsport."

He shook his head. "I didn't think she'd have gone that far. Besides, she'd never been there before." His face tightened. "But apparently she ended up there."

He would have tried friends and acquaintances first, Dinah felt sure. Most kids who ran away didn't go far on their first effort, maybe because they wanted to be found.

Mammi had come in a few minutes earlier, standing quietly by the door and listening. But now she spoke. "There is something—something I saw in the paper. About a group in that area that helps Amish kids who have jumped the fence. Maybe they would know something."

Jacob looked ready to jump on any clue. "Do you remember the name?"

"No." She went toward the jelly cupboard against the wall. "But I kept the piece. I'm sure it's here." She pulled out the drawer that held all the odds and ends the family saved just because they might come in handy.

The junk drawer, Daad called it, but sometimes it held just what was needed. Maybe it would this time. Dinah started to rise, thinking she could help look, but Mamm let out an exclamation.

"Yah, here it is." She turned with a piece of tattered newspaper in her hand. "I . . . I thought maybe sometime we'd . . . well, someone might need to know it."

Dinah's heart reached out to her mother. Did she worry about it, fearing that one day one of hers would run away? Probably so. There were few extended families that hadn't been touched by the pain of a member jumping the fence to the Englisch world.

"Denke." Jacob rose to take the paper from her. "That's certain sure a good place to try."

He stood frozen for a second, as if pulled in opposite directions and trying to decide what to do first. He was probably as worn out as she was, dealing with so many scary possibilities, afraid that he might choose the wrong path and lose Anna completely. Or maybe he was thinking about his little nephew.

"Don't worry about Isaac." Dinah pushed herself to her feet. "I don't open on Wednesdays, so I'll be here. And Mamm and Lovina. We'll take care of him. And Grossmammi will make sure we do it right."

With a small-scale business like her bakery, she could run it just a few days a week. Many Amish businesses ran that way, because they had to be squeezed in around farming and taking care of a family. She'd thought about expanding often enough, but that would mean hiring people, investing more money, and she guessed she was afraid to take a chance.

"Yah." Mammi glanced toward the living room, where it sounded as if the game was winding up. "Sometimes Lovina doesn't know what she wants, but she does love babies. She'll help."

Grossmammi claimed that if a person had more than one child, there was always one who needed worrying about. Just not the same one all the time. Right now it was Lovina. She seemed moodier than was accounted for by being fifteen, at least in Dinah's opinion. Mammi would be glad to have something to occupy her younger daughter.

"Denke." Jacob's face worked, and her heart reached out to him. He'd always been like a member of their own family, and there was so little they could do to help him now. "I guess I'd better go."

Mamm hurried to the counter. "You'll need some food. I'll pack it up for you."

"You don't need to do that." He moved toward the door, and she sensed he needed to be alone for a moment . . . maybe afraid his emotions were getting out of control.

"Go on out," Dinah murmured. "I'll bring it to you." Mammi was already fixing a plate for her and one for Jacob.

When Dinah stepped onto the back porch a few minutes later, she half thought he wouldn't be there. But he was, his hands gripping the railing, his whole body stiff with tension.

She touched his arm lightly, and he jumped.

"Sorry. I didn't mean to startle you. Here it is." She handed him the packet Mammi had made up. "Thanks for waiting."

He almost smiled. "I know your mamm. She'd have chased me home with it if I didn't."

"Yah. We . . . we all want to help you." *And we all feel helpless*, she thought. *Me most of all.*

"I know." He took the bundle, patting her hand. He turned to go, and she spoke quickly.

"One thing . . ." She hesitated, not sure how he'd take what she had to say. "I hope you find her. If you do . . ."

"You want to tell me how to deal with my sister?" He stiffened, ready to take offense.

"No. Just . . . just tell her that we love her, and we're waiting for her to come home."

Jacob let out a long breath, his tension draining away. For an instant she thought there were tears in his eyes, but it might be a trick of the long September twilight. "I will." He strode away.

She stood looking after him as he faded into the dusk. *Du Herr sie mit du*, she thought. The Lord be with you.

"THE PLACE SHOULD be somewhere along here on the right—maybe a mile or so."

Charlie Nelson, the Englisch driver Jacob had hired for the day, was always patient. That was probably why most of the Leit asked him first when they needed an Englisch driver to take them somewhere that was too far to go in a buggy. Charlie never cared how long it took his clients. He'd just settle back with the newspaper and wait.

Jacob nodded. "I'll keep watching for it. I just hope those directions were right." The woman in the thrift shop had told them where to find the group called Amish Assist . . . the folks who offered to help those Amish who'd jumped the fence and needed help. Or advice. He couldn't help wondering if they ever advised going back home.

This was the last place he'd come up with to try. If they wouldn't help him, he'd have to give it up, at least for the day. He couldn't leave the shop unattended for long, not when he now had a nephew to support.

Jacob's heart clenched at the thought of little Isaac. He'd do his best for the boy, but he didn't think he was cut out for parenthood. The baby needed his mother. He had to make Anna see that.

The day had been one failure after another. No one at any of the food pantries or food banks recognized his description of Anna. He could only guess at how she looked now, dressing Englisch, so that wasn't surprising.

He'd tracked down the thrift shop that matched the tag in the diaper bag, but no one there could tell him anything. Apparently they had a lot of customers in these hard times.

So this was . . .

"Wait, there it is. Ahead on the right." He leaned forward, hand braced on the dashboard as Charlie braked and then pulled into the gravel lane leading to a farmhouse with a barn and pastures beyond it. The sign was so small he'd nearly missed it.

They stopped at a turnaround a short distance from the front of the house. Jacob slid out and then turned to look at Charlie. "I'll try not to be long, but—"

"No worries." Charlie waved him away, pulling a folded newspaper out of his pocket. "Take your time."

"Denke." Jacob took a couple of steps away from the car and paused, stretching, and looked around.

This might easily be the area around Promise Glen, with the wide valley dotted with farms and the wooded ridge rising sharply beyond. There was a hint of fall in the air—not in the color on the trees, which were still the dark green of late summer, but in the golden swaths of fields cut and harvested and the orange and red that showed up along the roadside.

The farm itself looked well kept, with the barn freshly painted and the lawn a smooth green setting for the house. Beyond the barn, a couple of men worked at a fence, stringing wire.

If he was going to find out anything, he'd have to ask his questions. He headed for the front door, trying to keep his spirits up and knowing it would be a struggle.

He reached the porch, and as he lifted his hand to knock, a woman appeared behind the screen door. Youngish, wearing jeans and a flannel shirt, she smiled pleasantly, obviously recognizing him as Amish from his clothing.

"Hello. Are you looking for help?"

"Yah. But probably not the help you usually offer. I'm trying to find someone."

She grasped the storm door as if to close it. "Sorry. We can't give out information about the people we help." She started to swing the door shut.

"Please, wait. Just listen. I'm trying to find my little sister. Can't you help me?"

She didn't let go of the door, but she did wait, assessing him, it seemed. "No, you wouldn't be one of the fence jumpers. They tend to be younger."

"Yah." Bitterness welled in him. "My sister was only seventeen when she left. She's been gone two years."

The woman seemed to recede from him, even though she didn't move. "And you're just now looking for her?"

"No, no. I've been looking since she left, but lately— this week she sent her baby son home, wanting me to keep him. Saying she didn't want to take care of him."

"I'm so sorry." She reached out as if to comfort him. "Poor little thing."

He wasn't sure whether she was referring to Anna or the baby, but it could apply to both of them. He nodded. "Yah. The thing is, I know Anna needs my help. I have to find her."

"Don't you mean you have to make her go back?"

The voice startled him. The man had approached so quietly that he didn't hear a thing until he stepped up on the porch. It was one of the men who'd been working on the fence . . . sturdy, muscular, used to physical work. He was probably in his thirties, and he eyed Jacob without a trace of sympathy.

"She and the baby belong back with her family, with people who will take care of her."

"Could be she doesn't want taking care of. Maybe

she's happy the way she is." He glanced at the woman, possibly his wife.

"Anna," she said, in a way that seemed to mean they knew his sister.

The man gave a brisk nod. "Some people don't want to be taken care of," he said shortly. "We can't give out any information about the people we help."

"They count on that, you see," the woman added. Then she took a step back. "But I'll get some coffee for you and your driver."

Her husband, if that's who he was, looked after her with an expression of faint surprise, as if coffee wasn't usually part of their refusal.

"Don't bother, Lacey," he called. "He'll be going now."

Jacob's patience snapped, and his temper soared. "You can't keep my sister away from me. She's just a kid herself, and now there's a baby she can't look after. If you know anything—"

"We don't," he said. "And from what you say she's over eighteen now. Not a minor, so you can't claim she needs supervision."

"I don't want to supervise. I just want to help her and the baby."

He was already shaking his head. "Look, here's the way it is. Runaways come here, usually when they first leave. They need help, maybe getting a job, finding a place to live. They don't know how to get along among the Englisch."

Something about the way he said it brought enlightenment to Jacob. The man was Amish himself. Or former Amish now. He would have left his own family, and now he helped others to do the same.

"All the more reason they should stay with their own kind," he snapped. "Anna needs help, don't you see? And her baby needs her."

Something . . . maybe sympathy, maybe not . . . flashed across the man's face. Then he yanked the door open and stepped inside.

"Sorry. We can't help."

The door closed before Jacob could get out another word. He raised his fist to pound on the door and then let it fall. He'd promised himself he wouldn't lose his temper, and he'd failed, but at least he didn't have to make matters worse.

He took a deep breath and fought to control himself. If he made a pest of himself now, he wouldn't have another chance to gain their help. Funny, he could almost feel Dinah's approval at the thought. She'd told him nothing would be gained by losing his temper, or words to that effect, anyway.

He turned away from the door and spotted the woman, standing beside the car and talking to Charlie. She'd obviously brought the coffee, which was a friendly act. Maybe she was trying to encourage him.

Striding over to them, he managed a smile as he took the coffee. "Denke. This is kind of you."

"Not at all. You both look as if you've had a long day."

He nodded. "A discouraging one," he said, wondering if he should try again to learn something from her.

She looked at him kindly. "We really don't know where Anna is now. I'm Lacey Gaus, by the way. If I should hear from her, is there anything you want me to tell her?"

For some reason Dinah's words came into his mind. "Tell her . . . tell her the people who love her are waiting for her to come home."

To his surprise, the woman patted his arm. "I'll tell her. If I can."

She turned away, and with that, he had to be content.

DINAH SAT AT the kitchen table early the next morning, Isaac on her lap, trying to persuade him to have a little of the rice cereal she'd found in the diaper bag. A tea towel was draped across her to protect her dress. She looked at her mother, shaking her head.

"He doesn't seem to want it. I wish Anna had left a note in the bag telling us what we should give him when." She tried not to feel exasperated with Anna, but it wasn't easy when she thought about anyone not wanting such a sweet, beautiful baby.

Mamm leaned over her shoulder to watch. "What about the jar of bananas? Maybe if you put a little of each on the spoon it would work."

Willing to try anything, Dinah took bits of cereal and banana and touched the spoon to Isaac's lips. He turned his head away and then just as quickly came back to the spoon. They both laughed as he sucked it off greedily.

"He has a sweet tooth, that little one," Grossmammi said, watching. "He'll have a fine appetite before he's done."

"Yah."

Mammi stood back a little, looking at Dinah and the baby with a question in her eyes. Dinah knew exactly what the question was. Mammi still worried that Dinah would have her heart broken by little Isaac.

She couldn't reassure her, because it was already too late. "I've loved him since the moment I took him in my arms," she said, answering what hadn't been asked out loud.

Mammi nodded. "Yah. That's how it is."

"I just hope Jacob . . ." Dinah let that trail off and shook her head. "I don't see how he could consider passing him on to someone else."

"He probably feels helpless. Anyway, it's for him to say." Mammi's eyes darkened. "Not for us."

Lovina came in, yawning. "What's not for us? That boppli, I hope. He woke me up twice last night."

"Poor thing," Dinah said. "Did we ever tell you how many times you used to wake us up in the night?"

Grossmammi chuckled. "You had the loudest wail I ever heard in my life. We could have used you to call the pigs in when we used to raise them."

Lovina looked as if she didn't appreciate the comparison, but she wouldn't talk back to Grossmammi, thank goodness. Dinah hoped this wasn't going to be one of Lovina's pouting days. She could set the whole family on edge when she started.

"Anyway, who were you talking about when I came in?" She slid into the seat next to Dinah.

"Jacob. We wonder what he's going to do about the baby," Mammi said. "And how he made out yesterday."

"We'll know soon," Grossmammi said, looking out the window. "He's on his way over now."

"He got in late last night." Dinah realized they were all looking at her and hastened to explain. "I saw the light when I was up with the baby."

The yellow light from Jacob's bedroom window had looked lonely in the dark of night, and her heart had ached for him. If he'd brought Anna back, they would have come to the house, no matter how late it was. So it looked as if he'd come home alone and unsuccessful.

"Well." Mammi exchanged glances with Grossmammi. "I guess we'll know soon enough."

The marks of a sleepless night were clear on Jacob's face when he came in the back door, and Dinah's heart ached for him. "No news?"

He shook his head. "No one who could be sure they'd seen her except those people who help runaways. It seemed clear they knew her, but they don't know where she is now. Or if they do, they're not saying."

Mammi pushed a mug of coffee into his hand, and he took a large gulp, looking as if he needed it.

"We're that sorry about it, Jacob. And you know we're glad to help you however we can." Mammi patted his shoulder as if he were one of her own.

"I wish I knew what to do." His gaze met Dinah's, and for an instant his face lightened. "Ach, I'll keep him, that's certain sure. But how do I go about it?"

Dinah felt the tension in her ease. Maybe Isaac felt it, too, because he stopped turning his face away and accepted another mouthful.

Jacob was going to do his duty by his little nephew. Whatever happened, at least he wouldn't have another load of guilt to bear, and little Isaac would have a family.

"I'm glad," she said softly, trying to blink away the tears that wanted to form in her eyes.

He came around the table to lean over his nephew, and Isaac reached for his face. Jacob caught the small hand and dropped a kiss on it. "It's the two of us from now on, little Isaac. I just wish I knew a bit more about taking care of babies."

That made all of them smile, and the atmosphere in the farmhouse kitchen seemed to warm. "You'll learn," Mammi said.

"And we'll help," Dinah said again. "You know that." Quite aside from their lifelong friendship, there were all the things he'd done to help her with the business since Aaron died. Anything she could do would be small payment for his kindness.

"I've been trying to think of the best thing to do." Jacob straightened, including them all in his words. "If I took him with me to the shop every day, we'd be together, but I wouldn't get much work done with him around, would I, little man?" He cradled the baby's head for a moment, his large hand fitting around it easily.

"You might hire someone to take care of him during the day," Mammi suggested. "Someone who already has kinder at home might like having another boppli around, ain't so?"

"Someone like Ella Fischer or Betty Schutz," Gross-mammi suggested.

Almost without thought, Dinah shook her head, then reminded herself that she didn't have the right to say yes or no. It was up to Jacob.

He was still standing next to her, and he transferred his gaze from Isaac to her. "You don't think they'd do?"

She felt the color come up in her cheeks. "It's not that. They'd be fine with the boppli. But then you wouldn't be with him."

"What else can I do?" He was talking to her as if they were the only ones in the room, and she could feel his pain and indecision. "I'm trying to do what's best for him, but I don't know what that is."

Dinah hesitated, torn. If she offered to take care of Isaac herself, what then? To have the baby she'd always longed for but to know he wasn't really hers . . . She winced. Maybe Mammi was right. Maybe the pain of losing him would be worse than never having him at all.

"It doesn't seem so hard to me," Lovina piped up, earning glares from her mother and grandmother. "Well, I don't think it is. I could go to the shop and work for Dinah. With me there, we could help with the baby and keep both the bakery and the harness shop going, couldn't we?"

"Lovina, this is not something for you to interfere with." Mammi looked as if her younger daughter were a trial. "You shouldn't—"

"Wait a minute," Jacob said. "If that could work . . .

well, it would certain sure be me paying Lovina's salary, not Dinah. But it depends on Dinah. And you," he added, looking at Mammi. "It's too much to ask all of a sudden like this."

He stopped, because Dinah was shaking her head. "No. It's not too much or too soon." She looked down into Isaac's face and was sure of the answer. "I hate to admit it, but Lovina has the answer. We can do it. We'd love to do it."

Relief washed over Jacob's face, chasing the tiredness away. "Are you sure?"

Dinah cradled Isaac against her. "I'm sure." It might end in the sorrow and pain of losing him, but Grossmammi had been right. Loving him was worth the risk.

CHAPTER FOUR

D inah had expected preparing for the usual morning
rush at the bakery to be hectic with the baby, but to
her surprise, it went very smoothly. Isaac had fallen
asleep driving in from the farm, so Jacob carried his
basket right into the harness shop and settled him near
the connecting door.

"There," he said softly. "If he starts to fuss, one of the
three of us can reach him quickly."

"We can take him . . . ," she began, but Jacob waved
her words away.

"Go and get started before your customers are bang-
ing on the door. We'll trade later, yah?"

Dinah hesitated, but Lovina started tugging at her.
"Come on. We don't want to be late opening, do we?"

We? Lovina, who didn't usually take anything seriously, seemed eager to work. It was too good to last,
Dinah supposed, but she might as well enjoy it while she
could.

The rush hour was more rushed than usual, and it
was certain sure that more Amish came in than she had
expected. Many more. Clearly the news had spread about

Isaac's arrival, but how did they know he would be here, instead of at the house?

She was forced to conclude that the Amish grapevine was even more efficient than she'd thought, and she'd already had a lot of respect for it. Usually if a person sneezed at eight o'clock, people were offering home remedies by ten, but not this fast.

Her explanation that the baby was sleeping didn't satisfy anyone, of course. Some tiptoed to the connecting door and peered through the glass. Actually, they were easier to deal with than the ones who stayed at the counter and asked questions.

Lovina leaned across to murmur in her ear, "Why not let me work the counter? If you're in the kitchen, they can't get at you, ain't so?"

Dinah had to admit it made sense. She hesitated, but when she saw Ethel Gittler bearing down on her, she nodded in agreement and escaped into the kitchen.

Dinah stood for a moment by the door, listening. Lovina countered every question by saying either "I don't know" or "You'd have to ask someone else."

Her little sister, Dinah decided, had more poise than she ever would. She'd certainly never gotten the better of Ethel Gittler.

As it always did, the morning rush finally ended. Dinah exchanged glances with Lovina. "You did a fine job. Denke, Lovina. Will you take over while I deliver Jacob's morning coffee?"

Lovina's face lit up. "For sure. Whenever you want me to."

Carrying the coffee and a doughnut, Dinah went through the connecting door, wondering what Mammi would think about Lovina's accomplishment. If only her sister's good mood lasted until she got home, Mammi wouldn't even need telling.

Isaac still slept, his little hands over his head in the classic position of sleeping babies. She paused, looking down at him with a smile, and then headed toward the counter. Jacob was already coming around to take the coffee and jelly doughnut from her.

"I thought you might be out of doughnuts after the crowd you had in there this morning. What was going on?"

"Curiosity, that's what. Didn't any of them make up an excuse to come in here?"

He shook his head, his face tightening. "No, and it's a gut thing. I don't know what I might have said to them. How did you handle it?"

"I turned them over to Lovina. Honestly, Jacob, I never knew she had it in her. She was so polite and poised, and she didn't tell them a thing. It seems my little sister has hidden talents."

"I guess so." He relaxed a little. "Maybe we should have thought out what to say. Folks seem to know he's Anna's baby, ain't so?"

"I'm not sure how, but they do."

She felt sorry for him. It wasn't very pleasant to have the whole community gossiping about your family.

"Well, you couldn't expect to keep that from people anyway," she went on. "I'd just tell them the truth, only in a short version. Anna asked you to take care of her baby, and my family is helping you. And then don't say anything more."

"Not easy to do," he muttered.

She smiled, trying to cheer him up. "I'll lend Lovina to you if you need her." Before he could answer, she heard the unmistakable sounds of a baby waking up. She nodded toward his coffee. "Better finish that up. You're going to have a lesson in diaper changing."

He gulped down coffee. "I think I'll need it. From what I saw yesterday, you have to be quick."

In spite of his doubts, Jacob caught on quickly. She smiled, watching him fasten the sides. "There now, you see? Onkel Jacob is pretty good at it, right, Isaac?"

Isaac, as if in answer, gave a wide grin and then chortled when Jacob patted his belly. She had to laugh herself, and she realized Jacob was doing the same. For a moment they shared the amusement, but then Jacob's face sobered as he looked down at his nephew.

"How could Anna bear to leave him?" His blue eyes darkened as he looked from Isaac to Dinah. "Can you understand it?"

He seemed to be pleading with her to explain, and her heart twisted, knowing she couldn't. She reached out to put her hand over his where it now cradled Isaac's head. Would a touch express her concern, or did it need words?

"I'm sorry," she whispered. "I wish . . ."

His hand turned, clasping hers. "I know."

They stood close together, hands touching. Warmth and caring flowed back and forth between them, so strongly that it took Dinah's breath away. She felt . . .

The bell over the door sounded, jolting them apart. Jacob swung toward the door, and Dinah busied herself snapping Isaac's little outfit. She lifted him into her arms and then turned to see who was coming, hoping whoever it was hadn't been looking at them through the glass in the door.

Noah, her dear friend Sarah's husband, maneuvered a folding baby cot through the door. "So there's the little one." Shoving his burden into Jacob's hands, he strode quickly to Dinah, smiling at the baby in her arms. "Ach, he's a handsome boy, ain't so?"

"For sure." Noah, she suspected, was looking ahead to the baby that would soon join his own family. "He's just six months old."

Noah's face sobered as he exchanged glances with Dinah. "Sarah says anything she can do. But you know that, yah?"

She gave him a reassuring smile. "Tell her everyone is helping. And I'll see her soon."

Noah nodded, and it struck her that he was the one person who might fully understand what Jacob was going through. His late wife had left him and the twins when they were no more than babies.

"What is this thing?" Jacob set the cot down, starting to unfold it. "A bed?"

"It can be a bed or a play area for the boppli." Noah helped him open it and showed him how to fasten it securely. He slid the pad into place in the bottom, and it was ready. "We thought you could use it."

"It's just what Isaac needs." Dinah handed him the quilt from the basket, and he spread it in the bottom. "But doesn't Sarah want it?"

"Not for a few months, she says."

"Denke, Noah. It's wonderful kind of you." If Jacob had felt embarrassed by all the things he didn't know about babies, he'd recovered quickly. "Perfect for using here, ain't so, Dinah?"

In answer, she lowered Isaac into the cot. He lay still for a moment, surveying his surroundings, and then he rolled over onto his belly, looking pleased with himself. The men both chuckled.

"I guess that means he approves," Jacob said. "Maybe I should have some toys for him, ain't so?"

"There are a couple of things in the kitchen that would do. I'll get them." Guilt pricked at her. She'd left Lovina in charge longer than she'd intended. "I'll send Lovina over with them."

Jacob nodded. "You'll want to get back to work." He

reached out, as if he would touch her hand, but then snatched his own hand back, flushing a little. "Denke."

Dinah managed a meaningless smile and hurried off. He'd been embarrassed. Why? Because he'd seen her reaction earlier when they had touched? Because her emotions dismayed him? She felt her own cheeks getting hot as she walked through the coffee shop without seeing it.

JACOB MADE AN effort to pull himself together. What was he doing? Had he actually felt ill at ease with Dinah, after all the years they'd known each other?

Ferhoodled, that's what it was. He'd wanted to find a way to express gratitude to Dinah. That was all.

He felt as if an age had passed, but apparently it had only been a minute or two. Noah was bending over the cot, smiling down at little Isaac. He shook his head.

"I can't do it. I was trying to imagine when Matt and Mark were that small, and I just can't do it."

Jacob chuckled. "I'd say you'd best figure it out before long, ain't so?"

"That's certain sure." Noah put his hand on Isaac's back very lightly, and the baby responded by hitching his knees under him, rocking back and forth. "Look at him. Now that's something I do remember. He'll be crawling before you know it. Just wait."

Jacob didn't want to believe it, but he guessed Noah remembered. "This will be perfect, then. I sure can't have him crawling around the shop. But are you really sure you want to lend it?"

Noah shrugged. "Sarah says it's fine, and she ought to know."

"Yah, my cousin usually knows." He smiled, remembering the past. "She told me off one time for not supporting you more when . . . well, according to her, you needed someone to talk to. I guess talking about feelings isn't my strong suit. Or even knowing what my feelings are."

"Not mine, either," Noah said promptly. "But you know we're praying that Anna will come back."

"I know," he said, more touched than he'd expected. "I didn't see her, but Dinah said she wasn't ready . . . not right now, anyway. I guess you know what that's like," he added awkwardly, thinking about the wife who had left Noah.

Noah's face tightened. "Yah, but I was better off than you. I had plenty of family ready to jump in and help with the twins. I don't know what I'd have done without Mamm and Daad."

Jacob had a momentary longing for his own mammi and daad, but he shook it off. "Dinah's family has done the same, just like always. I couldn't have better neighbors."

"Yah. Sarah says she hopes it's not too hard on Dinah. Because she never had a baby of her own after she married Aaron, I mean."

That hit him right in the heart. Jacob tried to shove away a wave of guilt. He of all people knew about that. "Yah, I guess so," he managed.

"Still, seems like she's really cherishing this little guy."

"Everybody's cherishing him." Lovina's voice came first, and then Lovina herself, hustling over to the cot with a handful of things. "Who wouldn't?"

Glad of the interruption, he took a dangling plastic strainer from Lovina before it could fall. "Isn't this a little too big for him?"

Lovina made a face at him. "That's what my sister said. But he'll like that pretty bright yellow." Dismissing the strainer for the moment, Lovina leaned over, dangling plastic measuring spoons in front of Isaac. He promptly reached out, grabbed one, and rolled over onto his back. He looked surprised, but he didn't lose hold of his spoon.

Noah chuckled. "I'd best get going. I told Sarah I wouldn't be long. You take care, now."

When he'd gone, Lovina looked as if she'd be happy hanging over the cot railing to play with Isaac. Deciding he ought to take the moment to get on with some work, Jacob went behind the counter. He got out the order list he wanted to check, but his mind wouldn't stay focused on it.

Noah's comments had started a train of thought that wouldn't stop. Suddenly he was once again in the back storage room, getting down a box from the top shelf and hearing Aaron and Dinah talking through the partition that separated his storeroom from theirs. He'd started to climb down, and then he'd made sense of what he was hearing, and it had frozen him in place.

Aaron wasn't talking. He was practically shouting. "I don't want to hear what that stupid doctor said, do you hear me? He doesn't know anything."

"But, Aaron, it's just a simple test. If you took it, he'd be able—"

"He's trying to say it's my fault. And I'm not putting up with it. He's not going to go poking around trying to prove any such thing."

"The doctor—" she began. She didn't finish, because there was a sound as if Aaron had hit something.

"No!" It was almost a shout. "And don't you go telling everybody about it, either."

"I . . . I wouldn't." It came out in almost a gasp.

There was the sound of stamping feet, the slam of a door. He'd managed to breathe again. If they were gone . . .

But then had come another sound—the sound of Dinah crying as if her heart would break.

He hadn't done anything then. He couldn't have. And only a few days later an accident had taken Aaron's life. But of all people, he knew how much Dinah had been hurt by not having babies of her own.

DINAH MANAGED TO avoid Jacob for most of the day, not even sure why she was doing it. She couldn't decide whether she was imagining things or he had somehow sensed that emotional response of hers. Sensed it, and been embarrassed by it.

Forget it, she told herself. With Isaac's future at stake, she couldn't let anything else become a barrier between her and Jacob. The baby had to come first, because he was helpless and completely dependent on others. On them.

Early afternoon was usually a quiet time for the shop. People wouldn't come in for their afternoon break until about two. She'd sometimes thought she should change her hours so she was only open mornings, but she'd not convinced herself of that. Actually, with Lovina helping, she might be open more, not less. She filed that away to think about.

Dinah touched Lovina on the shoulder, distracting her from reorganizing the display case.

"Come and help me to bring Isaac and the cot in here. We can watch him until we get busy again. That'll give Jacob time to get some work done."

"Okay." That cheerful answer was a welcome change from the grumpiness Lovina usually displayed at home when asked to do something she didn't expect.

They found Isaac sleeping, sprawled on his back, looking as relaxed as a bowl of gelatin. "We'll take him for a while," she murmured to Jacob, seizing one end of the cot. "Then you can get some work done."

Jacob came from behind the counter. "Sounds good. I've been afraid to start the sewing machine. The noise might wake him. Need me to help you?"

He gestured at the cot, but she noticed he kept some distance between them.

"No," she said quickly. "Not necessary, I mean. Lovina's helping me."

Lovina, reminded, took hold of the other end, and they lifted the cot easily, carrying it to the door. Lovina opened it with a shove of her hip, and they took the cot, sleeping baby and all, into the bakery.

"Okay if I finish arranging the display case?" Lovina said the minute they'd settled the baby in a quiet corner. "I think the prettiest pastries should go on the top shelf. That way people see them first."

"Yah, for sure." She blinked at Lovina's enthusiasm. It had never occurred to her that some pastries were prettier than others, but if it kept Lovina helpful, she was all for it.

Dinah had plenty to think about when they finally headed for home. But with Lovina driving the buggy and Isaac falling asleep in Dinah's arms the moment it started moving, Dinah could feel herself relaxing.

The day had gone better than she'd expected, with the three of them sharing responsibilities. Even the inevitable questions weren't as difficult as they might have been. Most people seemed to accept it as normal that they would be caring for Anna's baby.

Well, most of the Amish, anyway. Offers of equipment came from all sides, along with offers of help. It was what she expected from the close-knit Amish of Promise Glen. And if her Englisch customers thought it strange that she suddenly had a baby, at least they hadn't said so.

Jacob's buggy had been following them, but it peeled off when it reached the lane to his place. He wanted to be taking care of the few animals he kept these days, but then he'd be over for supper at Mamm's insistence. Dinah had to smile at the thought. Mamm and Grossmammi had been trying to mother their neighbor since his own mother passed, and now they finally had their chance. Whether Jacob wanted it or not, circumstances, in the shape of one small baby, were sweeping him into the family.

"We might need to do more baking tomorrow if it's as busy as today," Lovina said as she turned in to the lane. "I can take care of the front while you're in the kitchen. We want to be prepared."

Dinah controlled the smile that tugged at her lips. *We?* she thought again. Lovina had jumped into the business with both feet, and before she knew it, her little sister would be trying to run it.

"Sounds gut," she said, and they went into the house while ten-year-old Will took over the horse and buggy. Will, coming at the tail end of the family, grabbed every chance he got to drive, and that certain sure made things easier for her when she got home from a day's work.

"Just look at what we got today for Isaac," Mammi exclaimed at the sight of them. She came to take Isaac, who woke up and gave her an engaging smile.

Mammi seemed to forget whatever it was she wanted Dinah to look at in the excitement of cooing at the boppli, and Grossmammi was just as bad. Dinah looked at Lovina, who grinned.

"Easy to see who's popular around here, ain't so?" Lovina put down the diaper bag she'd carried in.

"For sure." As it turned out, she didn't need Mammi

to show her the new arrival. It was a portable baby cot, similar to the one they'd left at the shop. It was set up in a corner of the kitchen, all ready for Isaac.

"Mammi, where did the cot come from? Sarah already sent Noah in with one to use at the shop."

"This one's from Cousin Lena. She says if she has her way, she won't need it until she has a grandbaby."

Dinah smiled and shook her head. Cousin Lena was a wonderful good mother who already had six under school age, including a pair of twins. But they all knew she was joking . . . she said that every time.

"That means we'll be giving it back soon," Grossmammi said, laughing a little. "Lena has babies as easy as—" She stopped abruptly with a look at Dinah.

"As falling off a log," Dinah finished for her, determined that Grossmammi shouldn't feel bad about such a simple thing. "Put him in the cot, Mammi, and he'll show off for you."

Isaac rolled over as if he'd understood her words, and Mammi and Grossmammi oohed over him so much that he rolled back again. Watching them, she knew that Isaac wouldn't lack love as long as he stayed near them. He'd already captured more hearts than just her own.

Dinah came down from changing her clothes to find that everyone had gathered in the kitchen, including Jacob. Her brothers were clustered around the cot. Will leaned over, dangling a small stuffed bird in front of Isaac, while the twins seemed to be trying to teach him how to crawl. And all the while Jacob sat quietly, looking from one to the other of the noisy gang.

Dinah's heart clenched. Jacob hid his loneliness under a cheerful grin and a ready laugh, and he did it so well that few people guessed there was anything behind it.

She had been as guilty as anyone else, even seeing

him as often as she did. But right now, watching the kind of family life he had lost, his face was open to anyone who looked at him with caring eyes.

Dinah glanced at the others. Mammi was starting to dish up supper, but she met Dinah's eyes for an instant, and Dinah knew she'd seen the same thing. Seen, and probably felt as helpless as Dinah did. How could Jacob give Isaac the kind of family life he needed when Jacob didn't have it himself?

Maybe Mammi would have some ideas. It was certain sure that *she* didn't, other than to continue doing what they'd been doing. That was fine for now, but Isaac would grow and change, and if Anna didn't come back . . .

She shook her head impatiently. There was no point in going over and over it. She'd find an opportunity to talk with Mammi, maybe after supper.

But the usually quiet time after the evening meal was interrupted by an abrupt flare-up. Lovina, who'd been so helpful all day, suddenly balked at drying the dishes.

"I don't see why I have to be the one." She threw down the dish towel with a final, dramatic movement. "Who says girls are the only ones who can dry dishes?"

Usually that was the sort of thing that Mammi dealt with calmly, but Dinah saw in an instant that she was at the end of her patience. Mammi turned on Lovina with a snap in her voice.

"You know perfectly well that every person in the family helps. If you can't—"

Dinah stepped in before both of them could say something they might regret, taking Lovina's shoulders and turning her away from the sink.

"I'd rather dry dishes than carry all this laundry upstairs," she said. "I'll trade you."

Lovina, looking as if she already regretted her hasty speech but didn't know how to get out of it, nodded mutely. She seized the laundry baskets, piled one on top of the other, and carted them toward the stairs.

Dinah dried a couple of plates and waited while her mother seemed to struggle with herself. Finally, Mammi smiled.

"Denke, Dinah. I don't know why I let Lovina make me snap. I didn't do that with you, did I?"

"No, but I wasn't anywhere near as . . . well, bold, I guess, as Lovina is. Or maybe *annoying* is a better word. Sass just seems to come naturally to her."

She meant that to be funny, but Mamm didn't seem to take it that way.

"She's so daring. Sometimes I'm afraid . . ." Mamm let that trail off as if she couldn't finish it, and her face worked as if she held back tears.

"Mammi." Dinah dropped the dish towel to put her arm around her mother. "What is it? Don't cry."

Mammi seized the abandoned dish towel and mopped her eyes. "Ach, I'm so foolish. But I couldn't help thinking about Anna, and it made me worry that Lovina might do what she did."

For a moment Dinah wanted to call for Grossmammi to handle this. She wasn't prepared to deal with giving her own mother advice. But Mammi had turned to her with the fear that must sometimes haunt every Amish parent—that of losing a child to the Englisch world.

"She's just being a sassy teenager, that's all." Dinah tried to sound confident. "I'm sure she's not thinking of any such thing. Besides, this situation with Anna and the baby must show her that running away isn't the answer to anything. Don't you think so?"

Mammi clearly struggled with herself. Then she turned to hug her close for an instant. "I'm sure you're right. I must stop worrying." She released Dinah and then patted her cheek. "I'm so fortunate to have a grown daughter to talk to. You make me feel better."

Dinah blew out a long breath. If she'd allayed her mother's worries, that was all to the good. But what about her own?

CHAPTER FIVE

One advantage of a large family, Dinah told herself later, was that you could usually find someone to help. Leaving baby Isaac with Mammi and Grossmammi, she went upstairs to arrange the bedroom for the night. She'd quickly figured out that the more preparation she did, the smoother things went.

She walked in to find that several things had been added to the room since the morning. Baby care equipment kept appearing—the crib last used for one of her brothers, cleaned and polished but still bearing someone's tooth marks along the top of the railing. Will's crib quilt had been hung on the bottom of the crib, ready for use, and she touched it lovingly. She remembered helping Grossmammi stitch the colorful squares together.

A changing table was a new arrival, and she thought she recognized it from her cousin Lyddie's nursery. It had a fresh pad on top, and when she pulled out the drawers, she discovered that they were already filled with baby clothes, also probably from one or the other of her cousins. She looked through the tiny outfits, taking out a soft pair of blue sleepers. Folks were so good, responding the instant they learned of a need. And they didn't just drop off bags of things—her cousins would have taken the time to set it all up so that it was ready to use. That extra thoughtfulness touched her.

Of course, everyone in the community wanted to help Jacob, understanding what a challenge this had to be for him. He'd had so much sorrow in his life that people would rejoice for this unexpected joy in the shape of one small baby.

Dinah took a last look around and then started down the stairs. Voices in the living room told her that Daad and her brothers were in from the evening chores, along with Jacob. Amusing herself by guessing who had claimed Isaac, she paused in the doorway, and her heart swelled.

Jacob sat in the rocking chair with Isaac on his lap, his big hands carefully supporting the baby's back. He was looking into his nephew's face with so much love that she couldn't possibly speak. All the love Jacob would want to shower on his parents, his sister, all the siblings who might have been part of his life . . . all of it was concentrated on one little baby. With Anna gone, there was no one else for him to love.

Jacob caught sight of her and raised his eyebrows. "Bedtime?" he asked.

"Yah, I think so. Once he has a bottle, he'll probably go right to sleep."

Jacob got up and handed him over, his reluctance to part with the baby clear in every movement. Her heart twisted again.

"If you come up in about half an hour, you can tell him good night."

"Yah, I will." His hand lingered on Isaac for another moment, and then he stepped back and Dinah moved away quickly. Fetching the warming bottle from the kitchen, she hurried upstairs.

"There we go, little man." She lowered him to the changing table and set the bottle out of his sight for the moment. "We'll get you all nice and clean and ready for sleep. And the longer you sleep, the longer I will, ain't so?"

She bent over him, smiling, and Isaac smiled in return and reached for her face. She probably looked just as infatuated as Jacob had.

"Now a fresh diaper and these pretty blue sleepers can go on for the night."

Continuing to talk, she distracted him while she got him ready for bed. He was tiring, she could see, as the dimly lit room and her soft voice had their effect. She picked him up and cradled him close.

The rocking chair waited, with the bottle close at hand. As soon she was settled in the rocking chair, Isaac tried to grab the bottle. Laughing a little at his greediness, she adjusted his position against her, his head seeming to fit perfectly in the curve of her arm. In an instant, he was sucking so hard that his round cheeks grew red.

Ach, what a sweetheart he was. No wonder Jacob had gone from shock to overwhelming love in less than two days. She had done the same, after all. It just hadn't taken quite as long. She'd been lost within the first moment of looking into his face.

Poor Jacob, facing so many questions. If Anna didn't come back . . . well, in that case Jacob would raise his little nephew no matter how many others volunteered to take him. She didn't have any doubt about that. But it would be difficult for him without any immediate family to jump in and help. The current situation worked, but it had to be temporary. Isaac would grow, and neither of them could have a toddler roaming around their businesses.

And what if Anna came back? Or worse, what if she came back and took him away? Or decided to do something else with him? Maybe she would marry the father and want him, or maybe she'd disappear into a new life. There were so many possibilities that it made Dinah feel dizzy.

No matter what happened, she feared for Jacob. He could be hurt so much by this situation, and she didn't see how anyone would be able to comfort him.

Isaac's eyes closed, and the nipple lay slack in his mouth. His head was heavy against her arm. Sated, he didn't react when she took away the nearly empty bottle.

She shifted him up against her shoulder and patted his back until he produced a burp. Once that was out, he sank back against her in total relaxation. Dinah held him close, and her eyes filled with tears.

She wished, so very much, that Isaac were her own baby. If she had had a child . . . She pushed that away, but it kept coming back. In those weeks after Aaron's death, guilt had piled on top of grief, seeming about to suffocate her. If she had been wiser, stronger, if she had handled the differences between them better . . .

Fiercely she pushed the memories away. Isaac, unaware of her inward struggle, was sound asleep against her. He had no regrets for anything, safe in his little world of warmth and love. She kissed his head and then the little roll of fat at the back of his neck, inhaling that sweet scent of baby. Her heart expanded with love.

Moving slowly so as not to waken him, Dinah rose and carried him to the crib. She lowered him gently, relieved when he made no complaint. He was miles deep in sleep, it seemed, far deeper than any adult could ever be. He had no worries to keep him wakeful . . . he just trusted, sure someone would take care of him.

Blinking away the tears that lingered, she backed away from the crib. As she turned toward the door, she realized that Jacob stood there, looking in. She gestured to him, and he came softly, tiptoeing his way to the crib.

They stood side by side, looking down at the sleeping baby. Jacob put out his hand, cradling Isaac's head against his palm so gently. Again she thought how much pain he risked in loving little Isaac. And thought that he was aware of it, but loved anyway.

Finally he drew back, and they went quietly out of the room. She left the door ajar so she'd hear if he cried, and then smiled at Jacob.

"We'll see how long he sleeps this time."

His blue eyes darkened. "I'm sorry you have to get up with him. I should . . ."

"Ach, I didn't mean that. I'm loving every minute of it. But . . ." She stopped, not wanting to voice her fears.

"But you're afraid this is going to hurt you," he said quietly. "I know. I should have realized sooner how this would pain you. Anna and I between us have set you up for being hurt. Not intentionally, but you will feel it just as much."

She was already shaking her head. "No more for me than you," she said. "And I'm not afraid. We both know we could be hurt, yah?"

He nodded, not speaking.

"Neither of us can stop loving him," she said, knowing it was true. "Like Grossmammi says, loving is worth the cost."

"Your grandmother is a wise woman." He seemed to speak with difficulty. "Denke, Dinah. For everything."

She could only nod without speaking. There was nothing else to say.

ON FRIDAY MORNING Dinah woke to find that a fall mist had filled the valley, creating a lacy veil over the pasture while the sun touched the top of the ridge outside her window. Autumn was on its way, even though the wooded hillsides were still a deep green. September was moving toward October, and evening drew in a little earlier each day.

By the time she, Lovina, and baby Isaac left for town, the mist had begun to dissolve, though it still hung on in the lower pastures. The spikes of the sumacs seemed to glow like the flames of torches along the road.

"Time for the fall tourists, ain't so?" Lovina clucked to the mare when she hesitated at a leafy branch extending into the road. "I'd think we'll be busy today, and even more tomorrow."

"Probably so. A few nice days like this will coax people out for a ride. We're not at the peak of it yet, not until mid-October, most likely, when the trees are at their most colorful."

Her thoughts went dashing ahead. Would they still have Isaac by then? Or would Anna reappear as quickly as she'd vanished? And if she did, would she stay? Or would she take Isaac and disappear again?

Her arms tightened around the baby, and his nose wrinkled up, even in his sleep. As usual, riding in the buggy had worked its magic.

She tried to focus on the baby's likely pattern of sleeping and waking today, but it was no use. Once she'd begun on Anna and Isaac's fate, she could only go around and around, trying to see a way in which everyone involved might be happy. She couldn't.

Grossmammi would remind her that we weren't put on this earth to be happy, but to do God's will. She should trust, but it seemed she didn't have the strong faith that her grandmother had achieved. Perhaps it came with age, but maybe for Dinah it never would.

Isaac still slept when they arrived at the shop, and Jacob came out to meet them. "I'll take him first so you're free during your busy time. Come see what I set up."

Nodding to Lovina to take the buggy around to the stable, Dinah followed him, carrying the baby while he took the diaper bag. Jacob led the way through the shop and into the storeroom at the rear. Bigger than the one at the rear of the bakery, it had been furnished with a small gas stove and refrigerator, and a table was covered with a quilt and a white pad. A box of diapers stood handy on the changing table he'd improvised.

"Wonderful gut, Jacob." She lowered Isaac gently into the portable cot that he'd obviously moved here. "Now I know why you came in so early this morning."

He nodded, coming to look down at Isaac, sleeping peacefully despite the changing environment. "This has been easier than I expected," he said softly. "Because you're doing the hard part at night, ain't so?"

"Just wait," she said, laughing a little. "Isaac's still sleeping a lot at his age, but Mammi always says no sooner do you get used to one schedule than the boppli changes to another one. The older he gets, the longer he'll be awake. And when he starts crawling and walking . . ."

Jacob threw up his hands. "Ach, I know. But maybe Anna will be back by then." He sobered suddenly. "If love and prayers will do it . . ." He let that fade away.

He was hoping Anna would return, picturing her moving back into the farmhouse, ready to be part of the family again. Poor Jacob. Last night he'd been resigned to the difficulties, but this morning he was trying to be hopeful, ignoring the other possibilities. She just wished she could believe it.

Fortunately the shop was busy enough that morning to keep her from brooding. Friday was usually a busy day, and Lovina had been right that business picked up as they moved into fall. Already today there were more Englisch in for coffee than normal. Two older couples were no doubt tourists, judging by the map spread out on the table. They seemed to be planning their morning drive.

Another, younger man had her a little puzzled. He was carrying a camera, true, but tourists didn't generally come singly. He came to the counter, taking his time making a choice from the glass case, and Lovina hovered, obviously eager to serve him. He must have asked her for advice, because she chattered away to him, pointing to one and then another of the baked treats.

Dinah felt a little misgiving. Would Mammi think she should intervene in their conversation? Before she could decide, Ethel Gittler claimed her attention.

"And where is that sweet boppli this morning? I hoped to see him. Does he look like Anna?"

Ethel was well meaning, Dinah reminded herself. She'd do anything to help out when people had trouble. But she had an intense curiosity and a very penetrating voice.

With a glance toward her Englisch customers, Dinah switched to Pennsylvania Dutch. "You won't be able to see him just now, I'm afraid. At six months, he just looks like any healthy baby, with blue eyes and a little yellow fuzz on the top of his head. Are you grocery shopping this morning?"

The question diverted her, as Dinah had hoped it would, because Ethel was also devoted to finding the best deals on what she had to buy, no matter how long it took. She went off into a comparison of specials at the various stores, and Dinah just had to listen and nod.

By the time Ethel had taken her coffee and settled down to check what was probably her shopping list, Dinah was relieved to see that Lovina's interested young customer had retired to a table as well.

Dinah's relief was short-lived, because as the morning rush subsided, she spotted Lovina standing at the young Englischer's table, one hand on her hip, talking vivaciously. Her heart sank. She knew exactly what Mamm would say about Lovina flirting with an Englischer—or anyone else, for that matter. It looked as if Lovina's career in the bakeshop was going to come to an abrupt end.

But before Dinah had to go to the rescue, if that's what it was, the man had gone out the door and walked off down the street. Putting off the talk she must have with Lovina for the moment, she collected coffee and a jelly doughnut.

"Lovina, will you take care of everything? I'll just run these over to Jacob and bring Isaac back here for a while."

"Sure I will." Lovina had been looking bored since her customer had left, but she brightened at being left in charge. Glad to have a reason to smile at her, Dinah hurried through the door to the harness shop.

No one was in the outer part of the shop, so Dinah walked through to the back room, where she paused in the doorway. Jacob, seemingly unaware of her, was in the process of changing Isaac's diaper. The baby's hands and legs were waving, but Jacob, talking to him in a low voice, didn't seem concerned. He fastened the little stretch suit deftly and then lifted Isaac to his shoulder, one hand on his back.

"There's a gut boy, all fresh and clean." Love seemed to flow through his voice. "Ain't so, Dinah?" He glanced at her.

"I thought you didn't realize I was here." She moved toward him, setting the coffee and doughnut on the cleared end of the table.

"I always know when you're here," he said, taking a bite of doughnut so that the jelly squirted out, narrowly missing Isaac's outfit, and leaving her in doubt as to what he meant. Was he saying that he heard her or . . .

Dinah pulled herself back from foolish speculation to help him mop up the jelly. She had to focus on the problem of the moment, not puzzle over what Jacob might mean.

"Best let me take him, or you'll both be covered with raspberry jelly."

She held out her hands to Isaac, who dived in her direction, trusting her to catch him. Laughing, she caught him and held him against her, cherishing the feeling of the warm, wiggly bundle.

Jacob stood still for a moment, watching them. "Will you be able to take him for a while?"

"Yah, for sure." She hesitated. Why was he looking so serious about it? "Was ist letz, Jacob? What's wrong?"

"Nothing, I hope. It's just . . . I had a message. The bishop wants to stop by for a talk this morning."

"Oh." She weighed that news. "He'll have heard about the baby. Maybe . . ."

Jacob shook his head. "He'll have questions that I can't answer, yah? He'll want to know about Anna. Is she married? Why isn't she here with her baby? Why—"

"Don't, Jacob." She took a step toward him to put a hand on his arm. It felt like an iron bar under her fingers. "Bishop John is wonderful kind. You know that. He's not going to blame the baby for any of it. And it's certain sure he won't blame you."

He pulled his arm away and seized the cot. "Maybe not, but I blame myself." He shook his head before she could say anything. "Never mind, Dinah. Just take Isaac for a bit. I'll deal with the bishop."

Obviously she couldn't do anything to shake his belief in his own guilt about his relationship with his little sister. But there was no need that she could see to anticipate problems with Bishop John.

Isaac, apparently deciding she should pay attention to him, reached up to pat her mouth and then tried to grab hold of her nose. Laughing in spite of herself, she caught his hand and kissed it, making him chortle.

"If the bishop seems upset about any of it, just bring him over and introduce him to Isaac. Isaac will capture his heart."

Jacob's expression eased, and he nodded. Then he pushed the portable cot toward her shop.

LATER, JACOB WASN'T sure why he'd been so apprehensive about seeing the bishop. Dinah had been right, just as she so often was.

Bishop John, still tall and lean even though his beard had turned to a snowy white, greeted him with a warm smile. "There is news of Anna, ain't so? That is a relief."

"Yah." Jacob's tension melted like snow in April. "It would be better if I had seen her myself, but at least we know she is well and safe."

Bishop John clasped Jacob's shoulder in a strong grip. "Dinah assured you. She wouldn't mislead you."

"No, she wouldn't." A vestige of his conviction lingered. "If I'd seen her myself, I might have gotten her to come back."

"Or you might have pushed her farther away," Bishop John said firmly. "We don't know the future. We must trust God to do what's best for His erring children."

Jacob struggled even harder to accept that, and it seemed impossible. Faith wasn't truly faith without trust in God. But for him and Anna to lose both their parents in such a short period of time . . . how did that fit into God's plan?

Bishop John seemed to read his heart, and his keen blue eyes softened with sympathy. "It is not easy, but it comes."

He nodded. "I have to admit that Dinah probably did a better job with Anna than I would have, that's certain sure." He struggled for words. "But I would like to hug my little sister again."

"Yah." Bishop John patted his shoulder. "I believe it will happen, one way or another. It's a gut sign that Anna wants her boy brought up as she was, ain't so?"

For an instant Jacob was too startled even to think. That had never occurred to him in all his thoughts about little Isaac. The bishop was right. Whatever had guided Anna to send the baby home was surely good. There would have been other possibilities open to her.

"Is there any help you need?" Bishop John went on as if he weren't aware of saying anything startling. "You know the whole Leit is eager to jump in." He smiled. "The women, especially."

He managed to chuckle at that. "I believe it. But not at the moment. My good neighbors are already doing all that's needful, and so much baby stuff has come in that I don't know what we'll do with it. Dinah says the bedroom is filled with clothes and toys."

Bishop John nodded, smiling. He would have no doubts about the generosity of his flock.

Jacob hesitated for just a second. "Do you want to meet young Isaac?" He sounded like a proud new father, he decided, but that was all right.

Bishop John responded with a smile and a nod, so Jacob led the way next door. Isaac was in the portable cot in a corner of the kitchen, surrounded by baby toys that had made their appearance today, as far as he could tell. Leaning over the crib and dangling the favorite plastic measuring spoons was young Will.

"Will, what brings you here?" Not that he needed to ask. Will was plainly fascinated by the baby.

Will, maybe thinking that wasn't manly enough for a ten-year-old boy, flushed a little, his always rosy cheeks turning red. "Daad had to go to the mill, so he dropped me off to help for a bit."

"That's gut of you, young Will." The bishop smiled, maybe pleased to see this additional sign of helpfulness from his flock. "And here is the little newcomer." He leaned over the crib, smiling warmly. "Ach, what a fine boy."

Isaac, seeming charmed by the long beard that fell toward him, reached up and grabbed for it. He succeeded and then looked as if he didn't know what to do next.

The bishop laughed. "You'll have a long wait to get a beard like mine." Before Jacob could reach to untangle Isaac's fingers, the bishop had done it, his gnarled fingers deft. He cradled Isaac's head with one age-worn hand, and his eyes closed. Realizing he was praying over Anna's baby, Jacob felt his heart swell. If only . . .

He shook the thought away. He'd be thankful for the blessings of the day without reaching for something else, hard as it was.

Bishop John left after greeting everyone in the shop, and Jacob realized Dinah was looking at him with a question on her face.

"Well?"

"I give up. You were right, as usual. Bishop John was as helpful as could be."

And hopeful, he added silently. He wanted to believe that the bishop was right about Anna's reason for sending Isaac home. Wanted to, but couldn't quite manage it. Wasn't it just as likely that she'd taken the easiest way? She knew there was no question but that he'd do as she wanted.

Shaking away the worry that gnawed at him, he reached toward the crib. "I'll take him . . ."

The bell in the harness shop rang, followed by the sound of the door closing and people's voices.

Dinah shook her head. "He's fine here for now, and it sounds like you have customers, ain't so?"

"Yah, denke, Dinah." He was already heading for the connecting door he'd left open. "I'll check back with you soon."

She waved him off, so Jacob hurried back to the harness shop. Four people had come in together—Englisch, a couple of women and two teenage girls. Horse people, he thought after a look. They most often came in early spring, getting ready for horse show season, but it wasn't unusual to have another rush this time of year.

He walked toward them and in a moment was swept up in their needs. All of them had horses, everyone wanted something, and one of the girls needed a custom-made leather headstall. Trying to answer several questions, he heard the door again and spotted another

Englischer, this one a young man in jeans and a denim jacket, a camera slung over his shoulder, stroll in and look around.

Jacob met his gaze, gesturing to the customers he was already working with, and the man shook his head. "I'll just look around. No hurry."

"No photos, please." Most Englischers around here knew enough not to take pictures without asking, but he didn't look like he was from around here.

Jacob pointed the others toward the pony harnesses and focused on getting the needed information about the headstall while answering questions about the harnesses and giving directions to the quilt shop to the other woman. They seemed to be on an all-day shopping expedition and probably ready to spend if they found what they wanted.

A busy half hour later he'd sold a pony harness, several utility halters, a lunge line, and, surprisingly, a leather belt he'd put on display for a friend. And he also had an order in hand for a top-of-the-line headstall as soon as he could make it.

After all that, he was surprised to find the stranger still waiting. He'd more than half expected him to have wandered off by this time.

"Sorry I kept you waiting so long." He moved toward the man, who was standing by a display of buggy whips. "What can I show you?"

"That's a good question." The man leaned back against the counter, looking at Jacob as if sizing him up. "I'm sure not in the market for whatever those people were looking for. No horses in my life."

Jacob frowned at him, puzzled and a little uneasy. If he didn't want what Jacob sold, why was he hanging around? He didn't, now that Jacob had a chance to study him, look like a horse person . . . he'd be more at home on a city street than in a stable.

"I don't understand," he said, trying to ignore the trickle of unease down his spine.

"It's easy," he said. "All I want to see is the baby. Anna's baby. And mine."

CHAPTER SIX

Dinah, hand on the connecting door to pull it open, froze at the words. Her mind refused to work for a moment, and then it spun into panic. Isaac's father? Could it really be?

If so, what were they going to do? Jacob wouldn't consider handing the baby over to a stranger, would he? But if the man really was Isaac's father, he might have no choice.

Common sense broke through the fear that gripped her. She closed the door gently, very aware of Isaac, cradled in her arms. She had to get in there to support Jacob, but first, Isaac had to be safe.

She grabbed Lovina before she could wait on the two men seated at a nearby table. "Take Isaac back into the kitchen, quick." She held the baby out to her sister, but Lovina didn't respond.

"I'm busy. Can't you—"

Dinah's temper flared. What a time for Lovina to revert to being a sulky teenager. "Do as I say," she snapped. "I'll explain later. Just do it."

She pushed Isaac into her sister's arms, not waiting for a response, and spun back to the door. A moment to catch her breath, a silent plea for help, and she was ready. She pushed open the door.

Jacob was staring at the man, his face unreadable to a stranger. But she could see the panic underneath the surface.

"I don't know what you're talking about," he said, his voice calm.

"Is something wrong?"

She knew it was a stupid question, but it might buy a little time for Jacob to think. She walked toward them, hoping the man wouldn't realize how odd it was for her to burst in.

He ignored her completely, focused on Jacob, but she could see his face now. It was the Englischer who'd been in for coffee and talked to Lovina . . . the one she'd thought out of place for a visiting tourist.

"You know what's wrong. Your sister Anna's baby. I know she sent the baby to you."

Studying him, Dinah compared him with the brief glimpse she'd had of the man in the car who'd picked Anna up. No, she didn't think so. This man seemed smaller, somehow—thin and wiry, not as big or broad shouldered, with a narrow, pointed face that reminded her of a fox.

Jacob's expression didn't change, but Dinah knew his heart must be pounding. "I have a sister named Anna, yah. What do you know about her?"

"Enough to spend plenty of time with her. Really personal time, you might say." He leaned a hip against the counter, looking ready to settle in for a stay. "Yeah, that's it. Personal."

His tone made it a slur, and Dinah had an urge to douse him with the dishwater from her kitchen.

Jacob was getting angry. It didn't happen often, but she could see it building in him at the man's words. The innuendos were enough to turn her stomach, and she could imagine what Jacob felt.

But he mustn't lose control. She felt certain of that. He had to find out what the man was really after.

She rushed into speech before Jacob could explode. "Why should Jacob believe you? You don't look like any friend of Anna's."

The man gave her a dismissive glance. "What's it got to do with you anyway? Stay out of it."

That sounded as if he didn't know that Anna had turned the baby over to her. She shot a look at Jacob, hoping to convey that information.

"I was like a sister to Anna from the time she was small," she said, striving for a calm she didn't feel. "Anything that involves Anna affects me."

"That's right." Jacob's glance told her he understood. It told her they were allied against this stranger. "If you were that close to Anna, surely you know who her friends and family are."

Dinah thought the stranger seemed to falter for a second. "We didn't talk about that. It doesn't matter. I have a right to see that baby."

"You say so." Jacob sounded more sure of himself now. "But I don't know anything about you. Not even your name. This could be a pack of lies."

"Yeah? Well, if this is my kid—" He stopped, as if he'd said something he hadn't intended.

"If?" Jacob pounced on it at once. "I think it's time you got out of here. We don't have anything to talk about."

The door opened, the bell ringing to announce another customer . . . Linda Markhan, one of the local horse people, who greeted Jacob cheerfully, smiled at Dinah, and sent an inquiring look toward the stranger.

"Can I do something for you today, Ms. Markhan?" Jacob turned to her rather deliberately.

"I can wait if you're busy," she said, waving a hand at the stranger.

"No problem." The man slouched toward the door. "I'm going, for now. If you hear from your sister, just tell her Nate Smith was here."

Jacob's face hardened, but he didn't speak.

The man didn't seem to expect an answer. He looked around the shop as if he were appraising it. "Nice place you have here. Worth a lot, I'd say."

He went out, letting the door slam behind him.

Shaking a little, Dinah leaned against the nearest counter. Of all the problems she'd foreseen, this had been the furthest thing from her mind. Was it possible this man really was Isaac's father?

Her instinctive reaction was to reject the notion. Anna wouldn't have been involved with someone like that. She didn't believe it.

But did she really know what Anna had become since she left her home?

She had to talk this over with Jacob, but they couldn't do anything with Ms. Markhan here. She struggled to contain herself and marveled at Jacob's ability to focus on his customer. She could only imagine what it cost him to keep a smile and a look of interest on his face until Ms. Markhan, satisfied with the repairs he'd made to her show bridle, had left.

"I don't believe it." The words burst from her the instant they were alone. "That man couldn't be Isaac's father."

"Why not?" Jacob turned a ravaged face to her for an instant. Then, just as quickly, he clamped his mouth shut. "I can't talk about it." He ground the words out through clenched teeth. "Just leave it for now, Dinah. I need to think."

Dinah went through her own struggle to contain herself. Her instinct was all for getting this out in the open. "We have to talk it over and decide what to do."

He turned away, his fist clenching around a bridle as if he'd pull it apart with his bare hands. "He's *my* nephew." His voice was harsh.

Dinah stared at him for a moment. Was he really trying to shut her out? He couldn't. She wouldn't let him.

"If you need time before talking about it, I understand." At least, she'd try to. "He's your nephew, yah. But Anna gave him to me."

Seized by an urgent need to see that Isaac was all right, she spun and rushed back to her shop.

IF JACOB HAD thought he could keep this new crisis to himself, he realized only too quickly that it was impossible. Not only did Dinah feel she had a stake in what happened with Isaac, her whole family felt that way. They considered Isaac a part of their family, too, and they weren't backward about saying so.

By the time Jacob had heard from everyone that evening, including young Will, who proposed to sleep on the floor by the crib to protect Isaac, he was ready to admit that he had to accept help. And that he certain sure wasn't alone.

Once the younger members of the family had settled down, Jacob found himself gathered into the group around the kitchen table. Dinah's mother and grandmother were vocal about what had to be done. Micah, at nineteen considering himself more worldly than the others, said they should go to the police, but Dinah's mother was firm in her insistence that the police could only mean more trouble and Isaac must be kept safe.

Jacob found himself watching John Stoltz, Dinah's father. John didn't say much—he'd always been quiet and given to few words, unlike Jacob's outgoing father. John was a born farmer, he'd guess, most happy when he was communing with his animals and his crops. Jacob had often seen him sitting back at ease, watching and listening to his lively family with a quiet smile.

Dinah was like him, Jacob realized. They both had a quiet enjoyment of life, a fund of common sense, and a generous heart. Dinah's confidence had been dented by her marriage, but beneath, she was the same.

John had sat listening to everyone's opinion, and now, Jacob thought, he was ready to speak. John put his coffee mug down on the table with a firm hand. As if it were a signal, the others grew quiet.

"Seems to me we need to start at the beginning with this fellow. Who is he?"

Jacob shook his head. "We don't know, ain't so, Dinah? He says his name is Nate Smith, but we don't know if that's true." Jacob considered that. "I guess there wouldn't be much point to using a fake name, anyway. The name doesn't tell us anything helpful."

"It might be a way to find out if he's staying in town," John pointed out, his tone mild.

"Sure," Micah said, brightening. "I could check around the motels and see if he's registered anywhere." He reached toward his pocket, which Jacob suspected harbored a cell phone like most teenagers, and then stopped before his father could see. Getting up, he gestured vaguely toward the door. "I'll go out to the phone shanty and check."

"I don't know—" Jacob began, but Micah was already out the door.

"Gives him something to do," John said easily. "If the man is sticking around, you'll have to be ready for him to show up again." He glanced at Dinah. "Does he know the baby was with you when he came in?"

"I'm not sure." Dinah seemed to picture the scene. "I don't think so, but it wouldn't be hard to find out. Almost anyone in town could tell him that much. That's why we need to think about keeping Isaac safe."

A shiver seemed to go over her as she said the words, and Jacob had to reject the impulse to clasp her hand.

"We will. I'm just sorry to have involved—"

"Don't be ferhoodled," Dinah said, and the others nodded agreement. "We were involved from the moment I heard Anna's voice on the phone."

"That's so." John paused in the process of filling the pipe he smoked in the evening. "Let's stick to the subject. The man claims to be Isaac's father. Do you think that's true?"

"No," Dinah said instantly.

"Maybe," Jacob countered. "How can you be sure he's not?"

She hesitated, as if arranging her thoughts. "He didn't seem to know enough," she said finally. "Not about you, not about Anna's life here. If they'd been . . . together, you'd think he'd know that. And anyway, he said *if* he was the father." She said that as if it clinched the matter.

"Maybe," he said again, sticking to his feelings. "But if he isn't, what would the point be in saying he is?"

"Money," she said, looking at him as if he were daft. "Don't you remember how he looked around the shop before he left and commented on what it was worth? Maybe he thinks you'd pay him to go away and not make trouble."

"Surely no one would do that." Dinah's mother, with

her innate belief in the goodness of people, looked distressed, but her father nodded gravely.

"Could be," he said.

Jacob considered. "If that's what it takes to make him go away and leave us alone, it might be worth it."

"No." John leaned toward him. "You can't do that. It would be like admitting he is Isaac's father. And that wouldn't keep him away. He'd come back for more."

Jacob saw his point. "Yah. I guess you're right. He was the kind of person I wouldn't give credit to if he wanted to buy something."

Dinah's tense face relaxed in a sudden smile, making him smile in return.

Micah, sliding his cell phone out of sight, came back just then. "He's staying at the Bluebird Motel out near the highway. Mike Foster's the night manager there, so he told me. Said the guy just registered for one night. They make them pay in advance."

Jacob caught on to what Micah meant. Smith, if that was really his name, wouldn't want to pay more than he had to.

"I was thinking," Micah went on. "Maybe he should take a DNA test, like folks do to see if their children might have some disease. That should prove it one way or another."

All the adults knew about the genetic diseases that plagued some Amish families. And about the clinic over near Burnside that did the test.

"I don't know," Jacob said slowly. "I mean, we couldn't make him do it. And the law might get involved. Maybe they'd say Anna abandoned him."

"They couldn't," Dinah protested. "She just asked us to take care of him for a time." Her voice faltered at the end, probably because Anna hadn't said anything about coming back. Ever.

Jacob's heart winced as he thought of Isaac, peacefully asleep in his crib upstairs. Anger with his sister jolted him. He should be sorry for Anna, not angry.

"Anna should have realized this might get complicated. You can't just hand a baby over to someone. We don't have anything in the way of papers. Not even a birth certificate."

Silence stretched across the table as they considered that.

"We know Anna wants him to stay here." Dinah's gaze met his, and she sounded as firm as a rock. "That's what counts."

"Yah, but we can't prove it." He spoke directly to Dinah, as if they were the only ones in the room. "If we could . . . if we even had it in writing . . ."

Dinah's green eyes sparked with an idea. "That woman—the one you talked to that day in Williamsport who knew Anna. What about her? If she knew what was happening, how serious it is, maybe she could get in touch with Anna. Someone has to tell Anna what's going on."

"Maybe," he said slowly, not sure he had much hope of that. Still, it was a chance, however small. "I could try, anyway. Lacey Gaus was her name. I'd best speak to her in person. I have the address."

That clearly encouraged Dinah. She wanted to believe it would work, of course.

He wanted to believe it, too, but he didn't know if he could.

Anna, where are you? You've left us with more of a problem than you even dreamed of.

BY SATURDAY MORNING, Dinah was struggling to hold on to the optimism she'd felt so briefly the previous night. True, Jacob had agreed to write a letter to Anna, and he planned to spend the day in Williamsport if necessary, talking to the woman he'd met and waiting around on the chance that Anna would be willing to speak to him.

But he hadn't looked very optimistic when he climbed into Charlie Nelson's car. She'd pinned a smile to her face and waved him off before she kissed Isaac goodbye, left him with Mammi, and headed into town with Lovina.

Midway through the morning, Dinah realized that all the customers in the world couldn't distract her from worrying. First she would picture Jacob's approach to the one person who might be able to link them to Anna. And when she succeeded in dismissing that, she'd start wondering how Mammi and Grossmammi were doing with Isaac.

Not that they didn't have far more experience than she did in taking care of babies. Isaac couldn't do any better than be with them. Because she was only open until noon, it had made sense to leave him home.

But what if that Englischer, Nate Smith, came to the farm? It was useless to try to convince herself that he couldn't know Isaac was there. A few questions asked around town would give the man any answers he needed.

Mamm had little experience dealing with outsiders, and none at all in handling someone like that man. Of course, Daad and her brothers were there. They wouldn't let anything happen to the baby.

"Dinah!" The tone of her sister's voice told her it wasn't the first time Lovina had tried to get her attention.

She blinked, shaking off her imaginings. "Sorry, Lovina. What is it?"

"I said, since it's so quiet right now, is it okay if I go out for a bit?" Lovina had her hands on her apron ties, as if ready to pull it off and plunge toward the door.

"Out where?" she asked, reminding herself that she was responsible for Lovina when she was here. At fifteen, Lovina wasn't as mature as she thought she was.

Lovina shrugged. "Just out. Maybe walk down the street and look in the shop windows. Nothing wrong with that, is there?"

Lovina was ready to take offense, and Dinah really didn't want to argue. "Yah, all right. Just be back in time to help me clear up so we can close at noon."

Half a day was plenty long enough to be open on Saturday, especially because not many of the hoped-for visitors had turned up in town this weekend. It wasn't surprising, as the leaves had just begun to turn and the weather had become rainy.

"Denke." Lovina had shed her apron and gone just as quickly as if she'd been sure of the answer.

Well, she was young enough that it was still a treat to walk along and window-shop, although fifteen wasn't really so young, either. She was wobbling on the boundary between girl and woman.

That reminded her of Mammi's concerns. Lovina would be sixteen and ready for rumspringa soon. So much depended on a girl getting into the right group at that time. Not that there were any Amish kids who were very wild in this area, but just one person who was discontented with Amish life and wanted to flout the rules could influence someone like Lovina, with her impatience and her volatility.

Dinah had already started to clean up when Lovina reappeared. She glanced at the clock but managed not to say anything about the time. Ten minutes here or there didn't mean a lot, but if Lovina started taking advantage, she'd have to deal with it.

"I'll take that." Lovina grabbed the tray from her

hands and carried coffee cups into the kitchen. "I'll have them washed in no time."

Her mood had certainly improved, making Dinah wonder if that was solely the effect of window-shopping. She walked into the kitchen behind her sister, carrying the coffee urn.

"Did you run into anyone you know?" she asked, trying to sound casual.

"No, why would I?" Lovina was instantly alert.

Dinah busied herself with the urn. "You might. Some people have errands in town on Saturday, especially if they work the rest of the week."

"Yah, I guess." She rinsed cups. "I did see Alma Esch and her mother looking at fabric. If she's making a new dress, I hope she stays away from pink. It makes her look as pale as a sheet."

Restored to a happier mood, Lovina chattered about dresses and fabric colors until they'd finished, and continued until they were most of the way home. As they turned into the farm lane, Dinah commented that Lovina would be able to buy material for a new dress herself with the money she'd earned this week.

Lovina pulled up at the back door, flushing a little. "I was thinking about that. Maybe a sort of medium green. That looks nice with my eyes, right? Do you want me to put the buggy away?"

Dinah shook her head. "I'm going over to Sarah's for lunch, remember? We're trying to finish up a wedding quilt for Dorcas Beiler. That wedding will be here before we know it."

After checking to be sure that Isaac was fine and no strangers had been spotted around the farm, Dinah drove the four miles down the road to Sarah's, where she found Noah and the twins eager to deal with the horse and buggy.

"Sarah's waiting for you, and you'll be happy to know that we guys already had lunch." Noah lifted the twins to the buggy seat. "We'll just put the mare in the shed in case it comes on to rain again."

"Denke." With a smile for each of the boys, Dinah hurried to where Sarah held the door open for her. "Don't stand there in the damp," she urged, drawing Sarah inside and shutting the door. "I'm sure it's not good for you."

Sarah, laughing, hugged her. "I'm not sick, Dinah. You sound like Noah. Komm, we'll eat."

The kitchen table had two places set, and Sarah quickly put out a basket of rolls, a bowl of chicken salad, and another of fruit salad. "I thought we could eat and talk first, then see where we are with the quilt."

"Lovely." She relaxed with a sigh.

"You've been worried, yah? Is it about the baby? He's all right, isn't he?"

Dinah held back for about a minute, and then the need to unburden herself swamped her. So she told Sarah the whole thing, reasoning that, as Anna's cousin, she had a right to know what was happening.

Sarah's face grew serious as Dinah talked about the stranger who'd shown up, and Sarah nodded when she heard about Jacob's attempt to contact Anna.

"Anna must make up her mind," she said finally. "If she truly doesn't want that precious boy, he'll grow up happy and loved here, ain't so? But she has to do her part to ensure he's safe."

"That's what Jacob thinks. I . . . honestly, I didn't think sensibly at all when Anna thrust the baby at me. But she didn't give me a chance to talk to her. I suppose she was afraid I'd try to get her to return." She paused. "I didn't have any choice except to bring Isaac back with me. I couldn't have gone to the police station, could I?

And I certain sure didn't give any thought to who the father was at that point."

"Who would in that situation?" Sarah's usually serene face was troubled. "Does Jacob think she'll come home?"

"I don't know. I'm not sure he knows what he thinks, other than to do his best for Isaac." She smiled gently, thinking of holding the baby close in her arms and feeling his soft breath against her cheek.

Sarah put her hand over Dinah's. "You're thinking about the baby, yah? I know that look. You wish he was yours."

Sarah had struck right to the heart of her feelings. Dinah swallowed with difficulty. "Yah," she murmured. "I love him. I'd do anything to keep him safe, but there isn't anything I can do."

"Maybe loving him is enough for now," Sarah said softly. "You and Jacob together—you'd make fine, loving parents for that little boy. Maybe that's the answer."

Dinah felt the heat rise in her cheeks, and she tried to evade the suggestion that she and Jacob might belong together.

"We . . . I'm sure Jacob doesn't think that way about me. And besides, I can't."

For an instant, she longed to tell Sarah everything—to pour out her pain over Aaron's attitude, to share what seemed his rejection. But she couldn't talk that way about Aaron. She couldn't tell anyone.

Realizing that Sarah was watching her with concern, she tried to find something to say. She sought to relax her tense throat.

"You understand, don't you? How could I marry, knowing I might never be able to give my husband a child?"

Sarah shook her head, a faint smile touching her lips

as if she was remembering something. "Men aren't all alike. You might find someone who will love you for yourself, not for any babies you might have."

The words soothed her aching heart, as Sarah had intended. But she couldn't convince herself that they'd come true.

CHAPTER SEVEN

By the time Jacob was nearing home on Saturday, he'd lost whatever optimism he'd had earlier. He felt as if he were groping in a fog, trying hard to find something secure to grasp. But there wasn't anything, no matter how he tried.

"Just let me off at the Stoltz lane, Charlie. And thanks. I appreciate it." He handed the payment to the driver as they pulled up.

"No problem." Charlie hesitated, looking embarrassed. "Listen, don't take offense, but my wife said to say we're praying for you. And the baby."

Jacob's throat tightened. "Denke. I could never take offense at that. The more prayers the better. Please tell her I'm thankful to have friends like you."

Charlie gave a short nod, and Jacob expected he was relieved to have gotten the words out. He didn't doubt that Elsie, Charlie's wife, would ask him about it as soon as he reached home.

The car moved off, and he started slowly down the lane. When he got to the house, everyone would want to hear what happened. They'd all be gathered in the kitchen at this time of day, waiting for him.

It didn't make sense to feel annoyed at that, but he couldn't stop. He'd had enough frustration without having to repeat it to other people.

They aren't just other people, his conscience reminded him. *They're good neighbors, and they love Anna and Isaac, too. If only . . .*

The sound of a buggy startled him, and he swung around to see Dinah driving up behind him. She pulled up when she reached him, and he knew she was studying his face. At least he didn't have to put on a good front for Dinah.

"No good news?"

He shook his head, realizing he didn't have to say more than he wanted with her. And knowing, too, that telling her wouldn't be difficult. It would be a relief. Even so, he hesitated.

"What are you doing out on the road at this hour?" he asked.

"Sarah and I are doing a wedding quilt for Dorcas. It's a good thing it's almost ready for the final quilting, because we're running out of time."

He nodded, not knowing whether she was referring to next month's wedding or Sarah and Noah's baby. But it didn't matter. It had been something to say, that's all. Dinah started to draw up at the porch, but he shook his head.

"Go on back to the barn. I'll help with the mare."

Dinah didn't argue. She drove on toward the barn, maybe realizing that he was putting off the moment of talking about his trip to Williamsport. But by the time they reached the barn, he knew he was ready.

"Wish I had better news." He pushed the buggy to its proper place and returned to the mare, taking the side of the harness across from Dinah automatically.

"You didn't talk to the woman after all?" Dinah

started unbuckling the harness, seeming just as glad to look at what she was doing.

"Yah, I did. It wasn't all bad, I guess. In fact, once they realized why I was there, she and her husband both were . . ." He groped for the word. "Kind, I guess. Not what I expected from him. He was antagonistic when I was there before."

"He's former Amish, ain't so?" She seemed to jump to the realization faster than he had.

He nodded, hesitating with his arm across the mare's shoulders. "I didn't mean to let it all out, not knowing how they'd react. I felt kind of foolish, letting strangers see how I felt."

"Maybe it was the best thing you could have done. Maybe that's what made them willing to help." Dinah's hand brushed his as she reached for a harness strap. "Ain't so?"

He had to admit that she was right. "The woman felt sorry for me . . . for us. Especially when I told them about that man—Nate Smith—and what he said."

"Did they know anything about him?" Dinah asked eagerly, and he realized she'd been worrying as much as he had.

"I'm not sure." He thought back over the conversation. "All they told me was that they'd heard the name. There might have been more but they didn't seem willing to say anything."

"Maybe it was best not to push too much. If you antagonized them, they wouldn't tell you anything."

His hand caught the strap and tightened on it. "It's so frustrating. If I make a misstep . . . if I say the wrong thing . . . it could make matters even worse."

"Don't, Jacob." Her voice went soft, and she patted his hand. "All any of us can do is our best."

"What if that's not good enough?" His anguish broke

through, and he grasped her hand, squeezing it as if it were a lifeline. "The baby . . ." His throat cramped, and he couldn't say anything else.

"I know," she whispered, and he realized there were tears in her eyes. It suddenly seemed the most important thing in the world to keep Dinah from weeping.

"It wasn't all bad," he said quickly. "Really, Dinah. I shouldn't have said so much. At least they promised to try and get my letter to Anna and to let me know right away."

"That's good, isn't it?" Her tears receded. "That must mean they know where she is."

"Maybe. Or think they can find her. They said they'd go into town and try a couple of people. They wouldn't let me go with them, but they had me wait at a park in case they could find her and bring her to me."

"It didn't work?"

"No." He clenched his teeth, reliving the disappointment he'd felt after hours of waiting, only to hear they couldn't find her.

The mare moved restlessly, maybe thinking this was going on too long. He forced himself back to the moment. "Let's finish this." He lifted the harness from the mare's back, and Dinah led her to the nearest stall. The mare stepped inside and immediately buried her head in the feed. By the time Dinah turned back, he'd hung up the harness and stood there, his mind blank, unable to think what to do next.

She came to him quickly, taking both his hands in hers. "Ach, Jacob, don't look so sad. Surely they'll keep trying to contact Anna, won't they?"

"Yah." He tried to shake off the wave of helplessness that had overcome him. "They said they'd try. They said they'd keep in touch. But if they don't—"

"Hush." She took a step toward him, their clasped hands linked between them. "You mustn't think that way. There has to be an answer. We have to trust, Jacob. Trust."

He wanted to reject that hope, but it was the only thing he had to cling to. And Dinah was the only person he could cling to.

As soon as the thought formed in his mind, he was horrified at himself. He couldn't rely on Dinah that much. He couldn't. She could be hurt so badly.

But her gaze met his, and her green eyes were filled with hope. He moved closer, unable to hold back, longing to close the space between them. For what seemed an eternity they stood, so near, and he could feel her caring and hope flowing into him.

Finally he let out a long breath, feeling renewed. He stepped back, trying to smile. "We . . . we'd best go inside. They'll be wondering."

"Yah." She gave him a bemused smile, and together they walked toward the back door. They were several feet apart, and yet Jacob imagined he could still feel her hands meeting his, keeping the fear for Isaac away.

They went up the steps to the back porch and on into the house. The whole family seemed to be waiting in the kitchen. As soon as they stepped inside, Dinah's mother burst into speech.

"At last you've come. Dinah, he was here. That man you told us about. He was here."

DINAH FROZE FOR an instant, and her mind flew to Isaac. "Is Isaac all right?" She was already moving toward the stairs.

"Yah, he's fine," Daad said. "Nothing happened."

She believed him, of course, but still, she had to see for herself. Dinah hurried up the stairs and eased open the bedroom door. Her little brother Will jumped to his feet, and when he saw that it was her, he sank back down into the rocking chair.

"Shh." He nodded toward the crib. "He's asleep. Nobody will get near him while I'm here."

"I know," she whispered, brushing the silky, straw-colored hair across his forehead. "Denke, Will."

Strange, how her little brother had attached himself so firmly to the baby. He couldn't have been more protective if Isaac were his own brother. As far as he was concerned, Isaac was part of the family. She could see it so easily because it was exactly how she felt, too.

Moving softly, she went to the crib and looked down at Isaac, sprawled on his back in complete relaxation. His cheeks were rosy, and breath moved audibly through his pink lips. She reached out to touch him, very lightly, just to reassure herself.

Then she stepped back, reality intruding. She'd best go down and get the whole story of what had happened. Maybe they should have expected it, but it seemed so unreal. Somehow there was a scary difference between a stranger entering the shop and one actually coming to their home.

Nodding to Will, who apparently intended to stay on guard, she slipped back downstairs to where the others were gathered in the kitchen. When she saw Mammi's distressed face, she felt upset all over again.

"I'm sorry, Mammi. I should never have left him."

"Ach, don't be so foolish," Daad said quickly. The others joined him in a murmur of agreement.

Except for Jacob. He just looked at her, face expressionless. So. Those moments when they were in complete harmony were gone already as if they'd never been. He blamed her.

Mammi glanced at the clock and got up. "Komm, Lovina. We must get supper on."

Daad's eyes twinkled at her. "You can talk while you work, ain't so?"

Mamm's gaze met his for a moment. That was complete harmony, Dinah thought, watching them. What she'd thought had happened with Jacob hadn't been real after all.

"Did he come right up to the door?" she asked, taking a stack of plates and beginning to distribute them automatically. "That takes a lot of nerve."

"He wasn't lacking that," Mammi said. "He drove right up the lane. Then he stopped and came to the front door." She paused, emphasizing the fact that in the country, everyone came to the back door.

"Just as well," Daad said. "Isaac was in his cot in the kitchen, so there was no chance he'd see him."

"I didn't even think of that," Mamm said, pausing in whatever she was stirring on the stove to stand, wooden spoon in the air, dripping. "I knew it must be him, and when he said he wanted to see Isaac, I was just so shaken I couldn't talk. He probably thought I couldn't speak Englisch." She laughed at herself. "Thank the gut Lord your daadi and the boys came right away."

"There was no fuss or trouble," Daad said quickly.

"You don't know what he might have done if I'd been here by myself," Mammi snapped. "He wouldn't have been so polite then."

"I wouldn't say he was polite."

Daad and Mamm seemed to embark on one of those meaningless spates of correcting each other that drove their kinder crazy. Mamm had been known to spend a half hour arguing about whether something happened on a Monday or a Tuesday, and Daad was just as bad. Silly as it sounded, she thought they enjoyed it.

"What happened?" she broke in before it could go on. "Did he try to convince you?"

"Didn't give him a chance," Daad said tersely. "I just said unless he could show us proof, he wasn't going to see Anna's baby. And I kept saying it no matter how he blustered until he went away."

Jacob nodded, seeming relieved. "I guess there's no other way to handle it. If he pushed too much—"

"Ach, no worry about that. I don't think he'd be any more anxious for us to call the police than we would be to do it."

"It makes me think he doesn't have any proof," Micah interjected. "He was just blustering. Maybe trying to get money to drop it."

"You don't know that." Lovina dropped a pan lid on the stove. "What if he really is Isaac's daadi? If he was, it would be terrible to keep him away from his little baby."

"It would be more terrible to let him cause trouble," Dinah snapped, her nerves stretched thin. "We have to take care of Isaac, just like Anna said."

In the face of the general acceptance of Dinah's statement, Lovina backed down, but the rebellious expression on her face made Dinah uneasy.

"We can't do anything until we hear from Anna." Jacob's tone was final. At the sound of a slight wail from upstairs, he stood. "Denke." He looked from Daad to Mammi to Micah. "Let's just pray it's soon."

He turned toward the stairs, and Mammi looked questioningly at Dinah. Dinah waited until she'd heard his footsteps recede up the stairs.

"It's not all bad news," she said quickly. "He talked to those people who help Amish runaways, and they understand the situation. They said they'd do everything they can to get in touch with Anna." She put her hand to the tension in her neck, trying to rub it away. "I don't see what else we can do."

Ach, Jacob. Her heart ached. *Won't you let me help you? That's all I want, just to help.*

And then she wondered if that was really true. Was that all she hoped for from Jacob?

SUNDAY STARTED EARLY, as it always did, with much to be done before they left for worship. Dinah fed and dressed Isaac, laughing at his efforts to roll away while she fastened his diaper.

They'd talked everything over the previous night. Should they take Isaac to worship or should someone stay home with him? Jacob had been reluctant to take him, and Dinah wasn't sure why. Everyone in the community had surely heard about Anna's baby by now, and the bishop's visit should have wiped away any doubts.

Grossmammi had finally settled it. Isaac was part of the Leit now, and he should be with his family for worship. That was what was right, whether Anna was here or not. She had looked firmly at Jacob, and he had nodded. So Isaac went to worship, cradled in his uncle's arms for the ride to the farm that hosted worship today.

When they reached the Fisher place, young Adam Fisher and several of his cousins came hurrying to take the buggies, obviously pleased with their role as hostlers this Sunday. Jacob handed Isaac to Dinah, got down, and then lifted them both down. He stood for a moment looking at them, tucking Isaac's little jacket firmly against the morning chill.

"You'll be all right?" A faint frown appeared, as if he still questioned whether they should be here.

"Yah, for sure." She trusted that she sounded confident.

Mammi moved beside her. "It will be fine, Jacob. This is where Isaac belongs."

His frown didn't altogether vanish, but he nodded. With a final look, he headed for the spot where the men and boys lined up to enter the barn, which had been cleaned until it shone for hosting worship. Because Lucas Fisher was one of the ministers, he'd have expected it to be spotless, and everyone in the family from oldest to youngest would have spent the last week making it so.

They took their places in the line of women and small children, just behind Sarah and her mother-in-law, who was clearly keeping a caring eye on the daughter-in-law who would shortly give her another grandchild. Soft-voiced greetings were exchanged, with much cooing over Isaac, sleeping in Dinah's arms.

Sarah seized the moment when they started to move into worship to whisper in Dinah's ear. "Was Jacob successful yesterday?"

She shrugged slightly. "He didn't make contact, but he talked to people who will try to find her."

Sarah's response was a gentle pat on her arm, but it was good to know Sarah was with her. They entered the barn, filing into benches on the women's side. Lovina, who had hurried away from her parents' eyes as quickly as possible, came in with the girls her age, just as her brothers would be with their age groups. Mammi frowned slightly at the boys, probably wondering how much she could trust Will, who had only recently been allowed to sit with the other boys instead of with Daad.

When they were settled on the bench, Mammi slid the diaper bag between them on the floor, and Dinah wondered again if she'd included everything baby Isaac could possibly need for the next few hours. Mammi was ready and eager to help; that was certain sure. At least he was asleep for the moment. How long he would stay that way was anyone's guess.

She snuggled him a little closer against her. The barn

was warming already from the press of bodies, and the bright sunshine was promising another mild day for the beginning of October. Isaac would be fine, and there was an extra blanket in the bag in case of need. Soon they'd be worshipping at the homes of folks who had sites more easily heated, but for today, the barn was a fine place to be.

The faint murmur of voices while folks settled died down, and Dinah glanced around the benches near them. Some quick, curious glances met her, but that was only natural. The test would come after worship ended, when people would either press near to welcome little Isaac or . . .

She dismissed that possibility. Where the bishop went, others would surely follow, wouldn't they? People would have heard that the bishop had visited. Word like that went around the community quickly.

Silence stretched out, and there was no sound but the whisper of the breeze through the barn loft. Then the song leader lifted his voice in the long, wavering note of the first hymn, and worship had begun.

Isaac slept on, as peacefully as if he slept in his own crib, right through the first part of the three-hour worship. Dinah let her gaze roam over the women seated in front of her. Dorcas sat with the other unmarried women, though she wouldn't be there for long. A little mental arithmetic told her that the marriage would probably be announced soon—probably at the next worship. By then, wedding season would be underway, and it would be a challenge to fit in all the weddings.

She glanced at Sarah, giving a slight nod toward Dorcas, and Sarah nodded, smiling. It wouldn't be long, but then, neither would the arrival of Sarah's baby. Sarah might well find that the decision to attend the wedding was made for her by the new baby. If it happened, she wouldn't mind, Dinah felt sure. So many joys were in store for them.

Isaac held his peace until the long sermon began, when he let out a wail. Jacob's face jerked toward them as if a string attached him to his small nephew. Mammi, always prepared, already had the bottle out of the insulated bag. She gestured, and Dinah transferred the baby to her arms as planned. Mammi, having raised as many kinder as she had, believed in planning just what they'd do throughout the service, with the possibility of taking Isaac out as a last resort.

Dinah stretched unobtrusively. Holding a baby that long while sitting on a backless bench was not so easy. But when she thought of all those years when she'd longed to be one of those mothers with babies in worship, it was pure joy.

Finally the service drew to a close. Dinah's nerves stretched thin as she prepared to rise, Isaac again in her arms. This would be the moment. They'd soon know how the congregation felt about having Anna's baby here. For what seemed an endless time, she stood holding him close. Then there was a rustle of movement behind her, and the bishop's wife, beaming, squeezed in next to her, followed closely by the wives of the ministers.

Almost instantly it seemed that every one of the married women crowded close, eager to coo over the new baby. Isaac, with a fine sense of what was right, burbled and cooed and smiled. No one, she thought, could resist smiling back, especially at the sight of the dimples in his chubby cheeks.

Jacob managed to squeeze his way next to her. Anyone else looking at him would probably only see his usual ready smile and cheerfulness. She saw the tension that gradually eased with each person who talked to him and admired Isaac.

"You see," she murmured in a quiet voice. "Everyone is happy to welcome Isaac home."

His smile was like Isaac's then—innocent and happy.

But a moment later someone mentioned Anna. Jacob's face tightened a little, but she was relieved to see that it was with caring and concern, not tension.

"We have hope that she will soon come home where she belongs," he said, his deep voice calm. "That is what we are waiting for . . . for her to take her right place as Isaac's mother."

Only the strongest of wills kept the smile on Dinah's face. She wanted Anna to return. Of course she did. But when she did, then neither Isaac nor Jacob would have any need for her. And she didn't know how she would bear it.

CHAPTER EIGHT

Dinah sat in the bedroom rocking chair that evening, Isaac a sleepy bundle in her arms. The room was quiet, but from downstairs sounds floated up, blurred to a gentle background rumble. She could make out Jacob's deep voice and her brothers' lighter ones, threaded with laughter as they came in from after-supper chores.

Jacob fit into the family as if he'd always been there, and his voice contributed to the soft music that meant home to her. She remembered hearing that murmur of voices from downstairs when she was a small girl, lying under the quilt in this same room. It had lulled her to sleep at night, making her feel cocooned in warmth and safety.

Isaac gave a soft murmur, his eyes drifting closed, his pink lips pursed as if he still sucked on his bottle. She could put him in the crib now, she knew, but still she lingered just for the pure pleasure of holding him. She'd cherish these moments, trying not to think about how soon they might end.

Guilt nibbled at the edges of her joy. She couldn't stop praying for Anna to come home, even though the prayer might not be as wholehearted as it should be.

When or if Anna appeared to claim her little boy, Dinah would lose him. And she'd lose the closeness to Jacob she'd begun to count on.

Now she knew why Mammi had seemed reluctant to have her take on the role of caring for Isaac. She had foreseen this result, and she'd known Dinah would end up being hurt. That hurt was inevitable, and she could already feel the pain. And yet, as her grandmother said, pain was a risk of loving.

It was worth it, according to Grossmammi. Sometimes she wanted to argue with that idea, but she couldn't. These moments were worth whatever she would lose in the end.

The door creaked, and Jacob appeared in the opening. He tiptoed across the room to her, his gaze fixed on Isaac. "Is he asleep yet?"

"Almost." She smiled down at Isaac's small face. "It's all right to talk softly. It doesn't seem to disturb him. Maybe it sounds like a lullaby."

"Good boy," he said softly, cradling Isaac's head with his hand. "He is, isn't he?"

"A perfect baby." She rose, nodding to the rocker. "Why don't you sit down with him for a few minutes? That'll give me a chance to finish getting the room ready for the night."

In another moment Jacob was settled in the rocking chair, holding Isaac just as close as she had. The rocker gave its familiar creaking as he pushed it back and forth. Isaac sighed and melted a little further toward sleep, and Jacob watched him with loving eyes.

If Anna should take him away, it would break Jacob's heart. Still, so far as she could tell, he sincerely longed for her return.

Dinah moved softly around the room, disposing of the used diaper, putting the daytime clothes in the hamper, and then smoothing the sheet on the crib. She hesitated for a moment, but then turned down her bed so it was ready to slip into when she came back up.

"It was a gut day, ain't so?" Jonah didn't look up as he asked the question. "The Leit certain sure welcomed him."

She didn't need to school her face not to show her feelings, but she did anyway. "I knew it would be that way. You shouldn't worry about his acceptance. He's part of the community the same as if he'd been born here." She paused for an instant, not sure whether to say the comment that was on her lips. "So many people remembered Anna as a baby and said he looked like her."

"Yah." He sounded at peace about it, maybe feeling that a hurdle had been leaped. "It's the dimples, ain't so? When Anna returns, they'll welcome her, too."

She hesitated, a crib blanket in her hand. *When*, Jacob said, not *if*.

"She'll have to confess, of course." She said the words cautiously, not wanting to hurt him. But he knew as well as she did that confession and repentance were part of being restored to the fellowship again.

"She will." He sounded confident, his gaze still on Isaac. "What else can she do if she wants Isaac to have a happy life?"

He didn't seem to consider the fact that Anna might come home only to take Isaac away with her. One part of her longed to protect Jacob's feelings, while another wondered if she should warn him that Anna's return wouldn't necessary end all the problems.

Jacob looked at her then. "You're thinking that I'm ignoring the other possibility. That I'm being too optimistic."

"No, I . . ." She flushed, realizing that he had known her thoughts.

He shook his head. "I know. I know that it may not work out that way. But I have to have hope, Dinah. I let my little sister down. That means I let down Mamm and Daad, too. If I can see Anna and her baby settled back here where they belong, I'll have made up for that just a little."

"Ach, Jacob, it wasn't your fault that Anna left. So many griefs came one after another, and that affected her. And she was always curious about the outside world, more than most girls her age. You couldn't have stopped her if she was determined to go."

But he didn't believe her. She could see that.

"Denke, Dinah. You're a wonderful gut person, but it can't change what I know." He said it with finality. "You understand, don't you?"

The saddest thing was that she did understand. She knew him well enough to understand his sense of responsibility. He had a fierce need to take care of those who relied on him. All she could do was nod.

She stood for a moment, clutching the baby blanket against her heart. Then she managed to turn back to him and smile. "All ready. Is he asleep?"

"I think so." He got up slowly, holding the baby close, and brought him over to the crib. There he stopped, looking from Isaac down to the crib mattress. "Just put him down?"

She suppressed a chuckle. "That's all. You won't drop him."

Jacob lowered Isaac carefully. "It's like trying to hold pudding in your hands."

She did laugh then. "Yah, it is. Sleeping babies feel that way. You can let go of him now."

He slid his hands out from under Isaac, and she tucked the soft blanket around the small body. Isaac seemed to melt into the mattress.

"There. He'll have a gut sleep." She was careful not to mention the fact that he'd probably be wakeful in the middle of the night.

Jacob straightened, standing close to her as they looked down at the sleeping child. Then he closed his hand over hers where it rested on the crib railing.

"How can I tell you how much you mean to me . . . to both of us. Denke, Dinah. I couldn't do this without you."

He cares because he needs your help, she told herself desperately. *You can't think he means anything else, because he doesn't.*

"It's all right." She stumbled over the words, very conscious of the gentle touch of his hand, of the warmth of his skin against hers and the sense of him so close. She didn't want this moment to end, even though she knew it had to. "We . . . we'd better go down."

"Yah." She felt his breath touch her cheek. He kept his hand on hers so that they walked toward the door with their fingers entwined.

For a moment, she was able to let go of all her doubts. For a moment, she could just be happy.

"ACH, YOU'RE A bright boy, ain't so?" Jacob leaned over the cot they'd set up in his back room on Monday morning, talking to his nephew. Isaac babbled back at him, batting at the plastic bird that dangled over his head. His fingers connected and he grabbed it, looking so surprised that Jacob laughed out loud. It was a good thing his shop wasn't busy on Monday mornings, because it would be hard to tear himself away.

Gratitude swept over him . . . for Isaac, for the link he made with Anna, and for Dinah and her family, who made this possible. He could have found someone else to care for Isaac, true, but not like this, not having him so close at hand all the time.

He couldn't be surprised. After all, they'd been there helping in every problem throughout his life. He couldn't have had better neighbors.

The bell on the shop door jangled. He moved another toy into Isaac's line of sight and then walked through to the shop. Thomas Fisher came toward him, carrying an armload of harness.

"Thomas, gut to see you. Have a harness problem?"

Thomas nodded, the harness thudding onto the wooden countertop. "One you can help with, I hope. This belonged to my grossdaadi, and Daad passed it on to me. I thought I could recondition it myself in time for visiting after the wedding, but then I got a big carpentry job over in Grover." He shrugged. "I'm running out of time. Any chance you could do it?"

"Should be no problem." He pulled it through his fingers, noting that a few of the buckles would have to be replaced. The leather was sound, though. It had been cared for, at least. "I'll have it finished in time to wave goodbye to you and Dorcas." He grinned. "Going away far?"

The custom of visits to friends and relatives by the newly married couple hung on in the community. And with Thomas's father being one of the ministers, he was a stickler for tradition.

"Not as far as we could have. I want to go out to my aunt and uncle's, but we're going to wait until later, maybe in the early spring, so we can stay longer."

Jacob nodded, understanding. Thomas had lived with the relatives for several years while he honed his carpentry skills in his uncle's business.

"Besides, Dorcas promised to help out at the school for a time. She trained the new teacher, but I don't think she's ready to let go entirely. You know how she loves those scholars."

"Yah, I told young Will how fortunate he was to have Dorcas for a teacher." He chuckled, thinking of the past. "Remember when we were stuck with Hannah Gross filling in for a month? She couldn't teach for anything."

Thomas grinned. "I remember how you always looked innocent after the pranks you pulled. You had her fooled most of the time."

"Never fooled my daad, though." His smile faded a little as he wished Daad were here now to give him some sound advice.

A burbling little voice echoed through from the back room, and Thomas's smile deepened. "Got the boppli here with you, ain't so? I had a chance to see him after worship yesterday when Dinah's bruders were showing him off."

"Yah, they've been as gut to him as if he were their little bruder. Will says he's better at taking care of him."

"He would," Thomas said. "Won't catch my little bruders saying anything gut about me." But he smiled, showing how little he meant it. "I'd best be off. Hope all goes well for you. That baby is lucky to have you."

Jacob shook his head, smiling. "It's the other way round."

He raised his hand in farewell as Thomas went out, and then carried the harness to the workbench, his smile fading. It was wonderful good to see the happiness Thomas felt, settling into Promise Glen and finding love after his time away.

As always, his mind reverted to his own troubles. If only he could do a better job with Isaac than he had with Isaac's mother . . .

Before he could start any work, Dinah came through

the connecting door, carrying coffee and a large slice of streusel coffee cake.

"No jelly doughnuts today?" he asked, smiling.

"You'll have to make do with walnut streusel, I'm afraid."

"You know I love walnut streusel, too."

Her answering smile was not convincing, and he hesitated before taking the cup and plate. Setting them down on the countertop, he turned back to her.

"Was ist letz? What's wrong?"

"Don't get upset," she cautioned, and immediately his nerves tightened.

"What?" he demanded, shooting a gaze toward the door. "Don't tell me he's back. I hoped we were rid of him."

"He came in for coffee."

Jacob took a step toward the door, but Dinah moved in front of him, her hand up.

"Don't, Jacob. All he's doing is sitting there drinking coffee. He's not asking questions or bothering anyone."

"He's bothering me just by being there," he snapped. "If you don't want to tell him to leave, I will."

"No, you will not." She could be just as sharp as he could, apparently. "I can't refuse to serve someone who comes into my business, and neither can you. It's against the town ordinances for businesses. As long as he's not causing trouble, we can't do a thing."

His frown deepened, and the urge to move was almost too strong to resist. Almost. "I guess you're right. But I don't like it."

"I know. I don't, either, but at least he's there, not here." Her glance toward the back room showed what she was thinking. "Remember, I'm only open until noon today, so he'll have to leave then. I'll take Isaac home with me, and we'll be fine."

He must have looked doubtful, because she took a step closer, holding out her hand as if to plead with him. "I'll shout if I need you. You're only seconds away, remember?"

He remembered. With her standing so close to him, he remembered something more, too—those moments last night when he'd nearly taken her in his arms. He'd held her hand, he might have . . .

She had moved, made an excuse, not let him do anything foolish. She'd been right. He shouldn't even touch her unless he was serious. They weren't courting teenagers. He couldn't make a move unless he was thinking of marriage.

To be together with Dinah, to know he could rely on her goodness, her caring, to be a family with Isaac . . . The thought was tempting.

No, he couldn't. He knew better than to take on another responsibility. Hadn't he told himself that marriage wasn't for him?

Isaac was the most important consideration now. Isaac was helpless. He depended on them. Jacob couldn't do anything that could upset the careful balance that kept Isaac safe, no matter what the cost might be.

"Yah, all right," he mumbled, turning so she couldn't see his face. "Just call if you need me."

She didn't speak. She just hurried through the door, and it swung shut behind her.

DINAH FOUND SHE was breathless when she hurried back to her side of the building. At least she'd kept Jacob from creating still more trouble by confronting the man. That would have been a disaster. Nate Smith might even have complained to the police.

She considered that, casting a covert glance to where

he sat at a table near the front window. No, she didn't
think he'd be eager to talk to the police. Instinct, maybe,
but that was how she felt. Still, the possibility was better
avoided.

If only he'd go. At the moment he was raising his
hand toward Lovina and then pointing to his coffee cup.
Obviously he was in no hurry to be off. At least he
wasn't saying anything. She could be thankful for that.

The coffee was getting low. She glanced at the clock
and then assessed the customers with practiced skill.
Not too many more were likely to show up, but she'd
need another pot, at least.

She put it on, vaguely aware of Lovina moving about,
refilling cups, chatting to customers. She ought to tell
Mammi and Daad what a fine job Lovina was doing.
Despite her occasional teenage sassiness, she had been
a real help.

Dinah smiled to herself. Lovina would hate the word
sassy, but it was a good description. Lovina at two or
three had been noted for temper tantrums, but they faded
when she discovered that they didn't get her what she
wanted. Now they were back, in a different form.

Poor Mammi. She was the one who had to cope. Daadi
generally dealt with the boys and left the girls to Mammi,
only intervening when the situation was truly serious,
like . . .

Like when she and Aaron announced they wanted to
be married. Daadi had been plenty serious then. Not that
he'd had anything against Aaron, as far as she could tell,
but he'd been convinced they were too young.

Maybe they had been. If they'd waited, would things
have been different? Or would they have turned out exactly the same anyway?

Shaking that off, she turned to survey the customers
again. Lovina again stood by Nate Smith's chair, nod-

ding at something he was saying. Dinah's jaw clenched. She couldn't kick him out of the shop, but she didn't have to expose her little sister to him.

She took a step toward them, but at that moment Lovina turned away, consulting her pad and jotting something down before stopping to refill the cups of two Englisch women who'd been shopping, she guessed. Relieved, she turned to calculate the amount of pastries she had left.

But she wasn't so relieved that she forgot about it. When Lovina returned to the counter, Dinah moved over next to her.

"Was Mr. Smith asking you something?"

Lovina turned a pair of innocent green eyes on her. "Smith? Oh, him. Just wanted to know why we close early on Mondays."

"What did you tell him?"

Lovina shrugged. "Like you always say, that early in the week it isn't busy enough to stay open afternoons. That Thursday and Friday are our busy days."

"Exactly," she said, pleased that Lovina had remembered what she'd told her.

All in all, she really should be giving Lovina more credit for her work. She'd definitely tell Mammi and Daad about it. Maybe . . .

"You know, if you wanted to stick around town on the early closing days, Jacob would give you a ride home. Would you like that?"

Lovina looked startled, almost embarrassed. "Mammi would never say yes."

"I could speak to her. You've been very responsible lately."

"Well, maybe. Not today, though."

Dinah nodded. "Another day, then."

The morning seemed to drag on, and Dinah thought

she'd never seen the clock move so slowly. But they stayed busy enough to make it worthwhile, and to her relief, Nate Smith drained his cup and left without speaking.

When they were finally cleaned up and ready to leave, Jacob carried baby Isaac out to the buggy and put him gently in her arms. "I won't be home until late tonight. Will you tell your mamm not to wait supper for me?"

"I will, but I'm sure she'll want to keep something hot for you."

He shook his head. "I'm going over to Noah and Sarah's to help with some repairs to the stable. You know my cousin won't let me leave without having some food."

"I'm sure," she said, laughing. "We'll see you whenever you get home, then."

He'd stop at the house, of course. She didn't need to ask that. He wouldn't go to bed without saying good night to Isaac.

BY THE TIME Dinah had settled in the corner of the sofa next to Mamm's rocking chair, she was beginning to wonder if she'd been right about Jacob saying good night to the baby. All the younger ones had gone to bed, and Micah was dozing at the other end of the sofa. Even Daadi, though he held the Amish newspaper in front of him, had half-closed eyes.

Ten more minutes, she thought. Ten more minutes and she'd give up and go to bed herself. He wasn't going to stop by this late.

She'd barely finished the thought when she heard the buggy come down the lane and pull up at the back door. A moment later there was a scuffling sound on the back porch and the door slammed open.

Dinah was already in the kitchen, Mamm and Daad right behind her, and Micah stumbling along behind them, half awake. "What's going . . ." His words trailed away at the sight that greeted them.

Jacob held Lovina with one hand on her arm while he clutched Isaac against him with the other. His face was a mask of anger.

For a moment they were all silent in stunned surprise. Lovina, outside this late at night, an hour after she'd gone up to bed. And the baby—

"What has happened?" Daad pulled himself together first. "What's going on?"

"Ask your daughter." Jacob grated the words out. "Ask Lovina. Ask her what she was doing running down the lane with Isaac, going to where Nate Smith was waiting for her with a car." He pushed Lovina toward her parents as if he couldn't stand to touch her. "Ask her."

CHAPTER NINE

Dinah froze in a moment of horrified silence. Then everyone started talking at once. All she could do was rush to Jacob, holding out her arms for Isaac.

Jacob stared at her, as if in looking at her, he saw Lovina. Then his eyes warmed, and he shifted Isaac to her waiting arms.

Holding the baby close against her, she managed an incoherent prayer of thanksgiving. He was here. He was safe. But what insanity had sent Lovina out into the night with him?

"Quiet." Daad seldom barked, but he did now. "Let us hear this without shouting. Do you want to have the younger ones running down here?"

He waited, looking from face to face grimly. Discovering that her legs didn't want to hold her up, Dinah sank into a chair, whispering to Isaac, her cheek against his head. Grossmammi sat next to her, patting her and Isaac both.

But Mammi . . . Mammi stared at Lovina as if her heart had been broken. Lovina couldn't meet that gaze. She stared at the floor, but her expression was stubborn and defiant. What was the matter with her?

"Now," Daad said, "Jacob, tell us what happened."

Grasping the back of a chair, Jacob gave a curt nod. "I was late getting back from Sarah's, but I wanted to tell Isaac good night, so I drove straight here. There was a car parked alongside the road just past your lane. As I turned in, I saw the driver. It was Nate Smith. And then I saw someone hurrying down the lane to meet him. Lovina. Carrying Isaac." His gaze was an accusation.

Dinah found herself shaking. "Lovina, why? How could you?" Her questions were drowned out by the others', but Daad's voice overrode them all.

"Jacob, I hope I don't need to tell you that none of us suspected anything like this. I promise we would do anything to keep Isaac safe." He looked at his errant daughter, and the disappointment in his face was more than Dinah could bear.

Jacob's expression relaxed slightly as he looked at Daad, and understanding seemed to pass between them. "Yah, I know that."

Daad turned to Lovina, his face tightening until it seemed the skin was stretched over the bones. "Well, Lovina. We're waiting."

"It's not my fault," she flared. "You're the ones who wouldn't even let Nate look at his baby."

"Nate?" Daad clipped the name out. "You've been talking to him. Where?"

"At the shop. When she was supposed to be helping," Dinah added, feeling as if Lovina's failure were hers. She should have kept a closer watch on the child.

"I was helping. I worked hard. You said so."

A memory slid into Dinah's mind. "I asked what you were talking about, and you said you were telling him about early closing. But it wasn't true, was it? You were talking about Isaac. You were planning . . ." She gestured, unable to describe Lovina's treachery.

Lovina shrugged, pulling herself inward. "I was just going to let him see what Isaac looked like. You wouldn't even do that. It wasn't fair. He said it wasn't fair, and I think so, too."

"What would you have done if he'd grabbed the baby and driven off in the car? Well?" Mammi had never spoken to Lovina in that tone of voice, and Lovina seemed to shrink.

"He wouldn't. He promised. He just wanted—"

"You don't know what he wanted." Mammi was outraged. "And you don't know whether he's Isaac's father or not. But you took his words against your family's."

"I didn't. Well, not exactly." For the first time, some uncertainty came into Lovina's face. "All right, I talked to him a couple of times. Down at the pharmacy that one day. He explained. He said he thought he was the baby's father, and he wanted to do right by him. But he had to see him first to be sure." Her words faltered as she looked around the circle of faces. "So . . . so I just slipped out the front with Isaac while you were all in the kitchen."

Dinah found her voice at last. "That's why you looked so pleased when you came back from shopping. You'd been meeting him."

"It wasn't . . . I mean, I didn't plan it exactly." But her face told Dinah she was twisting the truth.

"And you were embarrassed when I suggested you might be able to stay in town in the afternoon. I trusted you, and you were planning this." She snuggled Isaac close to her heart. "You should have been embarrassed. And ashamed."

"What about you?" Lovina glared at her. "You should be embarrassed—pretending Isaac is your baby. Everybody knows what you're doing. You—"

Her words cut off as Daad grasped her arm and swung

her around. "Enough!" he thundered. "Go to your room and stay there until we decide what's to be done. Go!"

Footsteps told her that Lovina was fleeing for her room, but Dinah didn't see it. She'd shut her eyes, trying to block out everyone and everything. Lovina was wrong . . . she had to be. If people thought that, it could not be borne.

She felt Grossmammi's arms around her from one side and then Mammi's from the other.

"Hush, now," Mammi soothed, tears in her voice. "Lovina—" She choked on the name. "Lovina doesn't know what she's talking about. She's striking out because she doesn't want to admit what she's done. It will be all right."

Would it? What if Lovina was right? What if people thought that of her? What if Jacob thought it?

JACOB SAW THE stricken look on Dinah's face, the women trying to comfort her. In another instant she was on her feet, struggling for calm.

"Isaac . . . Isaac belongs in his bed," she murmured. She hurried toward the steps, her face working. Her mother and grandmother exchanged glances and then followed her, leaving the kitchen to the three men.

John cleared his throat. "It's no good talking about how young Lovina is. She's plenty old enough to know that what she did was wrong." He shook his head slowly, his expression drawn. "Old enough, too, I'd think, to see that man was trying to use her. If not, she'll learn it now."

He slumped down into a chair. Jacob had never seen him look so defeated.

Jacob sat down across from him, knowing there were things that should be said, but not sure how to start.

"Thank the Lord I was coming back at just that time. If I hadn't . . ." It didn't bear thinking about.

"God had you in His hands. That doesn't excuse what Lovina did, though." John brooded, looking down at his hands, clasped between his knees. "I can't even ask you to forgive her now. I hope you will one day."

Forgiveness was the answer the faith demanded, but John was a wise man. All Jacob could manage now was to vow he wouldn't hold Lovina's actions against anyone else.

John straightened, looking at him. "If you want to call the police, Lovina will have to take what the law demands."

He didn't ask for anything or say anything about their long friendship and their kindness. If there were consequences to Lovina's actions, John would see that she faced them.

Rubbing the back of his neck, Jacob found himself wishing he had such a simple answer.

"No," he said finally. "If the police come into it, we have no way of knowing what will happen. Would it go to court? Would the court say I have no right to Anna's baby? Would they say she abandoned him?" He tried to force his mind to work, but it was like struggling through a fog.

Micah made a sound, as if he had something to say but didn't know if he had the right in this council of his elders. Jacob looked at him and nodded.

"Yah, Micah?"

"I was just thinking. You don't believe this guy is really the father, ain't so? Like I said, a DNA test would tell us. I know they do those DNA tests over at the clinic in Burnside. I . . . well, I've been seeing Ruthie King." He darted a glance at his father, his color rising. "Ruthie's cousin's family has had some cases of that maple syrup disease, so they've all decided to go and get tested. Just to be sure they don't carry it."

John looked as if he'd just received a shock, but he managed not to speak. He must not have known Micah was getting serious about Ruthie. Or maybe he hadn't known about the disease that showed up in some families.

"Anyway, that's how I know about it. I was thinking I could pick up some of their folders about testing. If this guy is a phony, he'd probably change his tune if you said he had to get tested."

Jacob could think of a couple of very good reasons not to do that, too. What if Nate was the father? Then what? Would Anna want him to take this step?

They were both looking at him now, and he wasn't sure what to say. Finally he found his tongue. "Denke, Micah. I guess it wouldn't hurt to have the information. I wouldn't have to use it unless . . . well, unless it seemed the only way."

"Yah," John said. "You wouldn't have to. And maybe you'll hear something from Anna any day now, ain't so?"

"Yah," he echoed. He pushed himself to his feet. "I need to see Isaac again."

John seemed to understand. He rose also. "I'll check and be sure everything is locked up tight. And, Micah, shut a couple of the dogs in the porch for the night. They'll raise a ruckus if anybody comes around."

Judging by his expression, he wouldn't regret turning the dogs on any stranger prowling around. And Jacob felt the same way. Forgiveness wasn't easy.

He went up the stairs as quietly as he could, not wanting to wake the rest of the house. But he had to see Isaac again. He had to know for himself that his nephew was all right.

The door was ajar, so he eased it open, tapping with

his fingers to let them know he was there. Dinah was alone with Isaac, though. Maybe her mother and grandmother had already said whatever they could to comfort her.

He was acknowledging the pain of what Lovina had said, he realized. Was it true? Did Dinah feel that way? He wasn't sure, and he guessed, for him, it didn't matter. Either way, she was hurting, and either way, she was intent on giving little Isaac what he needed.

Dinah tucked a blue blanket over Isaac, resting her hand on the sleeping bundle for a moment. Then she nodded to him, gesturing him closer.

"He's fine," she murmured as he bent over the crib. "I think he slept through the whole thing."

"He doesn't know. He doesn't ever need to know." He was fumbling, trying to find something to say to Dinah that would wipe the pain from her eyes. He patted the soft shape that was Isaac, sleeping peacefully.

"You know." Her voice was so soft it seemed to barely touch him. "And we know. Lovina . . ." She broke off, seeming unable to speak.

He glanced at her and saw the tears that traced down her cheek. With his other hand he reached out to pat her, much as he did the baby.

"Don't, Dinah. What Lovina did wasn't your fault. No one could have guessed that would happen. I thought it was a gut idea to have Lovina there, too." A flame of anger flickered up in him. "What kind of a man is he that he would try to turn a child against her family like that? Not someone who should be within miles of Isaac."

"I can't believe Anna would care for him." Dinah disengaged her hand slowly. "She wouldn't, that's all. She had more sense, even when she went away."

"Yah, I think that, too." If he had to, he'd insist Smith have a DNA test done to prove parenthood, and he'd pray his opinion of Anna was right.

Dinah couldn't know the direction of his thoughts, and he felt her mind was still on her sister.

"Lovina . . . ," she murmured. "I was wrong to think she was old enough to have more freedom. So wrong. I never knew she could have it in her . . ."

Was she thinking about Lovina's hurtful words? He ought to say something comforting, but he didn't know what. Maybe she *was* dreaming about Isaac being hers. Whether she did or not, she was still loving him and taking care of him.

"I know. But it wasn't your fault." He was repeating himself, but he didn't know what else to say. He was so tired and shaken that his mind had stopped working. Maybe tomorrow he'd be thinking more clearly.

Probably not, if that required getting a good night's sleep, because he doubted he'd be able to sleep that night. Most likely Dinah and her parents were in the same position. The happenings of this evening had rocked all of them.

He studied Dinah's face. None of them was as pained as Dinah was right now. And he didn't know how to make it any better.

One thing was sure: He wouldn't be going back to his house to sleep tonight. Even if he had to be content with a blanket on the porch with the dogs, he would be here.

DINAH'S BUGGY WAS completely loaded, so Dinah hurried through the cool morning air back into the warm kitchen. Isaac must have his soft knit hat on the way to the shop on a day like this. Jacob followed her, his own buggy pulled up behind hers. He hadn't said anything, but she felt quite sure he intended to stick close on the way to town, just in case he was needed. And she'd already noticed the dark circles under his eyes this morning. That made two of them.

"Isaac's hat . . . ," she began, but Grossmammi interrupted her. "He already has it on. We're ready to go."

And there was her grandmother, dressed in the black wool sweater and black bonnet she always wore when she went to town. She was holding Isaac and clearly intended to go with them.

"Grossmammi, there's no need for you to come." They hadn't even talked about someone taking Lovina's place, and she for sure didn't expect it to be her grandmother.

"Don't you think I can do it?" Grossmammi gave her a look that reduced Dinah to an errant six-year-old. "I can do it just as well as Lovina—probably better."

"I'm sure you can," she said quickly. "But I'm only open until noon, and I can manage."

"You can, but you're not going to. I'll bake and watch the baby while you take care of the front. Komm. It's time to be on the road."

She glanced at Jacob, who shrugged and nodded. "Yah, it's time."

They'd just gotten Grossmammi and the baby into the buggy when Will rushed out of the house, clutching his books and his lunch. He looked at Isaac, snuggled in Grossmammi's arms, and his face clouded.

"I don't see why I can't come and help," he muttered. "I told Daadi that. I was a big help before, ain't so?"

She had a mental picture of him hanging over the cot, practically upside down in his need to entertain Isaac. Her tension eased, and she tried to find the tactful thing to say.

"You're always helpful, that's certain sure. But what did Daadi say?"

Will's lower lip came out. "He said I had to go to school. He said we all have our jobs to do, and that's mine right now. But I could be a lot more help keeping Isaac safe than going to that dumb old school."

Dinah would have said that nothing could possibly make her laugh today, but she felt a bubble of laughter welling in her now at the look on his face. She suppressed it firmly.

"When you get home, I'd like for you to be on duty with Isaac. That way I can catch up on a little sleep." She put her arm around him and hugged him close, loving the little-boy feeling that clung to him in spite of his desire to do a grown-up duty. "There's no one I'd trust more," she whispered, and he hugged her back with a fierce grip.

"I would never do what Lovina did. Never."

"I know." Eyes stinging, she climbed into the buggy and picked up the lines. With a quick wave to Mammi, watching from the window, they set out.

Isaac, secure in Grossmammi's arms, snuggled against her. In another moment his eyes drifted closed, and he was asleep by the time they reached the end of the lane.

"Always works," Grossmammi said, smiling down at him. "Take a baby in a buggy, start moving, and the baby falls asleep. I wonder if it works in a car, too?"

"Probably," she said absently. "I appreciate this, but you really didn't have to come. It's such a short day, and we're never really busy early in the week."

"I know you could manage, Dinah." Her grandmother patted her arm. "But it's better to have an extra person keeping an eye on the baby, with you and Jacob working. Besides, if you think I wanted to stay home today and listen to your parents dealing with Lovina, you're wrong."

Dinah's fingers tightened on the lines, and the mare tossed her head in an annoyed reaction. Focusing, Dinah kept her hands steady.

"I don't know how she could do it. I don't. I've thought about it and thought about it. I'd never have dreamed . . ." Her words trailed off, and she was close to tears again.

Grossmammi was silent for a moment before she spoke. "I've lived long enough to have seen most things," she said, her voice sounding as if she was looking back into the past. "He probably appealed to her sense of fairness. It's strong at that age. 'It's not fair' comes easy to her."

"Yah. And usually about things fairness doesn't have anything to do with. Like wanting to be treated like her older sister and brother without having their age and experience." She shook her head. "Maybe I shouldn't have given her so much responsibility. And so much freedom. I thought it would be good for her, and instead, she does a thing like this."

"She'll learn," Grossmammi said. "She's never met anyone like this Smith person. She didn't realize he was using her to get what he wanted."

"What does he want?" she exclaimed. "I'm convinced he doesn't think Isaac is his. And even if he did think it, I doubt that he'd want to take on the responsibility of a baby. So what's he after?"

"Money, I guess. He probably believes those stories folks tell about the Amish keeping packets of money under their mattresses."

She had to smile at the derision in her grandmother's voice.

"You ever know anyone who did that? No, nor me," she said, answering her own question. "He's thinking he'll make Jacob nervous enough that he'll pay him to go away."

"Jacob mustn't do that." Everything in her revolted at the thought. "That man can't be allowed to trade money for a child. But what if . . ." She ran out of suppositions at that point. They'd considered everything, hadn't they?

"It's too bad Jacob won't go to the police. I understand why," she added quickly. "But if ever someone belonged in jail, that Smith does."

Dinah nodded, her thoughts revolving around and around and not coming up with anything useful.

"Are you fretting about what Lovina said last night?" Grossmammi asked, her voice gentle.

Dinah didn't need to ask which thing Lovina had said. It was clear to both of them. When Grossmammi and Mammi had gone out of the kitchen with her the previous night, they'd tried so hard to comfort her. She'd reached the point where she didn't even take in the words they'd said. She'd just listened to the comforting music of their voices.

"Maybe she was right." The words slipped out before she could stop them. Small wonder, as she'd been thinking them most of the night. "Maybe people are saying that."

"Maybe." Grossmammi didn't sound upset. "What difference does it make?"

"Difference?" Dinah was so startled that she nearly lost the lines. She swung to look at her grandmother. "What do you mean? Of course it makes a difference."

She cringed at the thought, her flesh shrinking away from hearing those words coming from her friends, her neighbors. From her sister.

Grossmammi touched Isaac's head. "Look at this child. Will you stop taking care of him because of what people say? Will you?"

"No, of course not." Her heart warmed just looking at that precious baby.

"Will you stop loving him because of what people say?"

Dinah could almost feel Grossmammi's wise old eyes studying her face. She knew what Grossmammi was doing.

"No. Nothing could make me stop loving him." She knew that was true, bone deep.

"Then it doesn't matter," Grossmammi said firmly. "Ach, I don't think they're saying it, not really. Except maybe a few people whose opinions I wouldn't give a penny for. But it doesn't matter if they are."

"It doesn't feel very good," she muttered, not liking to look at herself so closely.

"For sure it doesn't." Grossmammi patted her hand. "But you're doing the work God has given you. Taking care of this little one is more important than anything else right now. Even if it hurts, it's worth it."

"Loving is worth the risk," she said softly, remembering and knowing it was true. She wouldn't turn back from this, no matter how much it hurt.

She had been looking at the past too much. If other folks wanted to look back and talk about her, let them. She would let the past go and focus her eyes on the future.

CHAPTER TEN

D inah quickly found that her resolution to ignore the past wasn't as easy to keep as she'd thought . . . especially when memories of the past walked in the door in the shape of Aaron's cousin. Liva Hershberger lived ten miles away in Fosterville, and it had been while Aaron was visiting Liva's family that Dinah met him and fell in love.

And now here Liva was, almost the first person in the door on a Tuesday morning. She glanced at the three people ahead of her lined up at the counter for their usual takeout coffee and then sat at a table next to the wall. Her gaze skimmed over Dinah as if she weren't there. And yet, why would Liva be here if not to see her?

Dinah focused on her customers and found herself wishing that Lovina, despite her failings, were here to serve customers. Grossmammi was in the kitchen baking the sweet rolls they'd brought with them, and she wouldn't ask her to come out here anyway. She'd have to get to Liva as soon as possible and hope she hadn't come to be troublesome.

The bell jingled frequently in the usual morning rush. More people than ever seemed eager to pick up their morning coffee before heading to work. The aroma of baking rolls floating from the kitchen did its work, too, and when Grossmammi came out to the counter with a tray fresh from the oven, they were gone before she had a chance to put them in the display case.

Lovina had made herself useful in such a short period of time the she'd left a hole. Dinah found herself looking for her, then remembering why she wasn't here, and then feeling the weight of it settling on her shoulders again.

She couldn't just tell herself that Lovina was Mammi and Daad's responsibility. Dinah was the one who'd agreed to this, maybe even thinking that Mammi should be giving her a bit more freedom. She'd taken on the responsibility, and she should have taken better care of her little sister. The thought jarred her—it was such an echo of what Jacob felt about Anna.

Finally the rush slowed down, as it always did, and then petered out. Dinah took a deep breath, trying to relax. Arranging a smile on her face, she walked back to the occupied table.

"Liva, it's wonderful gut to see you. Will you have some coffee?"

Liva looked startled, as if that question didn't fit in with whatever she'd planned to say. "Yah. Yah, that would be nice."

She seemed ill at ease, Dinah reflected as she poured the coffee. Liva must be about twenty now, given how much younger she'd been than Aaron, the big, handsome cousin she'd idolized.

When Dinah returned with the coffee, Liva was looking around with what seemed grudging approval. "The family wasn't in favor of Aaron starting a business here in Promise Glen. I suppose you knew that. But as things turned out, maybe it was for the best. At least it's something for you to do."

It had never really been Aaron's business. It was always hers. That was what she wanted to say, but there was no point. How foolish it would be to react now. With Aaron gone, there wasn't a link between her and Aaron's cousin.

Not that there had been, not to any extent. As she recalled, Liva had burst into noisy tears when their marriage plans were announced, embarrassing everyone and making Dinah feel like an evil monster for taking her cousin away.

Dinah pressed the smile more firmly in place. "Yah, the shop is doing fairly well now. I'm only open in the morning on Tuesdays, and that's the busiest time anyway."

"I noticed you didn't seem able to handle the customers very well."

The grown-up air Liva put on didn't mask the dislike she still felt. Surely she should be getting over that by now. Whatever teenage Liva had felt about Aaron's choice of bride, Aaron was gone now.

"I'm afraid I'm shorthanded today." Her smile hid the worry that churned inside her over Lovina. "My grandmother is helping in the kitchen, but I wouldn't want her to have to wait on tables. Besides, she's a better baker than I am."

Keep it light, she told herself. There was no telling what had inspired Liva to show up this morning, but she wouldn't let it ruffle her.

"What's this the family hears about you having a baby?"

Dinah's breath caught. If she had ever dared to speak in that offensive way to anyone, she'd have had her mouth washed out with soap. Maybe Liva was a bit old for that consequence, but the church's discipline would be worse if word reached Liva's ministers.

"My family is helping to take care of Anna Miller's baby. They are our neighbors, you know."

"Your family? We heard it was you who went off to Williamsport and came back with a baby." She made it sound disgraceful. Dinah winced, Lovina's words still too fresh in her mind.

"Yah, Anna asked me to bring little Isaac back home for her. I suppose she thought I'd manage a baby better on that long bus ride than her brother would."

"If Aaron were here—" she began.

"Aaron and Jacob were good friends," Dinah said firmly, cutting her off. "Remember? I'm sure he'd have wanted to help Jacob if we could."

It seemed clear that Aaron's family had been talking to Liva. Had his mother encouraged this visit, or was it her own idea?

Dinah's temper began to fray, but she was determined to hang on to it. Reacting angrily would just add fuel to the fire. Thank the Lord there was no one else in the coffee shop right now to hear Liva. There'd been enough talk without adding her obnoxious behavior to it.

Liva's face reddened, and she opened her mouth, probably to say something more outrageous, when two things happened. Grossmammi came in from the kitchen and marched toward them. And Jacob appeared in the doorway, carrying Isaac in his arms.

Isaac was wide awake and looking around at his new surroundings. Then he turned back to Jacob and began patting his face, apparently trying to pry Jacob's lips apart.

"Sorry," Jacob said, giving Isaac the opportunity to push his tiny fingers in and grab Jacob's lower lip. "I didn't mean to interrupt."

Dinah relaxed, her smile becoming real. She was relieved at the interruption and amused as always by Isaac's lively actions.

"We'll take Isaac for a while." She started toward him, thankful for any distraction from trying to talk to Liva. "You remember Aaron's cousin, Liva Hershberger, ain't so?"

"Yah, for sure." He nodded. "You've grown up since I last saw you, Liva." He seemed to recall that the last time would have been Aaron's funeral, and his smile faltered.

Isaac suddenly caught sight of Dinah approaching him, and he spread out his arms and launched himself toward her. Fortunately Jacob was becoming accustomed to his nephew's quick movements, and he caught Isaac and swooped him into Dinah's arms.

Dinah held him close, laughing a little, her gaze catching Jacob's and sharing the laughter.

"I see what it is." Liva's voice cut through the moment. "You've found someone to replace Aaron. And the baby you couldn't give him."

A stunned silence greeted her outburst. Dinah didn't know which to react to—her possible relationship with Jacob or the slam at her childlessness. Before she could say a thing, Grossmammi took over.

"Liva Hershberger, what's got into you? If your parents could hear you, they'd be ashamed. And if the bishop heard you, you'd end up on your knees confessing your behavior. It would be a service to the church to write and tell him what you've said today."

Liva's eyes widened, and a flush mounted on her face. She opened her mouth as if to say something, but no words came out. Then she jumped up and ran for the door, letting it slam behind her.

"What's eating her?" Jacob looked from Dinah to her

grandmother with a baffled expression. "I know she always had a crush on Aaron, even though they were cousins. But isn't it a bit late to be coming after you now?"

Dinah held Isaac close, taking comfort in his warm sweetness. "I imagine her mother and aunt were gossiping and she decided to interfere. That's all." Jacob certain sure didn't need to start blaming himself for Liva's antics.

Grossmammi shook her head. "I shouldn't be surprised if you were right about it, Dinah. Those women were always terrible blabbermauls. As for Liva . . . well, she'll never find herself a husband with a temper like that."

Dinah found her tension dissolving in laughter. That was Grossmammi's inevitable response to misbehavior in a young woman.

"Maybe Liva doesn't want a husband."

"Ach, don't you be so foolish. Of course she does, and she's probably wondering why no one's turned up courting her yet at her age. I could tell her why."

Laughter continued to ripple through Dinah, chasing away the clouds for a moment, at least. "Grossmammi has an answer to everything," she told Jacob, holding on to Isaac and feeling him laugh with her. "Think of Liva coming all the way over from Fosterville for that." Something else struck her, making her laugh again. "And she didn't even pay for her coffee."

Jacob looked at the helpless laughter that had captured Dinah and her grossmammi, and shook his head, grinning. "If you ask me, it was cheap at the cost to get rid of her."

Isaac laughed out loud, gave a huge burp, and grinned with satisfaction.

"See?" Jacob said. "Isaac agrees with me."

RELIEF CAME OVER Jacob as he saw Dinah laughing at the nonsense. This morning she'd appeared so fragile that it hurt to look at her. Last night's trouble with Lovina had hit her hard, and most likely she hadn't been able to sleep much. For that matter, neither had he.

Remembering why he'd come over to begin with, he gestured toward Isaac. "All right if he stays with you for a bit? I've got a harness to work on, and once I start stitching, it's hard to hear him."

"Yah, of course," Dinah said, and her grandmother echoed the words.

"You bring the cot right back to the kitchen. Isaac and I will have a fine time together."

Her grandmother left no doubt about how she felt about Isaac. Her faded blue eyes were sparkling. He guessed she'd been waiting for one of her grandchildren to produce a great-grandchild for her, and Isaac filled that spot just right.

He'd pulled the cot over to the connecting door in anticipation before he walked in on the fuss Liva Hershberger was stirring up. So all he had to do was open the door and pull it through.

He trundled it across to the kitchen, followed by Dinah carrying Isaac, her grandmother supervising. The minute they reached the kitchen, Grossmammi was arranging toys in the cot and clucking over Isaac as Dinah lowered him into it.

Isaac, seeming to get the message that it was playtime, immediately rolled over onto his belly and grabbed for the closest rattle. His fingers closed on it on the first try, and he held it up to look at the toy before deciding to taste it.

"I think he's saying you can go and work on the harness," Dinah said as they walked back to the front. "I'll get your coffee and doughnut for you." She moved behind the counter to the coffeepot.

"Make it one of your grandmother's sticky buns." He grinned. "Nobody would pass them up."

For an instant she didn't respond, and then she seemed to concentrate with an effort before she reached for the sweet roll.

Dinah was brooding, that was certain. She'd managed to forget for a few minutes, but that quickly it had come back. Now it was hanging over her again. First Lovina, and then Liva had added her little bit.

But it was Lovina's behavior that would haunt Dinah . . . the little sister she loved and had tried to guide. Who would know that feeling better than he would?

He tried to find something to say, but there was nothing. He knew that, too. Nothing anyone had said to him about Anna had ever helped, that was certain sure.

Dinah put the coffee and sweet roll together on the counter. "There you are. You haven't . . ." She hesitated, letting it trail off.

"What?"

"I just wondered if you'd seen anything of him . . . Smith? Maybe what happened last night scared him off."

"I haven't seen him. Hard to believe he'd just disappear after that, but he couldn't be sure we wouldn't call the police. Trying to lure an underage girl away from her home has to be against the law."

She nodded. "Maybe we should have called them." She shivered and rubbed her arms. "When I think of what might have happened if you hadn't come along when you did, it makes me sick."

"Yah." He had to face it. He might have no choice but to bring the police into this if Smith continued to be a problem. "I wanted to give it a little longer to hear from Anna. She's the only one who can resolve this."

He grabbed the coffee and sweet roll. "Ach, there's no use talking about it. I'd best get to work if I want to get anything done before lunchtime."

Quickly, before she could say anything, he headed back to his own place. He and Anna between them had involved Dinah in their problems, and he shouldn't keep going over it with her, probably making her feel even worse about what Lovina had tried to do.

Jacob wasn't destined to stay away from Dinah's family very long, though. By the time he'd finished the initial stitching on the harness, the bell jingled on the door and Dinah's brother Micah came in.

Jacob grinned at him. "Don't tell me you're shopping for a new harness?"

"Not a chance," Micah responded, smiling. "Sorry to disappoint you. No, I stopped by to give you this." He put a brochure down on the counter between them. "This is the stuff I said I'd get about the DNA testing."

"Yah, denke." He hesitated and then picked it up, forcing a smile. "I don't suppose you minded having an extra excuse to talk to a pretty girl, ain't so?" He was satisfied to see a flush come up in Micah's cheeks.

"Ruthie was glad to pass it on to me. Her folks are really encouraging people to get tested. They say that knowing ahead of time saved her cousin's baby's life."

Jacob nodded absently, focusing on the leaflet. "I wish I knew what would happen if I told him he'd have to take this test before we'd so much as let him see Isaac."

Micah leaned on the counter, obviously giving it some serious thought. "Well, it might just be enough to scare him off entirely. I mean, if he knows he couldn't be the father, he wouldn't want to take the test."

"And what if he could? I don't want to think it, but I have to. Your sister thinks that's impossible. She says Anna would never get mixed up with someone like that."

"What do you think?" Micah studied his face, his own youthful face looking serious and mature.

"I don't know. I wish I could be as confident as Dinah is, but I can't. I thought I knew Anna once—thought she'd never run away from home. Well, I was wrong about that, wasn't I?"

Micah hesitated. He looked as if he were debating with himself. Finally he spoke.

"I knew Anna pretty well, being about the same age and all. I always thought she had a gut head on her shoulders. She got mixed up when your daad died and then your mammi passed so soon afterward. I remember her saying to me that her mammi missed him so much she couldn't wait to follow him, even if it meant leaving her without a mother."

"Anna said that?" He didn't really doubt that Micah was telling the truth. It just stung. "I wish she'd talked to me as open as that."

Micah looked embarrassed all over again. "Don't you think Anna meant . . . well, maybe she figured it would just hurt you worse than you were already hurting if she said anything. Maybe it was easier to say it to me."

Jacob nodded slowly. He could see that happening, especially if she had thought that telling him would result in a lecture. Maybe he'd let his sense of responsibility push too hard, to the point where he'd pushed her away.

"Right now, all I can do is wonder why she doesn't come back, especially when she knows we need her to keep her baby safe."

"She's always been a good person," Micah said. "Maybe a bit mixed up and eager for new experiences, but that's all."

"New experiences," he repeated. "She got new experiences all right. If only she'd give it up and come home." Jacob heard the desperate plea in his own words and knew he was repeating himself until people were probably tired of hearing it.

"Yah." Micah considered. "We'd certain sure hate to give up little Isaac, though. Especially Dinah. She really loves him."

Jacob nodded, pain gripping his heart. It seemed like no matter what he did or what happened, somebody would end up with a broken heart.

DINAH LOOKED UP in surprise when the connecting door from the harness shop opened, especially because she could hear the leather sewing machine operating. She was even more surprised to see Micah. He wasn't usually in town at this time of day.

She smiled at him and automatically reached for the coffeepot. "What brings you to town, and what can I get for you?"

"Coffee, good." He grasped the mug she held out. "How about one of those cream-filled doughnuts?"

"Coming right up."

Dinah studied her brother's face as she bent over the display case. Her little brother. That was how she always thought of him, but Micah wasn't so little anymore. He already towered over her, and he'd turn out to be the tallest of the family, she'd guess. His lean face and straight brows contrasted with the round, cheerful faces of the twins.

Right now his face was expressing concern, maybe even worry.

"Is something wrong? I mean, I didn't realize you were coming into town today."

"Oh, that." He took the doughnut, staring at it so absently that it alarmed her. None of her brothers had ever hesitated when faced with a doughnut. "I got that leaflet about the DNA testing and brought it in to Jacob."

"That was nice of you." But it wasn't all that was on his mind. She felt sure of that. "I'm sure he appreciated it." She hesitated, but if he wanted some big-sisterly advice, she'd have to probe a little, she suspected. "Is there anything else that's troubling you . . . about Ruthie, maybe?"

Micah looked up with a sudden flare of resentment in his eyes. "You sound just like Mammi. Everybody wants to know how serious it is."

She'd hit a sensitive spot, clearly.

"Micah, I'm sorry. I didn't mean that, really. I just thought you looked worried."

His face smoothed out after a minute, and he smiled, a little shamefaced. "Sorry. I didn't mean to snap. I just get tired of everybody butting in."

The little brother who'd looked to her for advice had grown up. The old confidence between them had slipped away when she married, and it hadn't come back since she'd been living at home. She'd like to have it back again, although the good Lord knew she wasn't all that wise.

"It's all right. You know Mammi asks questions because she loves you."

"Yah, I know. But a guy doesn't want to talk about his courting with his mother."

She had to grin. "Courting seriously?"

Now he looked more like himself, and his lips curved. "Thing is . . . well, I just don't know how serious I am about Ruthie. And now it feels like people are pushing me to move faster than I want to."

She considered. "Does . . . do you think Ruthie is pushing?"

"No. No, I guess not. I mean, she just told me that about the testing because she thought I should know before, well, before we saw any more of each other."

That was good of Ruthie, and her opinion of the girl rose. But they were both still young to be seriously courting.

"Now I'm sorry," she said. "If you hadn't offered that information about the DNA testing, all this wouldn't have come out, and you wouldn't have been in this pickle."

"Never mind. Mammi would have figured it out before long anyway, ain't so? I can never keep things hidden from her. Can you?"

"I'm afraid not. She always knows, whether she asks questions or not. But I wish it hadn't come into the open because of this situation with little Isaac. You were a help, though. It gives Jacob something else to use against this Smith person."

"Maybe he won't need it." Micah had the air of someone who was trying to look on the bright side. "Could be that business with Lovina scared him off. That's what Jacob thinks, anyway. I hope he's right." He hesitated. "It's funny. I mean, that I can help Jacob. When I was a kid, I always looked up to Jacob, sort of like a big bruder. Just like Anna always looked up to you."

She blinked. "Did she? I'm not so sure."

"Well, yah. For sure. I mean, look at who she called when she didn't know what to do. She'd turn to you for advice sooner than her bruder. Not that she doesn't love Jacob, but that's just how it is."

Dinah realized she was learning something new about relationships she'd always taken for granted. If Micah was right, maybe there was still something she could do to encourage Anna to stay. But Anna would have to come back for that to happen.

And in the meantime, there was Smith to be dealt with, to say nothing of Lovina.

Should they have called the police? That question continued to run through her mind. She understood Jacob's reluctance, but if the man would try to enlist a young girl in his schemes, what else might he do?

"I just wish we knew where this Smith person is and what he's planning."

"At least he's not at the motel anymore." Micah demolished the rest of his doughnut in a single bite and then realized Dinah was staring at him. "What?" He wiped cream off his face.

"How do you know he's not at the motel? And why haven't you told anyone?"

He looked blank for a moment, and then color flooded his face, making him look years younger. "I forgot . . . I mean, I just found out this morning, and I was going to tell you and Jacob, and then I started thinking about Ruthie and everything, and it went right out of my mind."

Dinah began to suspect that he was more serious about Ruthie than he'd been willing to say. Maybe even more than he saw himself.

"Well, how do you know that he's left?"

"I stopped by the motel, just to see what I could find out before I came here. Turns out Smith checked out this morning. They don't know where he went."

"Away, I hope," Dinah muttered. "That's good news, anyway. You'd best go and tell Jacob right now."

"Tell Jacob what?" Jacob had already stepped into the shop, and she hadn't even noticed that the sound of the machine had stopped.

"Ach, Jacob, you startled us. Micah found out something this morning."

She started to say it was good news, but restrained herself. Because they didn't know where the man had gone, she shouldn't assume it was good that he'd disappeared. He could be anywhere.

Jacob turned his gaze on Micah as he came toward them.

"Yah, I wanted to let you know," Micah said hurriedly. "I stopped by the motel on my way into town today. I thought maybe Smith would have been scared off by what happened with Lovina, like we were saying. And maybe it did, because he checked out this morning."

"Maybe he has given up on bothering us." Dinah hoped with all her heart that was true, but she found it difficult to count on, especially because Jacob was shaking his head.

"I don't think so." Jacob's face had tightened. "Because he's parked just down the street from us."

Somehow she'd known it wouldn't be that easy. Poor Micah looked crushed that he hadn't brought good news after all.

"What is he doing? If he's coming here . . ." She glanced toward the kitchen, where she could hear Grossmammi humming a lullaby.

"He's just sitting there. Watching the building, I think. I don't like the idea of you and your grandmother driving home with Isaac by yourselves."

Fear slid into her heart, but just as quickly, common sense chased it away. "That doesn't make sense. He's not going to try anything foolish in broad daylight. He must know he'd end up in jail if he bothered us."

"He was foolish enough, or daring enough, to try to get Lovina to bring him the baby," Jacob retorted, but some of the anger went out of him. "Yah, I see what you mean. It was Lovina who took all the risks, not him. But what did he want to do that for, anyway?" His hands clenched into fists. "He must know we'd have called the police if he'd driven off with them."

Dinah frowned, trying to make sense of what she knew about the man and what she'd sensed about him from a brief meeting. "I wonder if he's not just trying to scare us." She shivered. "If so, he's succeeding. Now I don't like the idea of driving home alone."

"You're not going to be alone," Micah said, his tone firm. "When you're ready to go, I'll follow right along behind you. And if he comes near us, I'll call the police." His smile flickered, and from under his jacket he pulled out the cell phone Jacob had suspected he had. He wiggled it in front of her. "See? You don't have to be afraid."

"You'd best be afraid your daad will find that," Jacob said, but he clapped Micah on the shoulder. "Denke, Micah. And I think it's time I had another talk with Mr. Smith. When you're ready to leave seems like a good time."

CHAPTER ELEVEN

Jacob followed Dinah and her grandmother out the back door, carrying Isaac in his arms. Micah was waiting with the two buggies ready, both his and Dinah's. He handed Grossmammi into the buggy and passed Isaac to her, and Isaac looked up into her face and chortled.

"Ah, you are the best-tempered baby ever," she said, snuggling him. "Ain't so, Jacob?"

"I think so, but I might be prejudiced, yah?" He turned to help Dinah as she climbed up, then held her hand for an extra moment. "You be careful, now. Maybe I should—"

"No, you don't need to go with us." Dinah read his mind before he could get the words out. "Micah is with us, and with you distracting Smith, what could go wrong? We'll be fine, and we'll be waiting for you when you get home."

Home, he thought. Dinah's whole family seemed to think of their home as his and Isaac's, too. In fact, he found himself doing it. His own house had been empty for so long that it didn't feel like anyone's home.

"Maybe I'll have some news, if I can get that man

talking. It's about time he came out and told us what he wants."

He wasn't looking forward to a confrontation with the man, but he was convinced now that he had to seize control of the situation instead of waiting for Smith to act.

Dinah squeezed his hand and then released it. "You will find the right thing to say. I'm sure of it."

"I hope so." He didn't feel quite as confident as she seemed to be. He could use some of Dinah's calm assurance right now.

Glancing back at the second buggy, he nodded to Micah. "Take care of them." Then he stepped away. "Give me a few minutes to get out front and speak to him. I'll try to keep him busy until you both get going."

Dinah nodded, picking up the reins. She murmured something under her breath, and he thought she was praying. Then he hurried back into the shop and strode through to the front.

Smith's car was just where it had been, and Smith himself stood next to it, leaning on a fender as if he planned to stay there all day. He walked toward him, seeing the man notice him and straighten.

"Don't tell me I can't stay here," he said belligerently. He jerked a nod toward the meter. "I'm feeding the meter, so I can park as long as I want."

Was it Jacob's imagination, or was the man on the defensive? His quick response gave Jacob a bit more confidence, anyway.

"Doesn't matter to me where you park, but we need to talk. Come inside." He gestured toward the shop and then started walking. Surely, Smith would follow him. Whatever he really wanted, he could only get it through Jacob.

Apparently his guess was right. They walked into the

harness shop, and Jacob flipped the sign on the door to *Closed*. Once Smith was inside, Jacob locked the door. He didn't want anyone overhearing this conversation.

Determined to hold on to the initiative, he plunged right in.

"You know we could have reported you to the police after what happened last night. I don't think you'd like our county jail much."

Smith didn't look impressed. "I don't know what you're talking about. It's not against the law to park along a county road, is it?"

He hung on to his temper with an effort. "Lovina is only fifteen. It's against the law to lure an underage girl away from her parents, and folks around here would feel strongly about that. And it's definitely illegal to try to steal a baby." The man's smirk faltered.

"But you didn't call the cops." He was trying to bolster his courage, Jacob thought. "I figured you wouldn't. Know why? Because Anna told me about how you people hate to be involved with the cops, that's why."

Jacob's hands clenched into fists, and he forced them to relax. He wouldn't give the man the satisfaction of causing him to break church law and his own moral code. But he was tempted.

"We can still call the police if you don't stop harassing us, and we will. The chief knows the Amish community well. He wouldn't like some stranger interfering with our children."

"Not yours." Smith thrust his face toward Jacob. "He's not your kid, and Anna left you people. Besides, I'd have plenty to say if you turn the cops on me. Ever think about that? They might get the idea of arresting Anna for deserting her baby. Or you for taking a kid that's not yours."

For an instant he couldn't breathe. He hadn't even

begun to think that Anna might be in trouble. Panic ripped through him, but then he seemed to feel Dinah's calming hand on his.

"That's nonsense," he snapped. "It's not against the law for Anna to ask her own brother to take care of her baby for a time. There's nothing wrong with Anna's actions."

He glanced toward the street, catching a glimpse of the two buggies disappearing from view.

Smith followed the direction of his gaze. "Yeah, I saw them going." Smith shrugged. "I wasn't going to follow them anyway. My business is with you."

"Business." He almost spat the word. "That's how you see it, yah? Just business. Well, it's no business of yours where Isaac is."

"The law wouldn't see it that way if I say he might be my son." He ambled to the counter and slouched against it. "They'd take me seriously, all right."

"Not unless you could prove what you say." It seemed the time had come to take a risk and trust his judgment of Anna.

Jacob leaned across the counter to pick up the brochure he'd slid under the cash drawer. He slapped it down on the counter.

"What's that?" Smith glanced at it, not touching it.

"DNA testing. Did you think the Amish were so backward we didn't know about it? The clinic isn't far away. If you're really Isaac's father, you can prove it by getting a DNA test. Come back with the test results, and then I'll listen to you."

Jacob held his breath. Should he have gone that far? What if the man took him up on it? What if he really was Isaac's father?

Smith's gaze slid away from the brochure. "I don't have to do anything I don't want to."

"You do if you want to come near Isaac. I know he's my nephew. You don't know if he's anything to you." Jacob's doubts vanished. "So prove it."

Shrugging, he moved back a step. "Maybe I'll do it. Maybe I won't. You can't make me."

Convinced he was on surer ground, Jacob pressed ahead. "If you want to see Isaac or have anything to do with him, you'll have to."

"So? I don't have to prove it to make it tough for you people. You don't like me hanging around, do you? Lovina's parents don't like it, either."

"We can put up with it if we have to." But it was poor to repay Dinah's family for their help by exposing them to this excuse for a man. "Meanwhile it's costing you money, staying around here, ain't so?"

He thought he sensed a quickening of the man's interest at the mention of money.

"Yeah, well . . . I guess there's that. If I'm hanging around this hick town, I'm not making anything."

Jacob waited. This was the way to get rid of Smith. He was suddenly sure of it. Money.

But the words of Dinah's father came back to him, telling him it was the wrong thing . . . it was like admitting there was something to the man's story.

Did that matter, if it got him to leave them alone?

"How much would it take for you to go away and not come back?" he asked bluntly.

Now there was a greedy gleam in the man's eyes . . . enough to make him stand up straight. He shrugged. "Can't put a price on a man seeing his son, can you?"

"Never mind the nonsense. You don't care a thing about that baby. How much?"

Smith glared at him. "Okay. Five thousand and I disappear."

"Where do you think I can get that kind of money?"

"Don't play poor with me. Everyone says you Amish have cash stashed away. Take it or leave it." He moved as if to go. "Maybe Lovina's father will feel different about it."

"Hold on." He didn't want to put John Stoltz in that situation. "Give me a little time to come up with it." He needed time . . . time to think, time to seek advice. Besides, he might still hear from Anna, or even from the woman who was trying to contact her for them.

"Tomorrow." Smith's tone was sharp. "Tomorrow noon. Have the money, or I go to the girl's father."

He didn't give Jacob time to reply. He swung around and slipped out like the weasel he was.

Tomorrow noon, Jacob repeated to himself. That wasn't much time.

MEANWHILE, DINAH HAD taken a quick look to either side as she reached the street with the buggy. It had been clear both ways. Smith's car still sat where Jacob had said, but it was empty. Good. She took a relieved breath and headed for home.

She still seemed to feel the warm clasp of Jacob's hand on hers, the feeling that they were together in this battle. *Together* was a fine word, much better than *alone*.

Appreciating their friendship was one thing, she lectured herself. But hoping for more would be both foolish and wrong. Foolish, because Jacob couldn't think of anything other than Anna and the baby just now. Besides, he was so convinced that he had failed in his responsibility to take care of his sister that he was hardly likely to want to take on a wife.

And it was wrong, because she could never marry.

Jacob might one day accept the fact that he wasn't to blame for Anna jumping the fence, but she still could never risk disappointing another person the way she'd disappointed Aaron.

Stop thinking about it. Going over and over it didn't change anything. She must stay focused on keeping Isaac safe. That was her duty now.

Reminded, she shot another glance behind them. Micah was right on their tail, so close, in fact, that if she stopped suddenly, he'd be in their laps. But there wasn't another vehicle on the road.

"Is anyone following?" Grossmammi asked.

"Just Micah. And he's so close behind us that he may as well tether his mare to the back of the buggy and be done with it."

"But no cars," Grossmammi persisted. "I was afraid that Smith wouldn't give up so easily."

"I don't suppose he will. But apparently Jacob kept him too occupied to notice us leaving. I just wish I knew what they are saying to each other. If Jacob loses his temper . . ."

"He wouldn't." Grossmammi sounded confident. "He knows how important this is."

She looked down at Isaac, who stared back at her with sleepy eyes. Dinah smiled at the sight. The buggy ride was having its usual effect.

"He'll be asleep in a moment," she said. "How was the morning for you? You're probably ready to take a nap, too, ain't so?"

"Ach, I'm not as old as all that, Dinah. I can still do a morning's work." Grossmammi sounded a bit offended.

"For sure you can, but you shouldn't have to." She smiled. "And before you argue, let me say what a big help you were. You kept the food coming and watched the baby at the same time."

"Easy enough after years of looking after a family. It was nothing in comparison to feeding the harvesters in the old days while your father was a babe in my arms. Now, that was a challenge."

Dinah suppressed a smile. "I know. But I still wish . . ." She let that trail off, not sure what she wanted to say.

"You wish it hadn't been necessary for me to come in this morning. That Lovina hadn't been so foolish, and your parents didn't have to punish her."

"I think I'm the one who should be punished. I should have looked out for her while she was at the shop."

"Now you sound like Jacob, talking about his little sister. It's time both of you learned you can't protect the people you love from growing up and making mistakes."

"If Lovina hadn't come in to help at the shop, it wouldn't have happened." She shook her head. "I actually thought Mammi was being overprotective of her. She knows Lovina better than I do, it seems."

"Ach, foolishness can strike anyone, even people who are all grown up. That's all it was with Lovina, foolishness. I'm sure of it. Lovina's softhearted. That's a good thing, but she doesn't have enough experience to go with it. She fell for the yarn that man spun for her, but she'll come to her senses soon enough. No need to worry."

She nodded, more to reassure Grossmammi than because she was sure of Lovina's motives herself. She'd begun to believe she didn't know her little sister at all. What had been happening at home this morning? Had Mamm and Daad had it out with Lovina?

She'd find out soon enough, she guessed. But whatever Mammi and Daad decided in regard to Lovina, she had her own struggles with her sister. It felt as if it would be easier to forgive a stranger than to forgive her own sister. She'd best remember what Grossmammi said, that it was a mistake caused by Lovina's softheartedness. Knowing Grossmammi, that's probably why she'd said it . . . to help Dinah see.

The mare turned in automatically at the farm lane, quickening her step at the prospect of getting rid of the harness and being turned out in the field with the other horses.

Dinah wasn't in such a hurry. The respite between what went on at the shop and what was happening at home was nearly over, and there would be things to deal with here.

"Lovina will have to see for herself how wrong she was," Grossmammi said, as if they'd been talking about it all the time. "All the punishment in the world can't do that . . . only her own conscience and her own heart can do it."

Dinah nodded. As usual, Grossmammi had it right.

They entered the kitchen to the overwhelming scent of apples and cinnamon. The table held bowls of apples at one end and two kettles of applesauce at the other, while rows of canning jars waited on the counter with Mammi and Lovina in attendance.

"Canning day, I see." Dinah tried to sound as if it were a normal day. "I'll help if we can settle Isaac somewhere. He slept in the buggy, so I don't think he'll go down for a nap until later." She glanced at Lovina without thinking, and just as quickly looked away.

Lovina was helping with the canning, her eyes red and averted, her face wearing the sulky look that tried Dinah's patience. No, she wouldn't pick Lovina for watching the baby; that was certain sure.

Will bounded over, holding out his arms to Isaac. "I'll take care of him, Dinah. Let me. Please?"

Exchanging looks with Mammi, Dinah nodded.

"Let's put a quilt down on the rug in the living room. He might decide he really can crawl if he has that much space."

"Great!" Will raced to the door. "I'll get a quilt." In an instant she heard his feet thudding on the steps.

"That boy never walks anywhere," Mammi said. "He sounds as if he weighs two hundred pounds when he goes up and down the stairs."

"He does, doesn't he?" She kept her thoughts on Will, not her sister. "Just let me wash my hands and I'll get busy."

Mammi nodded. "We can use your help if we're going to finish sauce this afternoon in time to make supper."

"Grossmammi should take a rest . . . ," Dinah began, only to be interrupted by a snort from her grandmother.

"I told you, I'm not that old yet. Let's get this boy settled on the quilt. Will can show him how to crawl, if he can slow down that much."

In a few minutes Isaac was established on the quilt with his toys around him.

"Look, Isaac. This way."

Will crouched next to him, and Isaac obligingly rolled onto his belly. Seeing the toys from a different angle, he got up on his haunches, rocking back and forth, just as if he understood Will.

"That's it," Will said. "Now move your hand and your knee like this."

Laughing at his demonstration, Dinah headed back to the kitchen. She was soon immersed in the applesauce production, keeping busy enough not to worry about the situation.

Lovina peeled, Dinah cut, and Mammi minded the kettles on the stove. It went with the smoothness of long experience, and her years in another house with Aaron seemed to disappear. By the end of the afternoon, they'd have most if not all of the applesauce they'd need. Then it would be time for apple pies, apple cake, apple fritters, and, eventually, apple butter. The trees were loaded this year, but nothing would go to waste.

Lovina continued to wear the sulky look throughout the afternoon. Did she know how annoyed it made others feel? Or was that really the only expression she could manage?

Having finished what she was doing at the moment, Dinah pulled the pail of apples closer. "I'll help you with these."

For an instant Dinah saw pain and thankfulness all mixed up together on Lovina's face. Then the peevish expression closed down again.

But it was too late. Dinah knew what she had seen. Lovina was hurting, and hurting would, she thought, lead to the longing for forgiveness. It was a step in the right direction, at least.

Oddly enough, knowing Lovina was hurting made a difference to her feelings, too. Maybe it wasn't going to be so hard to forgive, after all.

They worked in harmony for a few more minutes, and then they heard a shout from Will.

"Mammi, Dinah, come quick! Look at Isaac."

Not sure whether it was good or bad, they all raced for the living room. Isaac, seeming fine, was up on all fours, with Will next to him.

"He crawled. He did. Here, Dinah." He grabbed a small stuffed bear and tossed it to her. "That's his favorite. See if he'll come for it." Will was so excited that he was bouncing in delight.

"Look, Isaac." She held it out in front of her and wiggled the bear where Isaac could see. "Come get it. Just like Will showed you. You can do it."

Again, it was almost as if he understood. Isaac rocked back and forth. Then he lunged forward, landing on his face. But he was up again in an instant, undeterred. By now, they were all encouraging him and cheering him on.

"You can do it." Dinah wiggled the bear again. "Come get your bear."

For a moment she thought he was going to land on his nose again. Then somehow he got his knees and his hands to work together, grinning when he saw the bear come closer. Another step, and another, and then his tiny fist closed over the bear, and he rolled over onto his back, still holding on to the toy.

"You did it!" Dinah scooped him up in her arms, bear and all. "What a clever boy!"

He waved the bear triumphantly, and everyone laughed, even Lovina. She stopped, as if she hadn't meant to laugh but wasn't able to help it. Suddenly she looked at Dinah.

Two tears squeezed out of her eyes, and she wiped them away with her fingers. Dinah could see the pain and regret in her sister's face. But she didn't speak.

Dinah remembered Grossmammi's words. Lovina would have to see for herself how wrong she'd been, and they wouldn't know it until she spoke.

HARD AS IT was to believe, by suppertime, the kitchen looked as if the chaos had never been. The canning jars, filled now, had been carried to the basement by the boys, but past experience told Dinah that the jars were not yet on the proper shelves. She and Mammi would have to do that.

As supper was finished and the others scattered to do their chores, Dinah watched Jacob. Surely he would tell her what had happened with Smith. He must know she was on pins and needles, waiting. Naturally he wouldn't talk about it in front of the younger ones.

When the boys headed out, Dinah looked a question at Jacob. He understood, she realized, but he looked toward Lovina, who was drying the dishes while Mammi washed, and shook his head slightly.

Dinah carried the last of the dishes to the sink. "Mammi, I'll go down and put the applesauce on the shelves. I'm certain sure the boys didn't do it. They came back too fast."

Mammi gave a strained smile, and Dinah knew her thoughts were on Lovina. "Yah, you're right about that. Denke."

Dinah started down, trusting that Jacob would follow her. She heard him stop to say a word to Grossmammi, who was talking to Isaac just as if he could understand everything she said. Then his footsteps sounded on the wooden stairs.

When he reached her, she was sliding jars of applesauce onto the waiting shelves, putting them next to the last batch of string beans they'd canned.

"Sure is hard to get a word alone." He pushed another box closer to the shelves and began unloading it.

"You're not used to big families," she said lightly. "I like the busyness, but this afternoon I wanted to shoo all of them out of sight. And out of hearing, especially. What happened with Smith? Did you talk to him?"

"Yah, we talked." Jacob's expression settled into a frown. "If you can call it that. He wants me to believe that he is the baby's father, I guess."

Dinah's hands stilled. "What do you mean? Don't you think he meant it?"

"Not a chance, I'd say. He certain sure doesn't act

like a man who thinks he's a daadi. He's just trying it on."

"What did you do?" He wouldn't have paid off the man, would he?

"I got out the DNA test booklet Micah dropped off. Told him if he was Isaac's father, that was an easy way to settle it. He'd have to take the test and prove it."

She let out a deep breath. "I'm so glad you did."

And she was thankful to Micah, who had gotten himself entangled with his courting, if that's what he was doing, in order to help them. She knew very well he hadn't meant to reveal what he had to Mammi and Daadi.

"It took him off guard, I could tell. I suppose he thinks the Amish are so dumb they don't know about such things."

"Is he going to take the test?" She held her breath. If he knew he wasn't Isaac's father, he wouldn't dare, would he?

"He wouldn't say, but he certain sure didn't want to. Said he could cause us a lot of trouble even if he didn't." Jacob stared at the jar in his hand as if he didn't see it. "Which is true enough, ain't so?"

She nodded reluctantly. "I guess so. If he keeps following us around, someone's going to notice."

"If the police are the ones to notice, who knows what might happen." The frown was back, and she began to think the wrinkle between his brows would become permanent.

She nodded, not sure what to say. If only they'd hear from Anna . . .

"Anyway, he came out with what he really wants." Jacob set another two jars down so hard she was afraid they might crack. "Your guess was right. Money."

"He's definitely not Isaac's father," she said. "That proves it." She pictured Isaac's sweet face and felt him in her arms. "No father would do that."

"Probably not, but who knows with him. If I paid him off, at least he'd go away."

Her heart hurt at the look on his face. "But if you do . . . I mean, could you?"

She had no idea how much cash Jacob might have, although the harness shop seemed to be doing well.

"It'd be hard to come up with the amount he wants. Still, he might well come down if I dicker with him." He hesitated. "I know your daad thinks it would be wrong."

She nodded, remembering her father's feelings about it. But she understood only too well what Jacob was feeling, too. "If you need, I have a little in the bank . . ."

"Ach, Dinah." He turned, his face transformed by a smile. "I can't let you do that."

"Don't shut me out." Her breath caught. "Do you think the money means anything compared to Isaac? I love him, too."

He took her hands in his strong clasp. "I know. But only if I have to. I'd rather do almost anything else, but what? If only we'd hear back from that woman, Mrs. Gaus, in Williamsport. But if she'd been able to contact Anna, you'd think we'd have heard by now."

It wasn't exactly easy to think with his warm hands on hers, but she had to. "What about calling her again? Maybe she could still tell you something that would help."

His face tightened. "I was afraid if I bothered her too much, she wouldn't be willing to help. But I guess we're past worrying about that now. It's worth a try."

His expression eased, and his fingers moved on the back of her hand, sending little flickers of warmth through her. "You've always been the smart one, even when we were kids."

Say something light, she told herself. *Don't let him guess what his touch means to you.*

She forced a smile, thinking it probably looked like a grimace. "That's why you were always chasing me away when you played with the boys, I guess."

"I was dumb when I was young." He seemed suddenly closer to her, and her breath caught in her throat. "Now I know how much I rely on you." His eyes darkened suddenly, and he leaned closer so that all she saw was his face, and his breath touched her lips. The world seemed to stand still.

And then Mammi called down the stairs. "Do you need some more help?"

In an instant the spell between them was broken. Jacob took a step back.

"No, we're about done. We'll be right up." Her voice almost sounded normal, but it probably didn't fool her mother. Not daring to look at him, she pushed the empty boxes against the wall and hurried to the steps, feeling him close behind her.

Daad was sitting at the table when they reached the kitchen. Without speaking, he held out an envelope to Jacob. "You left the cellar door open. I heard what you said about the money."

Looking confused, Jacob opened it to disclose a wad of bills. "But . . . I don't understand. You don't approve of paying the man off. You said . . ."

"Yah, I know what I said. But Isaac means too much to hold back if that's the only way." Daad's lean, weathered face was solemn as he gave a decisive nod.

"I can probably come up with the money myself. I shouldn't take yours." Jacob's color deepened.

Daad shook his head. "Keep it for now. You might have trouble putting your hands on cash by tomorrow. Besides, I want to." He didn't invite any further talk about it. "I'll come to the shop tomorrow. To stand with you when you deal with the man."

"And I will, too," Dinah said quickly. He'd have to let her do that . . . he knew how much Isaac meant to her.

CHAPTER TWELVE

Jacob realized he'd been staring at the harness shop phone for most of the morning on Wednesday. He'd been willing it to ring, but like a watched pot refusing to boil, it wasn't cooperating. And that was his last hope.

He'd called last night, trying to reach the woman who'd been so helpful about getting in touch with Anna. Nothing. He'd left a message, begging her to call him back. Nothing. He didn't even know if she'd received the message.

Now . . . now Smith would be showing up shortly, and he had no additional information to defend Isaac from the man's plans. And little hope that any would show up.

He'd expected that John and Dinah would be here by now. He didn't doubt that they'd come. They weren't people who would break their word. He didn't need them, of course, but their presence would give him the extra confidence he'd appreciate when dealing with Smith.

And then he heard it—the back door of the shop next door opening. Footsteps told him that John was coming straight through, but Dinah had stopped in the kitchen.

Relieved, Jacob checked the cash drawer, making sure that the money was there—his own, as much as he could come up with in a hurry, the money John had pushed on him, and the small amount of Dinah's savings.

He had to smile, thinking of her insistence. For such a gentle person, Dinah could be very stubborn when it came to something she felt strongly about.

It would hurt him to have to take money from them to give to a man like Smith, but it would hurt much worse to lose Isaac. If only . . .

The door between the shops swung open, and John came through. He looked at Jacob right away, and then shook his head. "No news?"

"No. She hasn't called me back, so I don't even know if she got the message." He'd told the others everything that had happened, so they'd been waiting and praying, too.

"Well, they might be away from home. Could be she'll call you later."

John tried to sound optimistic, but they both knew if he hadn't heard by now, then it was unlikely he would. And it would be too late to be helpful, anyway.

The door swung open again, and Dinah came through, holding a mug of coffee in each hand. She let the door close behind her and handed the coffee to Jacob and to her father.

"None for you?" he asked.

She shook her head. "I think my stomach is too nervous to accept any caffeine just now." She glanced at the clock, her face tightening so that she looked as she had for so long after Aaron's death.

He felt the same, and he understood. It must make Dinah feel better to do something, even if she didn't want anything herself.

John downed a gulp of coffee, never one to reject it

when it was offered. At their house, the coffeepot was always on the back of the stove.

He glanced around the room. "The shop has supported generations of your family, yah? It won't let you down now."

"No, but I hate having to use money meant for the family to pay off a man like Smith."

Jacob looked around, remembering himself standing at the counter, barely able to see over it, but glad to be helping his father. He could see his grandfather sitting at the sewing machine, his back bent, his hands manipulating the leather easily as he worked.

This place was his heritage. If he had his way, it would be Isaac's heritage, too.

"Still, Daad and Grossdaadi would be the first ones to understand. Isaac is safe for now, and I have to keep him that way."

"You will," Dinah said, her voice quiet but confident. Then she glanced past him and stiffened.

He didn't need to turn to know what she'd seen through the front window. Smith must be here. A moment later the door opened.

Smith stopped, seeming surprised that Jacob had someone with him. Then he came forward, eyeing them. "Looks like you have some company. You want to talk in front of them?"

"We are involved," John said, not identifying himself and making Jacob remember what Smith had said about going to Lovina's father. Well, he was seeing him, but he looked a little intimidated at the stern, dignified figure.

"Doesn't matter to me." Smith shifted his focus back to Jacob. "Where's my money? Looks like me disappearing and leaving you people alone might be worth even more if these people care about the kid, too."

Jacob's anger spurted at the words. "You'll be fortunate to get anything. I think the police would call this blackmail."

Smith's face darkened. "You go calling names and the price might just go up."

"Why are you so shy? That's what it is."

He shouldn't taunt him, he knew, but the thought of this creature claiming to be anything to that sweet baby was infuriating.

"Yeah, well, you can't prove it without going to the police, can you? All I have to say is that I had no idea what that girl was doing, coming toward me lugging a baby. Then she'd be the one talking to the police. You want that?"

John took a step toward the man, his hands curling into fists, his face as stern and judgmental as that of an Old Testament prophet.

"If my daughter must talk to the police, she will. But you will be in the greater trouble, I tell you that."

Smith slid back a couple of steps. "Hey, I don't want to. I just have to get something for my time and trouble. You can't expect a man to give up his kid without getting something."

"We're not admitting that you have any claim." Jacob moved next to John. "We're taking care of my sister's child, and all we want is to live in peace."

Smith seemed to regain some of his bluster at that. "Well, like I said, it's going to cost you. Five thousand isn't much for peace of mind, right?"

Jacob was so intent that he hadn't even realized the door had opened until the woman shut it. Relief swept through him, so strong that it made him dizzy for a moment. He could see Dinah look at him strangely.

"Mrs. Gaus. You came."

She nodded to him, smiling a little. Then she looked

at Smith, and her smile vanished. "It sounds like I got here at just the right time."

DINAH HAD A moment of confusion, but then she understood. This was the woman from Amish Assist; she must be. She'd actually come. With good news? Surely it must be good, or she wouldn't have come.

She hesitated, and when Jacob didn't speak, she did. "My name is Dinah Hershberger." She gestured. "This is my father, John Stoltz."

The woman had a warm smile for Dinah. "Of course. You're Anna's friend. She asked you to bring baby Isaac home."

"Yah, she did." Jacob sent Dinah a grateful look. "Denke, Dinah. I'm forgetting my manners. Mrs. Gaus is the woman I spoke with before. And this—" He glared at Smith.

"This is Nate Smith," Mrs. Gaus finished for him. "My husband and I have seen him around Williamsport. I'd like to know what he's doing here, though."

"None of your business," Smith growled. "Nobody asked you to butt in."

"I did," Jacob said quickly. "I asked for her help and advice." He turned back to Mrs. Gaus. "What do you know about him?"

Obviously he hoped it would be something to use as a weapon against the man.

Mrs. Gaus looked from Dinah to her father and back again. "I should explain that my husband and I run a program called Amish Assist. We provide help for young people who have left the Amish and don't know what to do."

She paused, as if expecting a negative reaction, but

neither of them spoke, so she went on. "Sometimes we run across people who say they're interested in helping, but they're more interested in taking advantage of them."

"You can't say that about me. I'm not hurting anyone." Smith sounded belligerent, but his face was uneasy.

"What about us?" Jacob took a step toward the man, his hands clenching. "He claims to be Isaac's father. He wants money in payment for leaving us alone."

She didn't look surprised. "Seems to me the Williamsport police might like to know about that."

"Don't you threaten me with the police. You don't have anything on me. Besides, it would be harder on them than on me." But his eyes darted around the room as if he wanted to be sure of an exit.

Mrs. Gaus ignored him. "I don't know a great deal about him, but I do know what Anna thinks of him. She told me he was a creep she wouldn't touch with a ten-foot pole. And she asked me to give Dinah this."

She pulled an envelope from her bag and handed it to Dinah. Not sure why Anna had sent it to her rather than her brother, she opened it and pulled out the contents . . . an official-looking paper. Her breath caught in her throat.

"It's a birth certificate," she gasped. "Isaac's. It names Anna as the mother and—" she hesitated, to be sure she was reading it correctly—"Matthew Jacob Yost as the father." She looked at Mrs. Gaus. "Is he Amish?"

She nodded. "He was."

Smith took a step back, but he apparently wasn't giving up. "Just because she said that on the certificate doesn't mean it was true. That doesn't prove anything."

"Then take the DNA test," Jacob snapped. "Or just

disappear and consider yourself fortunate we don't call the police."

For a tense moment they glared at each other. Dinah couldn't stand it. She could see Jacob's temper rising. If he lost control . . .

She walked quickly to the phone on the counter. Once she was sure Smith was watching, she picked up the receiver. "I'll call the police station," she said.

Smith wavered for an instant. Then he turned and fled. The door slammed behind him.

Mrs. Gaus smiled at Dinah. "That did it," she said.

Her hand shaking, Dinah fumbled with the receiver and finally managed to hang it up.

"Denke. Thank you, Mrs. Gaus." Jacob's voice trembled for an instant and then steadied. "We are so grateful to you."

Her father nodded, echoing his thanks as Dinah moved across to join them.

"Denke," she murmured, her eyes filling with tears. She held out her hands to the woman. "You have saved us."

Mrs. Gaus smiled, and their hands and gazes locked as if the two of them were alone. "You'll take care of Isaac. Anna knows it, and so do I."

Dinah struggled to speak over the lump in her throat. "You . . . you will stay a bit and talk with us? Have some coffee, at least?"

"That sounds fine." She still held Dinah's hands, but her glance included all of them. "I'd like to do that."

Dinah led the way through the connecting door. Once Mrs. Gaus was seated at a table with the two men, Dinah hurried into the kitchen. After what Mrs. Gaus had done, Dinah was overcome with the need to serve her, and here it was, a day when she was closed and had nothing fresh ready.

Quickly she put yesterday's coffee cake into the oven to warm and started a fresh pot of coffee. As she poured a mug from the pot already made, her thoughts kept swirling with the same words over and over. *Thank you, thank you, thank you.*

She came back in with coffee and cake in time to hear Jacob speaking.

"About the boy who was listed as the father . . . ," Jacob began.

Mrs. Gaus had been telling them what work she and her husband did, but now her face changed. "Matthew was one of the people we tried to help, but . . ." Her gesture conveyed helplessness. "I think he'd already been in trouble even before he left his home. Then he got caught up in partying and drinking."

John nodded, his face sorrowful. "It happens."

They seemed to share a moment of regret before Mrs. Gaus spoke again. "Anna . . . well, Anna tried to help him. She said he was doing better, but they were out one night and he drank too much. She tried to keep him from driving, but he went off without her."

Dinah could read the rest of it in her face. "An accident?"

She nodded. "He was killed. And two older people also, in the other car."

"Thank the Lord Anna wasn't with him." Jacob's fingers whitened around his cup.

"I think . . . ," the woman said slowly, "that Anna blames herself. It wasn't her fault, but . . ." Again the gesture of helplessness.

Dinah began to see what a difficult job this woman and her husband had taken on, and her heart went out to them. And to Anna, who carried such a heavy burden.

They were all silent for a moment, and then Jacob set his cup down carefully, as if he feared he'd break it.

"Did my sister send any message to us?"

The words seemed to tremble in the air for a moment with the intensity of Jacob's need.

Mrs. Gaus nodded. "She asked me to say that she knew you and Dinah would love Isaac and take care of him like he was your own."

Jacob's gaze met Dinah's, just for an instant, and she wasn't sure what that gaze was saying. He turned back to Mrs. Gaus.

"Please tell her that we do and we will. And that we will go on loving her, too."

LATER IN THE afternoon, Dinah looked down toward the lane from the apple orchard to spot Jacob's buggy turn and pull up at the barn. He looked toward the orchard, waved, and a few minutes later was walking toward them.

She couldn't make out his expression from here, but he was walking as if he didn't carry such a load on his shoulders. She certain sure hoped he could hold on to his relief at getting rid of Smith.

She knew, only too well, that he could so easily slip back into his worries about Anna. Could he ever really be happy until she came home?

"Heads up, Dinah!" Will, above her in the apple tree, loosed a handful of ripe McIntosh apples, and it was all she could do to catch a few of them in her basket.

Chasing after the ones that were still rolling, she gathered them up and added them to the basket. "Next time shout *before* you drop them," she called back.

Will just grinned. "Better get that one that's rolling toward Isaac."

Startled, Dinah turned to see the apple bounce onto the rug where Isaac was playing, with Grossmammi sitting on a folding chair to watch him. She dived, getting there just before he focused on the rolling object, and sent his jingling ball toward him instead.

Isaac spotted it, tried to crawl toward it while still holding on to a rattle, and ended up landing on his nose. He didn't seem troubled—he just scooted forward until he could grab it and then rolled over, still clutching both objects.

Grossmammi chuckled. "If he keeps doing that, he'll flatten his nose. Now he'll try to put both things in his mouth."

"I don't believe his little mouth will hold them." Dinah plopped down on the rug next to them. "It's a beautiful day, ain't so?"

Grossmammi nodded. "A day to thank the Lord for our blessings. Even the ones we don't yet see."

Dinah blinked, not sure what her grandmother meant. Sometimes it wasn't easy to understand Grossmammi, but it was always worth trying. She had stored up a lot of wisdom over the years.

"I'm not sure how to be thankful for something if I don't know what it is," she said. "You'll have to teach me."

Grossmammi's smile was loving even as she shook her head. "Trust." Her voice was soft, and she seemed to look at something far away. "Things that seem hard are sometimes better for us."

Were they? Not having a baby of her own was hard; that was certain sure. Letting Aaron down was hard, too. And letting go of Isaac when the time came . . . that might be hardest of all. How could any of those things be better for her?

She was struggling again, wasn't she? She'd convinced herself that she wanted Anna to be reunited with her baby, but the very thought of losing Isaac set up a fierce pain in her heart.

Why did it have to be so hard? How could it be good for her to lose the baby she loved?

Rebellion surged in her, fighting against the very idea of accepting what everyone else agreed was right. Mammi had seen this coming, that first night when she'd brought Isaac home. She'd tried to warn her about getting too attached to Isaac.

The warning had come too late, she knew now. She'd loved Isaac from the moment she saw him. In that instant, it had already been too late.

Then Jacob reached them, and she forced the painful thoughts to the back of her mind to look up and smile in welcome. Jacob paused to greet everyone, but his attention was already on his little nephew.

Dropping on the corner of the rug, he leaned over Isaac, and his face filled with love. So much love made her heart contract and then swell again until it seemed ready to burst from her chest. If he ever looked at her that way . . .

That was another idea to banish from her mind. It wouldn't happen, and she knew it.

Jacob talked baby talk for a few minutes, pretending he understood the sounds Isaac burbled back to him. Then he glanced from her to Grossmammi. "You've told everyone?"

"For sure," Grossmammi answered him. "We're so thankful."

He nodded, and for a moment he seemed to be looking at something the rest of them couldn't see. "I just wish Anna had come, instead of sending the birth certificate."

Grossmammi reached out to pat him as if he were one of her grandchildren. "Yah, I know. We all wish that, but . . ."

"What?" Jacob looked up, startled and defensive, Dinah thought, at the hesitation in Grossmammi's words.

"Ach, Jacob." Her voice filled with love and regret mingled. "Sometimes the time isn't right. Sometimes people aren't ready."

His jaw set stubbornly. "Anna has a son. He can't wait for her to be ready to love him."

Dinah made an involuntary movement. "She does love him. She showed that by sending him here."

He seemed to struggle with that, and then he forced a smile. "Yah, well, at least we can stop worrying about Smith."

Relaxing back on his elbows, he looked around the orchard, where Mamm, Lovina, and Will were still picking. His gaze lingered for a moment on Lovina, whose eyes were suspiciously red but who still wore the sulky look.

"What's happening with all the apples? Your mamm isn't going to do apple butter already, is she?"

Accepting his change of subject was the only thing to do, it seemed. "Mamm's decided to make some apple pies for the curb market on Friday. And fill some small baskets of apples to sell, too," Dinah explained.

"When folks see her pies, they'll be inspired to make pies themselves," Grossmammi said. "So she sells the pies and the apples, ain't so?"

"What about some apple pies for the rest of us?" he asked hopefully. He turned to Dinah. "I remember your mamm's apple crumb pies from when we were kids. The best ever."

Dinah laughed, relaxing. "You tell her that, and I'm certain sure she'll be making some."

"I'll do that," he said. His gaze lingered on the apple trees as he rolled the jingling ball to Isaac. "Remember when we used to climb the trees and eat the apples, hoping nobody would see us?"

"I remember when you convinced me to eat a green one. I couldn't face another apple for a month." The ball got away from Isaac, and she bounced it back toward him.

"Ach, that must have been in my troublemaking period," he said, intercepting it and then rolling it to Isaac.

For a moment Dinah could see the two of them sitting on a thick limb of an apple tree, side by side. She'd shown him where she'd wedged a piece of wood between the branches and the trunk to make a seat, proud to share it with him.

They'd sat there swinging their legs, hidden from below by the thick foliage, her with her dress flapping between her legs and Jacob with his legs sticking out of the pants he was constantly outgrowing. His mother had declared that she no sooner finished a pair than he outgrew them.

They were happy memories, except for the green apple incident. They'd been good friends, each of them a few years ahead of their nearest siblings.

"Look," Jacob whispered, touching her hand.

She blinked. Isaac had gotten himself up on his haunches, but he wasn't attempting to crawl. He tipped to one side, recovered himself, and wobbled into a sitting position.

"Ach, look at you," Jacob exclaimed, as Dinah clapped her hands together.

Isaac looked up, laughed, and toppled over again, still laughing.

Jacob gave him a noisy kiss on his fat little neck, making him giggle. He turned toward her, as if inviting her to share his pleasure.

Jacob's blue eyes darkened for a moment as their gazes met. The air was so still that she could hear the distant droning of the bees. She didn't move, couldn't even breathe.

If only this moment could last . . . if only they could be together like this forever.

Chapter Thirteen

After that poignant moment with Jacob, Dinah wasn't sure how she was going to get through the rest of the day without revealing her feelings. But to her surprise, it was easier than she expected. She kept busy helping Mammi with preparing the apples. Jacob, other than coming in for supper, stayed occupied with Daad for what was left of the day.

At one point, Dinah looked out across the field that separated their farm from Jacob's next door. She spotted someone moving, and went closer to the window.

Daad and Jacob were there, talking busily and gesturing. She saw Daad's arm sweep out in a wave that must have included all of the upper fields that were usually given over to hay.

Not that Jacob had done much active farming recently. How could he, with the harness shop? When his daad was alive, he'd run the shop, and Jacob had divided his time between the shop and the farm. But now . . .

Poor Jacob. He tried to do everything, but it couldn't be done. If he had had brothers, or even if Anna had married in the church and her husband wanted to take over the farm, that would have worked. But Jacob simply couldn't do it all, and she knew his heart was in working with leather in the shop.

Her thoughts didn't become caught in an image of Jacob's face until she was moving quietly around her bedroom, getting ready for bed by the light of a single small lamp, with Isaac sleeping peacefully in his crib.

She paused to look down at him. He was sprawled out like a starfish, his arms and legs spread, and in its relaxation, his face had a look of Jacob's.

Jacob's face. She saw it again, looking at her with warmth and understanding and caring . . . and love?

No, she couldn't let herself think that. Jacob was too tangled up in his sense of having failed his little sister to think of anything else. And she . . . well, she couldn't, either.

Isaac's lips pursed, making sucking motions for a moment or two, and then he relaxed again. Was he dreaming? What did a baby dream of . . . warmth, milk, the beat of a mother's heart?

A small sound distracted her, coming from the hallway. Was someone still up? She listened more closely and almost thought she heard someone breathing on the other side of the door. A shadow blocked out the light that had filtered under the door.

Perplexed, she opened the door gently, turning the knob with care. There was Lovina, sitting on the floor, her arms wrapped around her knees over her white nightgown, her bare feet sticking out.

"Lovina." She whispered, not wanting to wake anyone. "What are you doing?" She was ready to scold, but when she had a look at the white face turned up to her, the words died in her throat.

Instead, she reached down to grasp her sister's arm and pull her to her feet. Lovina came up willingly enough. Her arm was cold to the touch, and she shivered, toes curling on the bare floorboards.

"You're cold," Dinah murmured. "Come in here."

She hauled Lovina into the bedroom, not sure what she was going to do with her. Realizing she was shaking, either with tension or with cold, she tugged her over to the bed and tucked her into one side, pulling the quilt over her. Quickly she slipped into the other side and put her arm around her sister, letting the warmth of her body do the work.

"Now," she said, still speaking softly so as not to wake the baby, "tell me what this is all about."

Lovina sniffled, trying without success to hold back tears. "I shouldn't have come." She made a half-hearted movement, as if to get up.

Dinah held her tightly. "Don't be so foolish." Remembering she didn't intend to scold, she spoke more lightly. "This is just like when you were a little girl, ain't so? When you'd had a nightmare, you'd creep in here and crawl into bed beside me. The first I'd know about it was feeling your cold toes against me."

Lovina made a sound halfway between a giggle and a sob. "I remember." She shivered again. "I . . . I liked it so much that sometimes I did it when I didn't even have a nightmare."

"I knew," Dinah said, laughing softly at the memories.

"I was so sad when you got married and moved out. I mean . . . I wanted to be happy for you, but I was sad for me. I missed you so much."

At the heartbreak in her sister's voice, a lump formed in Dinah's throat. "I wasn't that far away," she said feebly, knowing that hadn't helped.

Lovina didn't even bother to answer that. "But when

you came back, I thought it would be the way it used to. It wasn't, but when I started working at the shop it was better. I felt like I really belonged. And then I ruined everything." She moved, turning to face Dinah. "Did he really do what Daad was saying?"

Someone should have made sure that Lovina heard the whole story of their interactions with Smith. She'd have picked up just bits and pieces of what she'd heard Daad telling Mammi.

"We have Isaac's birth certificate now. Anna sent it with her friend. He wasn't Isaac's father."

"Maybe he didn't know?" She said the words tentatively, as if she didn't believe them herself.

Dinah shook her head. "He must have known that. He was just trying to get money out of us. He asked Jacob for money and said he'd go away if he got it."

She hesitated. Should she tell the rest of it? It would hurt, but maybe Lovina should hear it. "He was even going to threaten Daadi about what you did so he could get money from him, as well. He's not a good person, Lovina."

"I should . . . I should have known." The words were broken by a sob. "When I thought about what he said afterward it seemed odd, and maybe I didn't believe it, but when I was with him . . ."

Dinah rubbed her back, silently encouraging.

Lovina sniffled. "I thought he liked me. He said I was the only one who understood. The only one he could trust to help him. And all the time he was lying." She choked on a sob. "I'm sorry. I'm so sorry."

The tears took over, and all Dinah could do was hold her tight, pat her, and murmur soothing words that didn't mean anything. Poor Lovina. She'd found out painfully that not everyone could be trusted.

She'd been vulnerable to Smith, just because of her lack of experience. Guilt swept through Dinah. She was the one who'd made it possible for Lovina to work in town. She should have taken better care of her.

Eventually Lovina's sobs lessened, until she was finally able to mop her face and blow her nose. Then she looked at Dinah, her heart in her eyes. "Will you forgive me? Ever?"

Dinah cupped Lovina's face in her hands. "Do you understand that what you did was not just wrong, it was dangerous?"

She nodded, her eyes filling with tears again. "Yah, I do. I couldn't stand it if something happened to Isaac. Honest. I'm so sorry."

"All right," she said, and felt her little sister give a sigh of relief. She hurried on. "But there's something else you have to do."

Apprehension filled Lovina's face. "What?"

"You have to tell Mammi and Daad how sorry you are. And most of all, you have to tell Jacob."

And Dinah would have to pray that Jacob would say the right things to her.

"That . . . that'll be hard." Lovina was silent for a moment, but then she nodded. "Yah, you're right. I will do it."

"Good girl." She wrapped her arms around Lovina, holding her tight, and the whole time she was reminding herself that she should ask for forgiveness, too.

JACOB WALKED BACK to the house early the next morning, watching the sun begin to lift above the horizon and lighten the sky. John, coming from the barn, caught up with him.

"About time for breakfast." John rubbed his hands together against the morning chill. "I smell scrapple frying."

"Smells good. I haven't had scrapple since . . . well, I don't know when. I didn't cook much when I was on my own."

Just saying the words reminded him of how full his life was now in comparison to the months after Anna left.

And now, to have at least one burden lifted from his shoulders . . .

"John, are you sure you want to take on the extra work?" After all, John might have changed his mind after the casual conversation they'd had the previous day.

"Extra work will keep those boys of mine out of trouble." John clapped him on the shoulder as he followed the boys into the house. "Let's eat."

Dinah, sitting at the kitchen table with Isaac in a high chair next to her, must have noticed something in their faces as they came to the table. "You two look as if you're plotting something. What is it?"

Her father grinned, his lean face crinkling. "Maybe it's a secret," he teased.

"Secret?" The twins were on the word in a moment. "What's a secret?"

"Something to keep you out of mischief." He sat, looked around the table to be sure everyone was ready, and closed his eyes in the silent prayer asking God's blessing on the food.

The instant he raised his head, David stabbed a slice of scrapple and slid it onto his plate, while Daniel asked the question again.

"What? Anyway, we don't need to be kept out of mischief. We're as good as gold."

Will snorted at that. "Since when?"

Before the twins could retort, John was answering. "Jacob and I agreed we'll go in with him to farm his land. So you see, there will be more to keep you boys occupied."

"Don't worry," Jacob said quickly. "I'll still pitch in to help when I don't have to be at the store."

"The twins will remind you of that," Will said, eating scrambled eggs so fast that it was a wonder he could get the words out.

"Don't you worry," Daniel said, giving a mock punch to his younger brother. "We'll make sure you do your share, too."

Jacob thought how nice and easy it was to be here, with bowls circulating and silverware clinking on plates while the younger ones chattered. He had to reach far back in his mind, it seemed, to remember meals like these, when he and Anna were both small.

He realized Dinah was looking at him with a slightly troubled expression, maybe worrying whether he was doing the right thing. Isaac, growing impatient, grabbed at the hand with which she held a spoonful of cereal.

"All right, all right," she said, her voice lit by laughter. "You're a greedy little boy, ain't so?"

Isaac smacked his lips, seeming to agree.

His gaze lingered on them for another moment. Dinah leaned forward, smiling as she fed Isaac, and Isaac watched her eagerly, reaching for the spoon. They seemed to be in perfect unity.

Oddly, something almost like a cloud slipped through his mind, but it was gone again before he could pin it down.

He'd reassure Dinah that he was okay with his decision. They'd be driving in together this morning, as Thursday was one of her full days at the shop. He flicked a glance at Lovina. Apparently she wasn't going in.

Good, as far as he was concerned. His anger had vanished, swamped in more recent events, but once trust was shaken, it was hard to build it up again. He suspected she'd be staying under her mother's eye for a while longer.

Once the buggy was loaded, he helped Dinah's grandmother into the rear seat, and Dinah handed the baby up to her when she held out her arms.

When they were out on the main road, he sensed Dinah's gaze on him.

"Are you all right with what you've decided about the farm? I know Daad wouldn't want you to rush into anything."

"I'm sure." He glanced toward her, reading the concern that darkened her green eyes. "It doesn't have to be permanent, but it's the best decision for now."

"Yah, I guess." She still sounded troubled, and he realized she was reflecting his own feelings.

"It isn't the way Daad wanted it to be." He spoke slowly, sorting it out in his mind as he did. "He and Mammi must have pictured having a big family, with a son to follow in the harness business and another who'd want to run the farm. But it didn't happen."

He realized suddenly that she might think he thought about her own situation with Aaron, and that was the last thing he wanted to do.

"Mamm and Daad had a good marriage. They were happy together." A faint smile touched his lips as he thought of them teasing each other over the breakfast table. "With Daad and me working, we could manage the farm and the shop, but I can't do it alone. This is the best answer."

He didn't know if he had reassured Dinah, but he knew he'd reassured himself. This was the right thing to do.

"You're right." Her voice was warm with approval. "And the land is still yours. You'll be able to bring up

Isaac on the farm that's been in his family for three . . . no, four generations."

"I'd like to see that." He pictured Isaac climbing up to the barn loft, hiding a kitten in his bedroom, splashing in the creek and chasing lightning bugs in the summer twilight. "It will be a gut life for him."

Dinah wore a remembering smile, and he guessed that she was seeing the same things he was—the images of a happy, secure childhood with people who loved them.

They rode in silence for a few minutes except for the clop of hooves and the faint murmur of Dinah's grandmother humming to Isaac in the back seat. She seemed to see the baby as if he were her own great-grandchild. Just like all the Stoltz family, she accepted him without question.

"If Anna comes back . . ."

Dinah's words died away, as if she regretted having spoken. Still, it was natural enough that her thoughts would go to his sister. Where did she fit into their picture of Isaac's childhood?

"I've been telling myself that she will come back." He said the words with difficulty. "But every day it's a little harder."

And if she did? He thought of the love that had flowed between Dinah and Isaac at the breakfast table. Where did Dinah fit in if Anna came back?

He didn't need to look at Dinah to see her gentleness and her loving spirit. And he could sense, as well, the solid core of strength that lay beneath.

"Maybe it would have been better if we hadn't involved you." The words spilled out of him. "You love him."

"Of course." Her voice suggested that he said something so obvious it didn't need to be said.

"But if . . . ," he began, suddenly picturing a nightmare scene of Anna taking Isaac away with her, of them being helpless to stop her.

"No matter what happens." She answered the thing he didn't want to say. "It's like Grossmammi says. Loving is always worth the risk."

Jacob felt the words sink into him. He couldn't turn off his love for Isaac, and neither could she. Whatever happened, that was sure.

DINAH CHOPPED CARROTS in the respite after the morning rush. She ought to be taking coffee over to Jacob, but she needed to think first. She must talk to him about Lovina's apology before it happened. If he had a negative response . . .

Well, she really didn't think he would, but he'd be better able to deal with it if he were forewarned.

The carrot fell from her knife in round orange slices, and the rhythm of the blade against the wooden cutting board soothed her. There was always comfort to be had in ordinary, everyday tasks if you looked for it. The pot of beef stock was already simmering, sending its aroma through the kitchen. It would be ready for lunchtime. She didn't have an extensive lunch menu, but homemade soup was always popular.

Lovina should be talking to Mamm and Daad today, confessing her wrongs. Poor Lovina had learned the hard way that not everyone could be trusted, but there was no doubt in Dinah's mind that Lovina's rebellious spirit had made her ready to believe. That was what worried Mammi, she suspected.

Grossmammi looked up from checking on Isaac, who slept sprawled out in the cot. "You are worrying about Lovina, yah?"

She ought to be used to her grandmother's habit of reading her concerns by now. She scraped the slices into the kettle and picked up the long wooden spoon to stir the soup.

"Yah. How did you know?"

"I was wakeful last night, and I heard your voices."

"We didn't mean to wake you . . ."

Grossmammi brushed that away. "When you're my age, you don't need so much sleep. It's not a bad thing. I can listen to the night noises of the house, and I like to talk to God in the stillness."

Dinah's throat tightened. How many crises in her children's and grandchildren's lives had Grossmammi prayed them through?

"I told Lovina she had to apologize to Mammi and Daadi. And to Jacob. Now I'm wondering if that was wise. Not about Mammi and Daadi, of course, but Jacob."

Grossmammi considered. "It's needed, and Lovina won't be freed of her burden until she's done it. Why are you worried about Jacob?"

She stared absently at the bubbles breaking the surface of the soup. "He's all tied up in knots about Anna and Isaac, and his own guilt . . . well, I'm afraid that will make him too sharp with Lovina."

"Not if you prepare him first." Grossmammi's eyes crinkled. "Stop thinking about it, Dinah. Just go and do it. The soup doesn't need that much stirring."

Forced into a laugh, Dinah put the spoon down on a saucer to drip. "Right. I'll get his coffee and sticky bun first. That'll put him in a receptive mood."

Listening to her grandmother's chuckle, she headed for the coffeepot.

When she pushed through the door a few minutes later, juggling the coffee mug and the sticky bun, Jacob was standing at the workbench, rubbing a harness with neat's-foot oil. If he was busy, maybe she should wait.

Jacob exploded that feeble excuse by looking up with a smile and heading straight toward her. "Just what I need. Is that one of your grandmother's famous sticky buns I see?"

"It is." She shook her head. "I use the same recipe, but hers are always a little better."

"Experience," he suggested, leaning against the counter while he bit into the gooey confection. His face lit with pleasure. "Yum. I'll be sure and tell her how much I love it."

She barely managed to respond, because she was trying too hard to bring up the difficult subject. She'd just have to dive in, she guessed.

"I want to tell you something." She took a breath, needing a little more air for this. "Last night Lovina came into my room. She was feeling so guilty she couldn't handle it any longer."

To her dismay, Jacob's face hardened. "If you're going to ask me to be understanding, I'm not in the mood. Anything could have happened to Isaac, and it would be her fault. She should feel guilty."

"I've just told you she does, Jacob." She kept her voice calm with an effort. "She's still a child in many ways. She didn't know how to deal with someone like Smith. He was able to fool her so easily."

"Then she should have asked." He bit off the words, and then shook his head irritably. "Look, I'm not going to say anything to her. I owe your family too much for that. But it's best if we go on ignoring each other."

"That's not gut enough." The firmness of her words surprised her. "She needs to be forgiven, just like the rest of us do."

"You mean like I do, for not taking care of Anna better. You think I don't know that?"

"I think you dwell on it too much." Her voice sharpened. "We all did something wrong in dealing with Anna after your parents died. If I had tried harder to get her to talk to me that last year . . ."

A quiver broke the stiffness of his face. "You weren't to blame. Taking care of my sister was my job. My responsibility."

"Ach, Jacob, what I'm trying to say is that we all make mistakes. You did. I did. Lovina did, and she's sorry. Won't you let her tell you how sorry she is?"

He stood looking at her for a long moment. Then the blue in his eyes seemed to grow lighter, as if it reflected sunlight.

"I guess I can't tell you no when you put it that way. You know that. You're pretty good at turning my own words against me."

"I didn't . . . ," she began, but she knew it was true.

He grimaced, but the anger was gone. "I just don't think I'll be very good at this. I don't have a very good record of dealing with teenage girls."

"So long as you don't lose your temper." Her apprehension slid away. "Please, Jacob. She's my little sister, and she's hurting."

Just like your little sister is hurting, she thought but didn't say.

"Yah, all right," he grumbled.

"Denke."

"I don't know why you're so easy on her. After what she said about you pretending Isaac is yours—I know how much that must have hurt. Especially after the things Aaron said to you, the way he blamed you for not having—"

He stopped, as suddenly as if someone had slammed a door.

Dinah froze, trying to process what he'd just said. About Aaron, about what Aaron had said to her . . .

"How do you know?" she demanded. "Did Aaron tell you about it?" She cringed at the thought. "Or did you—"

She stopped, her eyes widening, her heart freezing. "You heard," she gasped. "That day at the shop. You heard him."

She didn't have to think it through. She knew.

CHAPTER FOURTEEN

Shock held Dinah motionless, and Jacob took a step toward her, his face pleading.

"Dinah, please, listen. It's not what you think. It's—"

Dinah's hands shot up, palms raised against him to hold him off. "Don't! I can't. I can't talk about it."

Jacob shook his head, his face contracted in pain. Before he could speak, the bell jingled on the door. Jolted into movement, Dinah fled to her own place.

She burst through the door and stopped, hand pressed against her chest as if she could stop the fierce pounding of her heart. Thankful no one was in the shop, she paused, listening to the rumble of Jacob's voice behind her as he took care of his customer. Swallowing hard, she fought to gain control of herself. She didn't want Grossmammi to guess what had happened.

No one knew. That had been the one thing that had comforted her in all this time. At least she held her humiliation to herself. People might guess, but no one knew of the painful things Aaron had said, of the terrible disappointment she'd been to him.

But now it seemed that Jacob knew. Not only that,

he'd known all along. Had he talked to Aaron about it? Had Aaron complained to him? Had Jacob, thinking of his long relationship with her family, kept silent?

"Dinah?" Grossmammi came through from the kitchen and stopped, looking at her with the wise gaze that seemed to see everything. "Was ist letz? What's wrong?"

"Nothing," she said quickly, relieved to hear sounds coming from the back room where Isaac had been sleeping. "There's the baby. I'll get him."

She walked quickly past Grossmammi, hurrying toward the storeroom, now a temporary nursery. If only her grandmother wouldn't ask any more questions, she might keep from breaking down.

Maybe Grossmammi knew what she was thinking. In any event, she didn't follow. Dinah was able to reach the storeroom and close the door behind her.

Isaac lay on his back, waving his arms and wailing. At the sight of her the noise stopped. He rolled to the sitting position he was trying to master and held up his arms, clearly confident she'd pick him up.

Dinah scooped him into her arms and held him close, loving the sweet, warm weight of him. When she was tending to him, she didn't need to worry about anyone else interrupting. Grossmammi would take care of anyone who wandered into the shop at this hour.

Her gaze wandered around the storeroom as she prepared a diaper change. That terrible argument had taken place here. Was it possible that Jacob had been in the matching room on the other side of the wall? But sound didn't go through the wall between her kitchen and his work area, so why . . .

Carrying Isaac, she walked toward the intervening wall. It only took a moment's inspection to tell her that behind the storage shelves, the wall was just a thin partition.

This space had probably been part of the harness shop at one time, maybe a workroom or a storeroom. Then, when they started renting out the adjoining shop, they had needed a storeroom for it. They hadn't bothered to put up an insulated wall, just added a partition.

So Jacob had heard. A flame of outrage flickered. How could he stand there and listen?

It must have happened that way. If it hadn't, then Aaron had told him, and that was even worse. Either way, she couldn't imagine facing Jacob again.

Well, she'd have to. She felt a moment of panic at the thought. How could she do it?

Isaac, getting bored with the inaction, started to wiggle. Bouncing him in her arms automatically, she took him back to the countertop they used for a changing table, putting him down on the padded mat. Isaac promptly rolled over, reaching for the bottle of baby lotion.

"Not that, you schnickelfritz." She set it out of his reach, turned him back, and put a rattle into his hands. He swung it violently, clipping her on the nose as she bent over him. "Hey, take it easy."

Isaac looked as startled as she felt, and she had to laugh at his expression. "You know what a schnickelfritz is? It's a mischievous little one, just like you." She tickled his belly as she slid the diaper into place.

Could it possibly be just a little over a week since he had come into their lives? It seemed impossible. Life could change in an instant, it seemed, sometimes for the worse, as when Aaron's accident happened, but sometimes . . .

She halted that line of thought. Surely the arrival of

Isaac was for the good. Even if Anna took him away again . . .

She had to stop there. If that happened, she'd hope she could still be thankful for the chance to love him, even if losing him broke her heart in pieces.

With Isaac dry and happy, she might be able to feed him some fruit and cereal before they got busy again. If not, of course Grossmammi would be happy to do it.

She couldn't help smiling at the sight of Grossmammi's eager expression as she came back to the kitchen carrying the baby. Grossmammi came toward them eagerly, crooning to Isaac.

It was obvious that both she and Mammi had just been waiting to get their hands on a baby again. Dinah must have been a disappointment to them, but they'd never let any whisper of it show.

Surrendering Isaac to Grossmammi, she set about mixing up his cereal. They now had a high chair at the shop, as well as one at home. Folks had been so generous, with someone turning up just about every day with something they thought would be useful.

The most recent thing was a stroller—nice for walks, if anyone had time for it. If Lovina were here helping, she could do that. But Lovina wasn't, and she didn't know how soon Mammi and Daad might be willing to let her out of their sight again.

"Ready for the high chair?" Grossmammi asked, pulling it toward the table.

"Here, I'll move it," she said, but it was too late. Grossmammi was more energetic than ever since she'd been helping with the shop, and she'd been plenty energetic before.

The cereal was about ready when the phone rang in the shop. Grossmammi, holding Isaac, nodded toward the front. "Go ahead. I'll hold him."

"You mean you'll take over," she said, smiling. "You know babies best of all of us, ain't so?"

Her grandmother waved her away, smiling, and Dinah hurried out to snatch up the phone. She'd hardly gotten through her greeting when the caller interrupted her.

"Dinah? Is that you?"

"Anna." She gasped the name and glanced wildly toward the door to the harness shop. "Anna, I'm so glad you called. I've been hoping you would."

"Don't get all excited, Dinah. I'm not missing home. I just wanted to check on Isaac."

"Of course you do."

She gestured wildly to Grossmammi, who'd come through from the kitchen holding Isaac in time to hear who she was talking to. She pointed to the connecting door. Grossmammi nodded and hurried to get Jacob.

"Well?" Anna sounded impatient, so maybe she guessed what was happening. "I don't need to talk to Jacob. You can tell me about the baby."

"He's fine, that's certain sure. He's grown, I think, and the way he's been chewing on his rattle, Mammi thinks he might be working on cutting a tooth."

"Really?" In that instant Anna sounded excited, like any mother with her baby's first tooth. But then she controlled it. "He's okay? You're sure?"

"Yah, certain sure." Dinah had a sudden thought. Would Anna come back if she thought Isaac wasn't doing well? But she couldn't lie about a thing like that. "He's trying to crawl, and he can sit himself up."

Jacob came hurrying, and all thoughts of not wanting to see him withered away to nothing. She had to get Anna to talk to him. If she said . . .

But she didn't have a chance to say anything, because Jacob snatched the receiver from her hand.

———

JACOB'S FINGERS TIGHTENED on the receiver. He wanted to burst out with all his worries and fears for his little sister. But Dinah's expression carried a warning.

Go slow. Don't try to tell her what to do.

He swallowed the words that wanted to burst out. Anna was already speaking, probably wondering if she'd been cut off.

"Dinah? Are you there?"

"Anna, how good to hear your voice." He didn't have time to plan, but the words came from his heart.

"Jacob." She sounded wary. "Is Dinah still there?"

"Yah, and her grossmammi. She's holding Isaac, and he's smiling."

"Oh." He thought her voice wavered. "Well, he's okay, Dinah says."

"Yah, he's blooming. With her grandmother helping, we've been able to have him here at the shop during the day, so I can spend a lot of time with him."

There was silence for a moment, and he wondered what Anna had pictured Isaac's life being like here. Or had she imagined it at all? He had to warn himself not to blurt that out—not if he wanted to keep talking to her.

"When he starts running around, we'll have to figure something else out, I guess," he went on. "Too many things here that he might get hurt on."

He held his breath. She might say that Isaac's stay here wouldn't be that long. Oddly enough, the picture in his mind was of Dinah and him caring for and loving Isaac for good. But that wasn't what he wanted, or what was going to happen, was it? For an instant he felt dizzy.

"Okay, well, that's all I wanted to know."

He couldn't let her hang up yet, and he could see Dinah scribbling something on a pad, hurrying.

"Do you have a nice place to live? Some friends around you?" If Anna didn't want her family, that was one thing; she must at least have someone.

"It's okay." She sounded suspicious. "I'm not going to tell you where it is, if that's what you want."

Dinah shoved the paper into his hand. *Tell her we'll need her written permission if Isaac has to go to the doctor.* He looked at Dinah questioningly, and she gave an emphatic nod and pointed to the phone.

"You don't have to tell me anything you don't want." That sounded false even to him, and he could imagine what Anna would make of her big brother sounding so reasonable. "Dinah says to tell you that we should have written permission from you, though, just in case Isaac should have to see a doctor."

"You said he was okay." Anna's voice rose. "You're just trying to get me to come back."

"No, really. Dinah says . . ."

"Let me talk to Dinah." The snap in her voice said she was on the verge of hanging up, so he surrendered the phone, hating to lose even that small link with her.

Dinah took the phone, her face strained with the effort to say the right thing. He understood what she was doing. She was trying to keep Anna entangled with her baby and her home. To keep open a pathway through which Anna might come back.

"No, no, Isaac's fine." Her voice was warm and reassuring. "But you know he should be having regular checkups at his age. And inoculations. And what if he did get sick?"

"If you took him to the doctor . . ."

"I'm afraid the doctor wouldn't be able to treat him

just on our say-so." She pushed on. "We should have signed permission from his mother to seek treatment for him."

Anna said something he couldn't hear, and he watched Dinah's face for a clue.

"I think it just has to be a signed statement that we have permission to arrange medical care of him. But it would be a help to have a list of any doctor visits he's already had. Maybe your Englisch friend can help you with it."

She must be agreeing, because Dinah was smiling and nodding. Then her expression changed suddenly. "Wait, don't go until you say goodbye to your brother." She thrust the phone at him.

"Anna? Listen . . ." All the things he wanted to say crowded into his mind.

"Goodbye, Jacob." Anna was gone before he could say any of them.

He wanted to throw the phone down, but he handed it quietly to Dinah. The pity and pain in her expressive face cut to the heart.

"What does she want?" The words burst out of him. "I tried, didn't I?"

"Yah, of course." Dinah reached out as if to touch him in sympathy, but he stepped away from her hand. "Listen, Jacob, at least she's not breaking with her home entirely. As long as she's in touch, there's still a chance, ain't so?"

What chance? He wanted to rail at Dinah, but none of this was her fault. Every contact with Anna led no-where, and each one just emphasized his failure.

"Here." Dinah's grandmother held Isaac out to him, and Isaac's arms reached eagerly. "Take him. He'll make you feel better."

Before he knew it, Isaac was close against him, his

little face inches from Jacob's and his hand patting Jacob's face. He felt the warmth of his love for the child sweep through him.

Dinah's grandmother was right about the healing effects of holding the baby. But what did the future hold for this sweet boy? Would he be able to protect him? Or would he fail Isaac as he had failed Isaac's mother?

For the rest of the day that loving look battled in Dinah's mind with the anger she still felt over the revelation that Jacob knew the painful truth about her marriage. Maybe she was being unfair to him; maybe she should hear him out; but she couldn't. She couldn't talk about it; she never had. She didn't want to talk about it to Jacob, and she didn't want to listen to his excuses, either.

So she'd been avoiding him all day, hoping he'd get the message. Now, as the sun slipped toward the ridge, Dinah desperately needed some peace, so she moved from the kitchen to the back porch. Isaac was asleep, and most of the family was occupied in a noisy board game in the living room, so they wouldn't know she was out here.

The porch swing rocked as she sat down and then settled into a comfortable rhythm at the pressure of her feet, creaking a little on each swing. It had been a warm day, but by this time there was a coolness in the air. The shadows were long, and peace settled over the farm. It was a good time for considering where she was and what the future might hold.

Where they were, she supposed she should say. All of them had a stake in what happened to Isaac. He hadn't taken any time at all to work his way into their hearts. And Anna . . .

The telephone call had been troubling. Anna didn't know what she wanted to do, that was certain sure. But when you had a baby to care for, you had to know. Whatever decision she came to, someone would be hurt.

Dinah was suddenly aware of someone walking into the kitchen from the living room, and it didn't take a moment for her to identify the footsteps. Jacob. If he was looking for her, she didn't want to be found.

Quickly, without thinking, she jumped from the swing, leaving it rocking, and hurried from the porch. She headed for the garden, praying he wouldn't follow. He ought to realize by now that she certainly didn't want to discuss it.

Before she reached the end of the garden, she saw Jacob pause on the porch, look around, and then step off. Not sure if he'd seen her or not, she hurried behind the barn. If she was acting like a child . . . well, she had a right to privacy, didn't she?

Leaning against the barn wall, she felt the heat that was stored in the weathered wood from the afternoon sun. Her great-grandfather had built the barn, and it still stood, square and strong, sheltering. Sheltering her, at the moment. She pressed her palms against the planks.

"How far do I have to chase you?" Jacob's voice, and Jacob stood at the corner of the barn, not advancing, but looking ready to do so if she moved.

Dinah buried the moment of embarrassment and let her temper flare. "It should be obvious that I don't want to talk to you. Can't you understand that? I won't talk about . . . about my marriage. Not to anyone."

"Fine. You don't have to talk. Just listen." He took a couple of steps toward her, his expression softening. "Come on, Dinah. You know it's not fair of you. You can at least hear me out."

She let out a breath she hadn't realized she was holding, feeling her anger draining, leaving in its place a deep well of sorrow. "Sorry," she muttered, not looking at him. "All right, if you insist. Go ahead, say what you have to. I'll listen."

"Denke." He moved closer, and she looked up at his face, then looked away, knowing she'd made a mistake. He was watching her with such tenderness. Not pity . . . she couldn't have stood that, but as gentle as if he were looking at the baby.

"I never meant it to happen, just be clear of that. I was already in the back room, up on the stepladder getting some boxes down. You and Aaron must have come into your storage space, thinking you were alone."

He paused, waiting for comment. Finally she nodded. "All right. You didn't mean it. But you didn't go away, either, did you?"

"No, I—" He stopped suddenly. Alerted by the change in him, she glanced around.

Lovina had just come around the corner by the garden, her lips open to say something. Her eyes widened as she took in the two of them, and something about their expressions and the way they were standing must have alerted her.

"Sorry, I . . . sorry." She shook her head and then turned and fled.

Jacob touched her arm lightly to reclaim her attention. "Lovina is growing up. She realizes when she's butting in."

"Yah." She thought of everything that had happened since she came home with Anna's baby. "She is. It hasn't been easy."

Poor Lovina had learned something about trust the hard way, but she was slowly managing to turn disappointment to maturity.

"All right. I'm not mad at her any longer. I'll talk to

her when she's ready. But right now I just want to have my say."

She gave a sharp nod, knowing she couldn't stop him.

"The thing was, Aaron was already angry, already saying things I shouldn't hear. Believe me, if I could have vanished in that moment, I would have. But there was no way I could put down the boxes, get off the ladder, and get away without being heard. That would have been worse."

She nodded, suddenly exhausted. "All right. I know. Aaron was too upset to care just then who heard him." She put her hands to her head, wishing she could close her eyes and be in her own bedroom. "Is that all?"

"No." His voice was low, and he was closer than she'd realized. He clasped her hands gently and drew them away from her face, holding them between his palms. "I'm sorry. But I couldn't go away then, even if I could have done it silently. I was afraid he was going to hurt you. Thought he had already hurt you. Did he strike you?"

"No. No." She met his eyes and read the caring and concern there. "I . . . I tried to touch him, wanting him to understand about the doctor and the test he wanted Aaron to take. Aaron . . . he pushed me away with a sweep of his arm. I stumbled, that's all. He couldn't . . . he couldn't even listen."

He was silent for a long moment, but still he held her hands pressed between his. "I knew Aaron pretty well, you know. He was a good guy in a lot of ways, but he never could accept that something might be his fault."

"It wasn't. I mean, it wouldn't have been a question of fault. It would just have been an accident if he hadn't been able . . ."

She let that drop, astonished that she'd said as much as she had.

"I'm sorry." His fingers moved on her hands, comforting her with his gentleness. "I never told anyone I heard. Not even Aaron."

"Not my mother?" The question slipped out, and she saw the surprise and shock in his eyes.

"For sure not your mother. But you mean you haven't told her?"

"I couldn't, don't you see that?" She looked up at him, pleading with him to understand, and knew there were tears in her eyes. "I can't talk about it to anyone."

"Ach, Dinah, you're such a smart person, and you don't see how hurtful that is? That makes it worse, holding it in all this time."

"It's not . . ."

"You taught me that," he said, cutting her off. "I couldn't believe I could talk about Anna, until you made me. You . . ."

His eyes seemed to darken, and he studied her face with such intensity that she felt it like a gentle touch on her skin.

"Dinah," he whispered, "I can't bear to see you hurt so much."

And then his lips claimed hers, lightly at first, then with more assurance.

And she . . . she should have pulled away, she should have done anything other than kiss him back. But she didn't seem to have any control of herself, not now.

Jacob drew back after what seemed like an eternity. His hand cupped her cheek so gently, and then he took a step back.

"Well . . ." He didn't seem to have any words.

She wasn't much better. "I . . . I think we'd better go in before someone else comes to look for us."

"Yah, I guess we'd better." He turned, but he took her hand and held it clasped firmly in his as they walked until they came within sight of the house. He smiled, just a little, and they seemed to communicate without the need for words.

She didn't need anything else, not now. Just a tiny bit, a glimpse, of what might be.

CHAPTER FIFTEEN

Friday morning meant that they were in for a long and busy day. Dinah glanced at Grossmammi, still concerned that she was doing too much by helping at the shop. But if her grandmother felt that, she wasn't showing it. She went briskly to the refrigerator, where the two big kettles of soup they'd started were waiting.

"I'll just simmer these—"

"Wait." Dinah reached past her to take the first kettle. "Remember, you promised Mammi you wouldn't go lifting anything heavier than Isaac. Ain't so?"

Grossmammi didn't like being caught. She made a face, and then her eyes twinkled. "Isaac's with Jacob, so we can't compare his weight with the soup kettle."

Dinah suppressed a laugh. "You're getting as bad as the twins for talking your way out of things. Just let me move the soup." She put the second kettle on the stove. "Then you can take over. I'll get the coffee started."

She had tried not to show anything when Jacob's name was mentioned, but she didn't know how successful she'd been. Since those tender moments together the previous night, she'd alternated between the warmth of hope and the chill of despair.

How had it happened? She had been so angry with him . . . for knowing, for keeping his knowledge a secret from her all that time . . . well, she had to confess that he couldn't have done anything else. If he had told her at the time, how horribly embarrassing it would have been, making it impossible for her to continue running the shop next to him.

And since Aaron died, he'd probably felt it was best forgotten. Only she'd never been able to forget. She had forgiven Aaron, she was sure of it. Whatever he'd said or felt, death really did end it.

So why hadn't she succeeded in forgetting it? And how was it possible that a quarrel about her late husband could lead to anything like that kiss?

She relived the moment when his lips had touched hers and seemed to feel again the featherlight brush of his fingers on her skin. She'd responded; she couldn't deny that.

If . . . if he had feelings for her . . . was it reasonable to hope they could find a happy ending in this tangle of hurt and loss?

Reasonable or not, she held on to hope, praying that the hint of a fulfilling future with Jacob might be realized. If only . . .

Grossmammi had said something, and Dinah realized she hadn't heard a word of it. She was still standing there, staring at the coffeepot as if she'd never seen one before.

"I'm sorry, I didn't quite hear . . ."

"You mean you weren't listening." But Grossmammi smiled, not offended. "I said it will be hard to have Isaac here once he starts to walk. And judging by the way he tries to pull himself up, that won't be long."

"Yah, I know. I keep thinking we should make plans, but then I remember it's not up to me. It may not even be

up to Jacob." The ever-present fear of losing Isaac un-
curled inside her.

Her grandmother rattled a kettle lid. "It's not fair of
Anna to leave everyone hanging this way."

"She's young yet. I don't think she knows what she
wants."

Grossmammi sniffed. "Not so young as all that. I'd
think she'd have grown up since she's been living in the
outside world."

Dinah still looked blankly at the coffee, starting to
burble in the pot. "If we have to lose Isaac, it will be like
losing my own." Her throat tightened. "Like finding out
there won't be any babies."

"Ach, Dinah, you don't know that's true. Just because
you and Aaron didn't—well, you weren't married that
long."

"Long enough."

The desperation of that time came flooding back as if
it had happened yesterday. All the things she'd kept to
herself all this time . . . but Jacob knew, and they had
actually talked about it.

As if that had unlocked a door inside her, she wanted
to speak the truth about it to her grandmother.

"Aaron blamed me." She said the words out loud, and
then she couldn't go any further.

But she didn't need to. Grossmammi was there,
wrapping her arms around her. "My poor sweet girl."

Comforting, crooning to her as if she were little Isaac
until she gained control of herself. Dinah wiped her face
with her fingers.

"Denke," she whispered.

Grossmammi nodded. "I thought, but you never
spoke. And how could I comfort you when you wouldn't
speak?"

"It took me a long time." She managed a watery

smile. "I didn't want anyone to know, and then I realized that Jacob had known all along."

"Jacob's a good man. A man to be counted on."

Dinah's cheeks grew hot. Her grandmother seemed to know everything. Did she know what had happened between them?

Grossmammi was carefully not looking at her, as if to spare her embarrassment. "The best thing for little Isaac would be for you and Jacob to raise him."

She couldn't speak for several moments. When she finally did, her voice was husky with strain. "The only way for that to happen would be for Anna to stay away. How could we possibly wish for that to happen?"

Grossmammi patted her back. "Trust, my sweet girl. That's all we can do."

Clearing her throat, Dinah nodded. "It's almost time to open. Now you be careful. No more lifting kettles, right? This long day might be too much for you."

Grossmammi's usually twinkling blue eyes grew serious. "I like to feel useful, and that's the truth, Dinah. That's the hardest part of getting older, I think. Now, if your parents would let Lovina could come back to work, we could share the time. The responsibility would be good for her."

"Mammi and Daadi may not think so."

She knew their worries. How much to protect? How much to trust? That was a difficult challenge for parents.

With a last look around, she headed for the door to open, but her grandmother had one more thing to say.

"We all have to make our own mistakes, Dinah. Nobody can help that. And we all have to learn to live with them."

Her grandmother's words resounded as she reached for the *Open* sign. Mistakes like hers, like Aaron's, like Anna's . . . yah, they'd all made mistakes. But each one's mistakes affected others, especially the people who loved them.

And in the closely knit community of Promise Glen, that meant that if one was hurt, they all hurt, one way or another.

Jacob lingered in the back room, leaning over the cot. Isaac slept with as much determination as he seemed to do everything else, diving into it in an instant. He sprawled in the cot, so completely relaxed that he reminded Jacob of a bowl of jelly, but he was frowning slightly, as if concentrating on sleeping.

Jacob touched him lightly before turning away. When had he lost that ability to plunge into sleep so easily? He could vaguely remember it, after a long day of satisfying work. But that had ended, and he didn't know when. These days, too many worries crowded his mind to make relaxation simple.

He headed reluctantly to the shop. Funny, he hadn't been in the least surprised by Dinah's loving reaction to Isaac or by her mother's and grandmother's instant love for him. After all, women tended to fall for babies.

What did surprise him was his own reaction to Anna's baby. Isaac had been in his life for such a short time, but he held Jacob's heart clasped tightly in his small hand. And when Jacob picked up the headstall he was making, he found he was picturing Isaac standing at his elbow, learning the craft in the same way Jacob had learned it . . . standing next to his father. It was the Amish way, and his legacy, as it had been Jacob's.

The door opened simultaneously with the jingle of the bell, and Noah, entering, smiled at Jacob's expression when he gave the bell an annoyed frown.

"Relax," he said, coming back to the workbench. "As

the father of two boys, I can tell you that it will take more than that to wake Isaac up. That's what you're frowning at, isn't it?"

Jacob chuckled. "You know me too well. So how is my cousin? Any signs that something is happening soon?" He and Noah had always been friends, but they'd become much closer since Noah married his cousin Sarah. Close enough, anyway, for him to admit knowing that Sarah's baby would arrive within the month.

"I'm no expert, but I think the boppli is going to get here before that wedding she's so eager to attend. I think we're ready, anyway."

"You should be an expert—after all, you managed the twins' arrival." The twin boys seemed as excited as could be at becoming big brothers. He hoped it would last.

"Yah, well, we were so baffled to have two babies at once that we didn't know which way was up. According to the midwife, we don't need to prepare for that this time around."

"Is Sarah relieved or disappointed?" He considered his cousin capable of managing just about anything, no matter how many babies arrived.

"Just waiting. She looks . . . serene. Happy."

He wondered for a moment how Anna had looked when she was expecting. If only she had come home so they could help her. Had she been alone then? He didn't even know that about his own sister. The familiar feeling of failure crept back.

"Jacob?"

Noah was looking at him questioningly. He must have been quiet for too long. He made an effort to shake off his feelings, and movement outside the front window caught his eye.

"Isn't that your daad coming?"

Noah swung around, startled, just as his father came in the door. One look at his face said he had news, and he didn't bother with greetings.

"Your mamm says to come home now. Sarah needs you."

"The baby? Have you called the midwife?" Noah was already on his way to the door.

"Not yet, but soon. Komm. I'll fetch the midwife whenever the women say."

Noah's father had his priorities right, it seemed to Jacob. The women would take over now.

He followed them to the door. "God bless. And I'll tell Dinah. She'll want to know."

Jacob suspected that Noah didn't even hear that. He started to climb into his daad's buggy before Noah's daad pointed out Noah's own buggy standing next in the row. In another minute they were both pulling out onto the street.

Smiling, Jacob came back inside. It seemed even an experienced daad like Noah could get rattled when the time came. He should tell Dinah . . . Before he'd taken another step Dinah came through from the bakeshop, carrying his usual morning coffee and a cruller. Her gaze was on the front window.

"Wasn't that Noah? And his daad?"

"Yah. Sarah wants him at home." He tried to suppress his grin, but he couldn't.

"The boppli is coming?" Her voice lifted with joy. "Ach, I'm so happy for them. I wonder if it will be a girl. That would be nice after two boys."

He took the coffee mug she held out. "Noah's fortunate, having the twins and now a new baby. Things have worked out so well for him."

Dinah gave him a measuring look. "Don't forget that Noah had his troubles," she pointed out. "Like everyone else. It's grace that brought him and Sarah together at last."

"Yah, you're right." He could feel his cheeks grow hot and knew it was shame at having said such a self-pitying thing in front of Dinah. What would she think of him, especially after what had passed between them the previous evening?

How had he come to embrace her? He couldn't find it in himself to regret it, but still, he shouldn't have. He had no business trying to fix Dinah's interest in him. Not when his own life was such a tangle between Anna and the baby. Who knew what the future held for them?

He wanted to say something that would take them back to normal, but the words wouldn't come. Just as Dinah set down the plate with his cruller, a tentative cry came from the back room. Isaac was up.

"I'll get him," he said quickly, seizing the opportunity to escape from his own fumbling.

The now-familiar feeling of love and attachment flowed through him when he picked Isaac up. "There now, that was a short nap. You slept in the buggy coming in, didn't you? And now you're ready to go."

Still talking to Isaac, he changed the baby's diaper as if he'd been doing that for years. He paused, amazed at himself.

The truth was that Isaac had already changed everything in his life. Having the baby thrust on him challenged all his earlier assumptions. He'd told himself he could never again take on responsibility for another person after messing things up with Anna.

And yet here he was, taking on Isaac and wanting to go on doing it. If he could do that, maybe it wasn't such a long stretch to think he and Dinah might have a future together. They already knew each other. Already cared for each other.

But what if Anna showed up again and took Isaac away? It was already going to break Dinah's heart as well as his. What kind of a future could he offer Dinah then?

The usual chatter around the supper table soothed Dinah's sore heart. This was real—this love that flowed back and forth effortlessly among the family, extending to include Isaac and Jacob. Dinah's smile caught her mother's across the table, and it was almost as if Mammi saw her thoughts.

The more people around the supper table, the better, as far as her mother was concerned. She never seemed to think of it as extra work, just as extra pleasure. If she ever had a home of her own again, Dinah hoped she might be able to do the same.

Not that it seemed very likely at the moment.

At a break in the chatter, Daad lowered his head for the short after-meal prayer. *Please.* Her thoughts were incoherent. *Please let this situation work out for the best.*

That was all she could say, because she didn't see any possible way for everyone to be happy.

Lovina hopped up from her place as soon as the prayer finished, stacking used plates on one another with a rush of energy. Dinah's gaze met her mother's again. Lovina's campaign to be the kind of good, helpful, honest girl who could be trusted was lasting longer than anyone could have expected.

Lovina grabbed her plate, pausing only long enough to bend over Isaac in the high chair, making a silly face and dodging out of the way of a sticky spoon.

"I don't want your applesauce, baby boy. You eat it."

Isaac appeared to find that funny, and he let loose a

belly laugh that had everyone smiling at him. Will immediately came over to see if he could coax another one from the baby.

Dinah looked over his head at Lovina as she balanced a bowl on top of the stack of plates. "Careful, Lovina. If you get any more helpful, you're going to burst."

For an instant Lovina didn't seem to know how to take it. But then, seeing the love in Dinah's face, she relaxed in a smile.

"Dinah's right." Mammi reached across and wrested the plates from Lovina. "I'll do this. What do you want tonight . . . washing or drying?"

Because Mammi usually insisted on washing, considering that no one else in the family was as particular as she was, that was a gift.

"Washing," Lovina said instantly. "Denke, Mammi. I . . ." Her eyes glazed with tears. "I will never make a mistake like that again. Honestly."

"No." Mammi patted her cheek. "You'll make another one, just like all of us."

"Denke," she whispered again. She looked toward Jacob, as if wondering whether the forgiveness extended from him, as well, and Dinah held her breath.

At last he smiled. "Don't think about it any longer, Lovina. I've done worse and been forgiven." Still smiling, he lifted Isaac from the high chair, snuggling him close.

"Let's take a walk outside." He dropped a kiss on Isaac's chubby neck. "Some fresh air, and you'll be ready to sleep tonight."

When the door had closed behind him, Grossmammi gave a satisfied smile. "How quickly he has become comfortable with the baby. I wouldn't have believed it."

"He loves Isaac," Mammi said, as if that explained everything.

Probably it did. Dinah bent over to pick up the spoon Isaac had knocked on the floor, hiding her face as best she could. She had stood there, watching Jacob's face come alive with love, and she'd recognized the truth.

He would never be happy without a family. She loved him, but that wasn't enough. She couldn't give him the family he longed for. So even if he loved her, she could never make him happy. That was the risk she couldn't take—not that she'd be unhappy, but that he would.

Dinah moved through the after-supper chores in a daze of unhappiness, trying not to let anyone see and knowing that she wasn't succeeding. Even Lovina saw it, and touched her arm in silent sympathy when she walked by.

When Jacob and the baby came back inside, Dinah exerted herself to smile naturally. To talk naturally. And to pretend that her heart wasn't breaking.

"Did Isaac have a gut walk?" she asked. She held out her hands to him. For an instant he clung to Jacob before he broke out into a big smile and dived at her.

She caught him, surprised into a real laugh. "Careful, little man. Make sure someone is ready to catch you before you jump." She held him close and spun him around. "I think it might be bedtime for you."

Jacob nodded, his big hand spread out gently on Isaac's back, just touching her own. "You go ahead. I'll come up in a bit to say good night."

She felt her smile grow stiff at the thought of being alone with him. Grasping the bottle that was warming on the stove, she hurried away.

It was quiet upstairs, and Dinah felt the tension slipping away as she moved through the familiar routine of getting Isaac ready for bed. Maybe she was just numb, but at least it wasn't so painful.

She couldn't have what she wanted, so she'd have to

settle for what she had. Her family loved her, and there was always work for willing hands to do. Isaac reached out, hands waving, and almost caught one of her kapp strings.

"Ach, no, you can't have that." She pushed the kapp strings out of reach and held up a squeeze toy instead— a rubbery kitten that made a sound that could be a meow if you didn't expect much.

She squeezed it, and Isaac cooed in return and snatched it from her hand. Immediately he stuffed it in his mouth and began to chew on it.

"That's gut," she murmured. "You exercise your gums on that before you have your bottle, and you'll soon be off to dreamland."

He stopped chewing for a moment, his huge blue eyes suddenly serious. He looked at her as if she'd said something very important. Then, with a sudden change of mood, he chuckled and threw the toy so that it bounced off Dinah's shoulder and fell back on his own head.

For an instant Dinah thought he'd burst into outraged crying, but instead he laughed again, that belly laugh that sounded so large coming from such a small baby.

Dinah snapped his soft nightshirt and picked him up, laughing, too. "You are such a funny boy. All the girls are going to love you."

Would she be around to see that? Probably not. But for the moment he was there, in her arms. She sat in the rocker and picked up the bottle. Instantly engrossed, Isaac snatched at her hand and stuffed the bottle in his mouth as if he'd been starving. He started sucking so vigorously that not only his face but the top of his head turned red.

Dinah held him close, listening to the satisfying sounds of a baby being fed, feeling his warmth, inhaling the sweet smells of milk and baby.

He was here, in her arms, she thought again. She would treasure every moment. The slightest push with her foot set the rocker moving, soothing her as much as it soothed little Isaac.

He was down to the last ounce or so and nearly asleep before an alien sound intruded on her peace. Dinah's head lifted and she frowned, listening, trying to interpret what she was hearing.

The purr of a car's engine and the rattle of tires on gravel gave way to silence and then to the slam of a car door. Footsteps downstairs, and a gaggle of voices she couldn't understand.

Then one voice rang out clearly, and she knew who it was. It was Anna.

CHAPTER SIXTEEN

Dinah, shocked into silence, stopped the gentle rocking. She had an instinctive desire to remain still and quiet, like a mouse when it spots the cat.

She fought that impulse until it crept back where it had come from. Anna was Isaac's mother and her neighbor. She had to go and greet her.

Still, there was no reason to take Isaac down with her. He was already asleep . . . she shouldn't disturb him. Moving softly, she lowered him into the crib, smoothing the blanket over him. Assured that he was settled, she slipped from the room.

Pausing at the top of the stairs, Dinah listened to the sounds from below. No raised voices . . . just the murmur of slightly stilted conversation and the clink of cups. Mammi was probably easing the situation with offers of food and drink.

So far, so good. She took a relaxing breath and walked steadily down.

"Now, you'll surely have a slice of cherry pie," Mammi was saying, wielding the knife with nervous energy. She glanced at Anna and then looked away.

Dinah had seen Anna looking like an Englisch

woman already, so it didn't shock her the way it obviously had the others. Mammi coped by sneaking quick glances, while most of the others were staring openly, Grossmammi with shock.

As for Jacob, his face was frozen into an expression that said nothing at all. She glanced at Anna and felt instantly sorry for both of them. They'd been as close as any brother and sister could be, which probably made the breach between them even more painful.

"Pie sounds wonderful, Mamm." She broke the awkward silence, trying her best to sound normal, and she went to give Anna a quick hug. "Wilkom, Anna."

She could hardly say she was glad to see Anna, because her deepest fear was that Anna had come to take Isaac away. But she could make sure that Anna knew she was welcome here.

"Thanks, Dinah."

Anna shot a resentful look at her brother, and Dinah felt a spurt of exasperation. Couldn't Jacob see that he'd get nowhere with Anna while he wore that disapproving expression?

"Did you drive yourself?" She glanced through the window at the dark car pulled up by the porch. There didn't seem to be a driver waiting.

Anna nodded. "I have a car now, so I figured I'd drive down when I finished work. Since you both seemed to think I needed to come and settle some things."

Jacob looked as if he'd explode into speech, so she shook her head at him vigorously. Whatever he thought to say, it didn't look conciliatory. He'd seemed to understand the importance of going slowly with his sister, but now he'd apparently forgotten it.

"Would you like to see Isaac?" She forced out the words. "He's just gone to sleep, but if you want to go up and see him we can tiptoe . . ."

Anna made one unguarded movement, as if to spring from the chair, but just as quickly sat back again. "No. Thanks."

"But . . ." She had to remind herself to go slowly, too. She couldn't begin to understand why Anna had refused, Dinah thought, baffled. Anna had turned into someone she couldn't fathom at all.

Mammi, still trying to take control of an unwieldy situation with food, put a slice of pie down in front of Jacob. Then she switched her focus to the boys.

"You boys go along and finish your chores now," she said, ignoring the fact that they'd just come in.

"But, Mammi—" Will began to protest.

Micah grabbed him by the shirt and pulled him toward the door. "Komm." He frowned at the twins, and they followed with a reluctant look back. Clearly, Mammi wanted the ground cleared if there were going to be fireworks, and Micah had gotten the message.

Jacob seemed to think that was a sign to talk, and maybe it was. She just hoped he'd approach Anna gently. Telling her what to do wasn't going to help.

"Anna, it's time you came home. This is where you belong, with your family and your baby. Please. We all want you here." Jacob's voice softened on the last words, and Anna, who'd stiffened, seemed to ease a bit.

But she didn't answer him. Instead, she reached into her bag and pulled out a long envelope, which she put on the table between them.

"I talked to Lacey Gaus, like you said, Dinah. She told me what you said was right, that if Isaac needed medical care, you'd have to have something to show you have the right to make the decisions."

She opened the envelope, drawing out a typed sheet. "Lacey checked with a lawyer who works with Amish Assist, and he helped her write this up. So it should cover everything." Maybe giving up on Jacob, she slid the document over to Dinah.

Dinah read through the typed words quickly. It was fairly simple, basically giving either Jacob or her the right to make decisions about Isaac's care, as if they were his parents.

The phrasing made her pause. His parents. But how could they ever be that?

"You can see I've already signed," Anna went on. "All you have to do is show it."

In response to Anna's words, Dinah passed it to Jacob. He took it automatically, not looking, his mind somewhere else, it seemed.

"Anna, please." He pleaded now instead of insisting. "You must want to be with your baby. Can't you stay? Even for a few days. We can go back home, and you can have your old room, just the way you left it."

Jacob was trying harder to show his loving concern than Dinah would have believed possible, but a look at Anna told her that it wasn't doing any good. She tried to imagine why, but it was impossible.

Anna shook her head with a quick movement. "No. I told you I wasn't coming home, and I meant it. Look, I'm grateful to you for taking Isaac, but I can't come back. I don't want this life any longer. You'd better try to understand that." She pushed back her seat. "I'll be going now."

"You can at least stay the night with us," Mammi said quickly, moving toward her. "Surely you don't want to drive that far in the dark. It's late already, and we have plenty of room."

"That's right." Daad came to life at the question of hospitality, at least feeling on solid ground there. "We're happy to have you, Anna."

Anna looked from them to Dinah. Whatever she saw seemed to reassure her. "I guess it is pretty late."

"Wonderful." Mammi clapped her hands together. "Are you hungry? I can warm up some chicken potpie for you in a few minutes."

Smiling, Anna shook her head at the mention of the traditional food. "I stopped along the way. But you're right, I am tired. I'm not used to driving this far. If it's okay, I'll just crash . . . I mean, go to bed."

Mamm nodded. "Whatever you want. Lovina, she'll have your room. Run up and get it ready. You can go in with Dinah and the baby."

Without a word, Lovina slipped out and up the stairs.

What was she thinking? Dinah knew very well that Mammi was afraid . . . afraid that one day Lovina would follow in the path that Anna had taken. There were always some, from every community, and not many of them came back.

An awkward silence ensued. Jacob clearly wanted to say something to Anna . . . something that would carry weight with her, that would convince her. For the first time, Dinah saw helplessness on his face when he considered his little sister.

This was not the time to give up. She wanted to tell him that. At least Anna had agreed to stay overnight. He wouldn't think that was progress, but it was better than having her storm out the door. Perhaps in the morning she'd be more ready to hear him.

Dinah held out her hand to Anna. "Komm. I'll show you where everything is."

Anna went with her to the door and hesitated, looking back at the table. "Good night, everyone. Good night, Jacob."

His face was transformed by a gentle smile. "Good night, little Annie."

If she reacted to the childhood name, Anna didn't show it. She went up the stairs in Dinah's wake.

Dinah paused at the door to her room, half wishing she could keep Anna out, knowing she couldn't.

"Do you want to peek in at Isaac? It won't wake him." Her hand was on the knob when Anna shook her head.

"No. Not now." Anna didn't even look at the door. "It's better not."

Midway between relief and grief, she took her on to Lovina's room. "Here we are."

Lovina flicked the quilt into place. "All ready," she murmured. She swept items from the top of the dresser into her apron and slipped out of the room without even looking at Anna.

Dropping her handbag on the quilt, Anna wrinkled her nose. "Lovina doesn't seem too happy. I shouldn't have put her out."

"It's not that," Dinah said, but she didn't really know the key to Lovina's attitude. "She's fifteen. It's a challenging age, remember?"

"Yah." Anna's face closed down. "I was fifteen when Daad died."

"I'm sorry, I didn't mean . . ." Dinah reached out to her, but Anna shook her head.

"It's okay. Bad things happen." Her tone didn't leave any room for discussion.

Moving the battery lamp a little nearer the bed, Dinah gestured to it. "You can use this. It'll be simpler for you."

Not sure what else she should say, she looked at Anna again. Suddenly she saw her as that grieving fifteen-year-old, not knowing which way to turn. Her heart filled.

Almost as if she knew what was going on in Dinah's heart, Anna was deliberately calm. "You've been taking care of Isaac, Lacey said. She seemed impressed with you. She said you love him."

"How could anyone help but love him?" she said simply.

For a moment Anna looked on the verge of tears. But then, just as quickly, she became again the woman she'd turned herself into. "I'll see you in the morning."

JACOB SAT WHERE he was, letting his head sink into his hands. Had he messed things up again? Talking to his little sister in person was completely different from the talks he had with her in his mind.

He was vaguely aware of the boys coming back in from their exile and the younger ones trooping upstairs. He felt a hand on his shoulder and looked up, startled.

Micah stood still, seeming ill at ease. "I was thinking you wouldn't want to go to work tomorrow, since Anna's here. I can go open up for you. I know only as much about harnesses as any farmer, and I can read the price tags, ain't so?"

All sorts of objections formed in his mind, but none of them were of importance next to the fact that his sister was here. Even if it was only to tell her goodbye, he had to be here.

"Denke, Micah. That would be helpful. If anything comes up you don't know how to handle . . ."

"I'll tell them to come in another day when you'll be there," Micah said promptly. "Don't worry about it. I'll take care of the shop."

Someone came in from upstairs, and he swiveled to see that it was Dinah.

"You're taking the harness shop tomorrow? Sehr gut. You can put a *Closed* sign on my shop door for me."

Jacob stirred. "I don't want you to lose a day's business just because Anna's here."

"Ach, don't be ferhoodled. For sure I'm staying. Maybe . . . maybe Anna will want to see the baby."

It didn't take much imagination to see that she was torn. Dinah loved Isaac. She longed to have him for her own. He'd seen that from the first day, but he'd been so obsessed with his own problems that he hadn't thought about the effect on her. He'd just been thankful for her help.

He got up suddenly, feeling that he had to make some movement forward, even if it turned out to be the wrong one.

"I'd best get off home. Will you come out on the porch with me for a minute?" He watched Dinah's face closely, looking for any key to her feelings.

But she just nodded. Walking steadily to the door, she led the way out.

No moonlight tonight, it seemed, but the gleam of yellow light from the kitchen was enough for him to see her face. She stood by the porch railing, waiting for him to speak.

"Anna could have mailed the paper, yah?" His sister was at the top of his thoughts. "She didn't have to come. So why did she? Wouldn't you think it was to see her baby?"

Pain seemed to flicker across Dinah's face. "I don't know her anymore." Her shoulders moved, as if to shake off that fact. "I should, ain't so? But I don't. She's like a different person, and I don't know what to make of her. The baby . . ."

She seemed unable to go on. She turned away from him, probably to hide her pain.

"Dinah, I'm sorry." He covered the distance between them in a quick stride. "I shouldn't have let you in for this."

"Ach, will you stop trying to take the blame for everything?" She swung on him, anger spiking in her face and her voice. "I came into it with my eyes open. I was the one Anna called, and I think I knew from the first moment I held Isaac in my arms that it was going to hurt."

The longing to comfort her overcame him. He put his arms around her and drew her close. "I'm sorry." He patted her back. "Anna won't talk to me, but it seems she still wants Isaac to stay here, ain't so?"

Her head moved as she nodded, and she took a deep breath and seemed to pull herself together. "It looks that way."

"She's not going to stay." He forced his voice to be calm. "I have to accept it." Remembering what she'd said about blaming himself, he forced those words back. "You won't desert us, will you?"

"No." This time she managed a slight smile. "I won't."

"I knew you wouldn't." He surged on, intent on settling one thing, at least. "I've been thinking maybe we should get married. We could make a good life together, and Isaac needs to have two parents, ain't so?"

She was still for so long that he thought he'd offended her or taken too much for granted.

"Shouldn't you wait until you're sure Anna is leaving him here before you make that offer?"

She was within the circle of his arms, but he felt sure she'd increased the distance between them without even moving.

"I didn't mean that. Even if Isaac isn't with us, I still think we could be happy together."

Didn't she understand that his proposal wasn't conditional?

But Dinah was shaking her head. "It's all right, Jacob. Whatever happens, I will still help you. I don't need a consolation prize."

"That's not what I mean." His temper flared. "You must know that."

She'd moved away before he got the words out, and an instant later she was gone.

He took one hasty stride toward the door and stopped himself. He couldn't very well chase her through her parents' house, trying to explain what he meant. His timing had probably been terrible, but how could it be an insult to ask a woman to marry you?

AFTER A RESTLESS night, Dinah woke early. There was little point in trying to sleep when her mind was going around and around in circles over what Jacob had said the previous night. If she'd had any suspicion that it was coming, she'd probably have handled it better.

It wasn't that she hadn't thought about marrying Jacob. Every time she saw him lately, in fact, especially after that kiss. If he loved her . . . well, that would be a different story . . . a wonderful one. But she couldn't marry him just because he thought he owed her marriage for all she'd done. Not when she loved him so desperately, and all he felt in return was gratitude.

Trying to shake off the thought, she slipped out of bed, realizing that Lovina had gone out already. She probably should have tried to talk to her last night. Someone needed to find out what Lovina was thinking.

But Dinah had been so upset it was all she could do to hold back tears. If she'd tried to find her voice, she didn't know what would have happened.

She dressed quickly, knowing Isaac would be awake at any moment, and somehow, this day had to be faced. At the slightest whisper of movement from Isaac, she turned toward the crib. The faint sound was followed by a jingle from the crib mobile that Will had put up for him—the same one Will himself had batted at what seemed such a short time ago.

For a moment she thought Isaac would go on playing, but apparently that wasn't his idea. He pushed himself up on his hands and knees and let out an experimental cry. Then he spotted her, his face clearing in a smile.

He attempted to hold out his arms to her and promptly fell over. But before he could cry, the sight of his feet distracted him. He grabbed for them while she put her kapp in place and secured it with hairpins.

"There now, you silly boy." She picked him up, nuzzling him until he chortled. "You don't want to cry just because you woke up. You're my happy boy."

Distracting him while she changed him, she continued to talk, loving the way he responded, studying her face so seriously as if trying to understand. She heard the door open behind her and glanced around.

Anna stood there, hesitating as if unsure whether to come or go.

"Come in." She forced a smile of welcome. "Everybody's awake in here."

"I see." Anna took a couple of steps toward her and then halted.

What was Anna thinking? If Dinah could only see what was going on in her mind and heart, she'd know what to do. But she couldn't, and she was groping in the dark, trying to find her way into understanding.

"Isaac is always such a happy boy when he wakes up." Trying to talk normally seemed her only choice. "Aren't you, Isaac?" Bending, she kissed his neck, making him laugh again.

Anna had moved a step closer. Keeping her voice calm, Dinah continued to chatter to the baby, telling him what a fine boy he was as she changed his clothes, dropping the used ones into the basket by the changing table.

A quick glance told her that Anna was leaning nearer.

"Would you like to take over?" She held out the small blue sweater she'd intended to put on him.

Anna shook her head, but at least she didn't pull back. "You're a natural with babies, aren't you?" Even here, alone together, she didn't let herself slip into speaking in Pennsylvania Dutch. "Considering that . . ."

"Considering that I never had any?" She held on to her smile. "Yah, we always hoped to have a baby, but it didn't happen." She found she was thinking of Aaron without pain. "But there were always plenty of babies in the family to practice on."

"Not for us." Anna's tone was flat, but she shrugged. "Still, that's no excuse."

It was the first bit of revelation as to Anna's thoughts, and she caught at it before it passed.

"Why do you need an excuse, Anna? You've done what you could in a difficult situation." She could only hope that was the right response.

"Have I?" Anna sounded lost, just for a moment, before she went on. "Maybe, if things had been different . . ." She shook her head, shaking off whatever she might have confided. "Well, anyway, I did the right thing in the end, didn't I? When I sent Isaac home with you?"

"We were all wonderful glad that you did," she said carefully, seeing that she had to walk the line between showing how much Isaac was loved here and reassuring Anna about her decisions. "And we'd be even happier if you came home, too."

But that was, it seemed, too far to go. Anna shook her head. "About Isaac." She seemed to struggle with the words she wanted to say, and Dinah held her breath.

"I wasn't a good mother to him." The words burst out on a single breath. "I really wasn't."

Dinah struggled to find the right thing to say. "The

first few months can be hard for any new mammi, especially when there's not enough help around. And you had other problems, too." She didn't know if she should mention the young man Lacey had told her about—the boy who'd died.

"Yah." Just that, and Anna's face closed down. That was clearly all she intended to say about it. "I'm going down," she said abruptly.

She headed out, and then Dinah heard her steps on the stairs. Snuggling Isaac close to her, she tried to believe she'd been helpful to Anna, but she couldn't.

"Breakfast," she told Isaac, trying for her usual cheerful voice. "Let's go have some cereal."

When she reached the kitchen, she found Will and Jacob still at the table. The others had apparently scattered to their chores already. Jacob looked from Anna to her, the glance obviously questioning. All his thoughts were for his sister. It was as if what had happened between them had never been.

She gave the slightest of shrugs as he took Isaac, holding him up to make him laugh before putting him in the high chair, while Will waited impatiently for him to finish so he could give Isaac his usual raspberry to make him laugh.

Lovina was giving Anna a cup of coffee, while Mammi dished up the cereal for Isaac. The silence was as odd as it was uncomfortable. Mealtimes were never quiet in this kitchen.

Jacob, apparently agreeing, cleared his throat. "I hope you had a good night's sleep, Anna."

"Fine." She sat down across the table from him, putting her cup down, her gaze on Isaac. Dinah could read the longing in it, and her heart clenched with pity and grief.

Two mothers and one baby—that was what it came

down to for her and for Anna. It was a problem worthy of Solomon, except that in his case, he just had to find out who loved the baby best. That wasn't something she could judge.

"I thought you usually took the baby to the shop with you, Dinah. Isn't it about time to leave?" Anna gulped some coffee and shook her head at the cereal Mammi offered.

"Yah, usually." She risked a look at Jacob but didn't see any guidance in his face. He was watching his sister with a strained expression, as if still trying to figure her out.

Nothing to do but go on with it. "We decided to stay home this morning, since you're here."

"To keep an eye on me?" Anna flared, but the annoyance, if that's what it was, was for her brother.

"No," Jacob said steadily. "To have your company a little longer. You know I wish you'd stay, but it's your decision."

"I'm glad you admit that."

"Anna, why are you trying to pick a fight with your brother?"

Grossmammi's voice came as a surprise. She'd apparently been standing in the doorway to the daadi haus. She spoke as if Anna and Jacob were two of her own grandchildren, but then, she always did.

"I . . . I wasn't." Anna, surprisingly, reacted as if she were. "Well, maybe I was, but . . ."

"But you mean I deserve it." Jacob reached out a pleading hand toward her. "I kept trying to tell you what to do, instead of listening to you. But it's because I really do think you'd be happier here with your own people."

Anna shook her head, standing up. "Don't you see it's no good? Too much has happened." Her voice was impassioned. "I can't turn back into the girl I was. I have to keep going."

Dinah could hear the ring of truth in Anna's voice. Whether what she said was true or not, she believed it. If only Jacob could hold on to this new understanding he seemed to have gained . . .

"But you don't, don't you see?" Jacob stood, facing her. "I'm your family. I'll take care of you and Isaac."

"I don't want you to take care of me." Her voice rose in frustration. "And as for Isaac, I can take him right now if I want to. He's my son, not yours and not Dinah's. Mine!"

CHAPTER SEVENTEEN

Dinah froze in shock, a laden spoon halfway to Isaac's mouth. Everyone else seemed unable to speak, but Isaac grabbed at the spoon, spilling half of it before getting it to his lips. Her attention jerked back to him, and her heart broke. She would lose him, and she'd never be the same again.

A chair scraped. To her astonishment, it was Will who shot from his seat, his face an image of pain. "No! You can't take Isaac away. It's not fair. We love him."

She seemed to see pictures—Will on the floor with Isaac, trying to teach him how to crawl; the twins putting the crib together; Will setting up the mobile and showing it to Isaac; Daad leaning over to talk to him; Mammi and Grossmammi rocking him to sleep. Will had it right—they did all love him.

Mammi put her hands on Will's shoulders, holding him tightly. Lovina was looking at Anna in disbelief. Then she stood, too.

"I know what a mother is. It's someone who loves you in spite of all the mistakes you make and puts what you need first. That's what Dinah is like."

Dinah's heart was taking such a pummeling, she

didn't know how it could keep beating. "Lovina . . . ," she began, but Anna was shaking her head. The anger slid out of her face, and her eyes filled with tears that she didn't shed.

Anna went slowly around the table, touching first Will and then Lovina. When she reached Dinah, she bent to embrace her. Dinah felt the intensity of her embrace and the way she trembled even as she did it.

"Yah," she murmured. "That is you. Lacey told me, and she was right. I didn't want to admit it." She blinked the tears back. "Keep on loving him, okay?"

"I couldn't stop." Her own tears brimmed over.

Anna turned to her son. She dropped a kiss on his forehead, and then caressed his head with her hand. With what seemed a wrench she turned back and went to Jacob.

He stood, seeming to struggle for words, but she shook her head before he could speak.

"Listen, it wasn't your fault I went away. Even if . . . if Mammi and Daadi had been there, I'd still have gone. The pull was too strong. I can't stay. I can't be at home here any longer. It's not right for me."

He started to speak, but she shook her head.

"But this is home for Isaac. I couldn't give him the life he should have. But you can. You and Dinah."

He stood like a statue for a moment. Wordless, he held out his arms to her, holding her tight for a long moment. Then he let her go. "Stay in touch with us. And I'm sorry."

"I told you, it isn't your fault. Don't be sorry. I have to make my own mistakes and figure out my own life. Now that I know Isaac's in the right place, I'll get on with it."

She wiped away tears and smiled at Lovina. "You're right," she said.

Jacob made a move to follow her when she went to the door, but she stopped him. "Don't come out." She glanced around the table. "Denke. To all of you."

She left quickly then, not looking back. Jacob clutched the back of his chair as if he needed that to keep from going after her.

Dinah sat quite still until she heard the car go out the driveway. When there was no more sound of it, a tremor went through her. She stood, holding out her hand to Jacob, longing to soothe the pain that tormented him.

He stepped back, shaking his head. He muttered something about work to be done and hurried off, and she was just wise enough not to follow him.

"WHERE'S JACOB GOING?" Once again, Will broke the momentary silence.

Mammi patted his shoulder. "He's feeling sad because of his sister leaving. He just wants to be by himself for a bit. You understand, don't you?"

Will nodded solemnly. "But . . . it's okay that we're happy Isaac is staying, ain't so?"

"Yah, Will," Grossmammi said. "It's okay." She looked at her grandchildren. "That's what life is like," she added softly. "Happy things and sad, good things and bad, all jumbled up together."

Mammi nodded in agreement. "Now you had best be off to see what Saturday chores Daadi has for you, ain't so?"

"Okay." He detoured past the high chair to make a silly face at Isaac and went out smiling.

Dinah found herself exchanging glances with Lovina. "Denke, Lovina. You said the right thing . . . the thing that mattered."

Lovina flushed, looking away. "Guess a person has to get smart sometime."

With an abrupt return to normalcy, Mammi and Lovina went to collect laundry from upstairs, leaving Dinah with Grossmammi and the baby. Grossmammi put a hand against Dinah's cheek.

"Don't worry. He'll come back. He's been so sure that his sister belongs here that he couldn't see past it. But we both know that there are some from every generation who aren't going to stay, and maybe they do belong in the outside world."

"I know." She busied herself wiping Isaac's cereal-covered face. "I just wish he'd let somebody comfort him."

Grossmammi shook her head. "He's the kind that needs to crawl away and grieve by himself. You should know, because you do the same."

She started to object, and then thought about how long it had taken her to confide in anyone about Aaron's hurtful attitude. Maybe her grandmother had a point.

"He'll come back. And when he does . . ." Grossmammi reached out to touch Dinah's cheek. "When he does, you can't be so afraid to ask for what you want."

Dinah considered that. She certain sure hadn't done any such thing the night before with Jacob. How could she? Maybe . . . maybe now there would be another chance. Maybe.

Dinah managed to keep herself busy with Isaac throughout the rest of the morning, and eventually out in the garden with Mammi. Isaac, on a blanket spread in the grass, seemed to enjoy this new adventure, although he must have wondered why every time he reached that pretty green grass, someone turned him around and headed him the other way.

As for Dinah, while she didn't go looking for him, she kept a sharp eye out for any sign of Jacob. Where had he gone? She'd caught a glimpse of him outside the barn at his place, talking to Daad, but then he'd vanished again. Whatever it was he needed just now, it didn't seem to be her.

When Mammi had picked everything she wanted for soup, she headed inside, but Dinah lingered, not wanting to give up her vantage point.

"I'm going to take Isaac for a walk to the orchard," she said, scooping him up and then gathering the blanket and toys together with the other hand. "We'll be back soon."

The orchard, mostly apples now that the peaches and cherries were done, was always a welcoming spot to her, and she seemed to head there whenever she needed solace. She went back to the spot where she had sat on the blanket with Jacob and Isaac and talked about the past.

From the orchard she could see her family's place and Jacob's spread out before her like a child's map. If . . . when Jacob came, she'd see him. She spread out the blanket and toys, put Isaac down, and sat on the edge of the blanket.

"There now. You have a fine view from here, although I think you're more interested in the grass." She plucked a long piece and tickled his chin with it. He responded with a chuckle and grabbed futilely at the wisp of grass, which keep eluding him.

It seemed a long time, but it probably wasn't much more than ten minutes when she saw Jacob emerge from the barn and start across the small pasture that separated the farmhouses. As he got closer he must have noticed them, because he veered and came toward them.

Once Jacob was close enough to make eye contact, she shifted her gaze to Isaac, studying his efforts to get his knees and hands working together to crawl off the blanket. He still hadn't reached the edge when a shadow fell over them.

She looked up with no idea what to say to him. He was a dark silhouette against the sun, so she couldn't make out his expression.

"Are you all right?" It probably wasn't the best thing to say, but it was all she could manage.

"Yah." He dropped onto the blanket next to her. To her relief, his expression had cleared. It was no longer drawn with loss and pain. Maybe, after his long struggle, he had come to some sort of peace with himself.

"Sorry I went off like that."

She shook her head. "I guess it's natural. Grossmammi thinks you're the kind of person who wants to run into a hole and grieve by yourself. She's probably right. She usually knows about people."

"She does," he agreed. He paused, staring down at Isaac's efforts to go where he wanted.

Dinah felt as if everything waited, depending on what he'd say next.

"Still, I could change, maybe. If someone wanted me to."

Her heart seemed to quiver, waiting for more.

Jacob wrapped his arms around his knees and clasped his hands lightly, his gaze intent on Isaac's fingers exploring the blanket's binding.

"I made a lot of mistakes, I guess."

Before she could find an answer, he went on.

"I thought coming back here would make everything all right again. That it would make Anna happy and satisfied, that it would give Isaac his mother, that it would fill my house with love and laughter. But I was wrong. Anna wouldn't be satisfied here. Isaac already has a mother in you. And the only way to fill my house with love and laughter is to do it myself."

She couldn't breathe. She could only wait. She had never heard Jacob express himself so fully, so openly.

He put his hand over hers where it lay on the blanket. "I was going the right direction last night, Dinah, but I did it all wrong. Sure, Isaac needs to have two parents who love him. But he also needs parents who love each other."

Dinah's heart was suddenly thudding so loudly it seemed she couldn't hear anything else. But she could hear Jacob's voice.

"I love you, Dinah. I always did. First as a little neighbor and then as my friend's wife. I don't know why it took me so long to see that now it's much bigger than that." He turned more fully toward her, his eyes intent. "You mean everything to me, Dinah. Can you possibly love me enough to marry me?"

She tried to speak, not sure whether to laugh or cry for the joy that soared through her. "You must know the answer to that." She reached to touch his face with her fingertips, her breath catching. "I love you."

Jacob leaned toward her and her heart raced. But at the last instant, she drew back.

"Jacob, you're forgetting. It means so much to you to have a family. I . . . I might not be able to give you that."

"Ach, Dinah, you know better than that, don't you? It's you I love, babies or not."

He reached out to catch Isaac, who was trying to stuff a handful of grass in his mouth. He grinned, setting him in front of them.

"Besides, we have this guy. And there are a lot of babies in the world who need someone to love them. We have a lot of love to spare, ain't so?"

Tears filled her eyes, but they were tears of happiness.

"Now can I kiss you?"

He didn't wait for an answer. His lips closed on hers, warmth and tenderness and longing pouring through her.

This was what had been missing in her life. Jacob

was right—they had enough love for each other and to go around for a dozen children.

She didn't know how long it was, but it seemed to go on forever. And then someone bumped into them—Isaac, trying to pull himself up with a hand on her apron and one on Jacob's shirt.

Jacob's laugh was wholehearted, with nothing held back. He held her close with one arm and wrapped the other around their baby.

"You don't want to be left out, do you? Don't worry, you won't be." He looked from Isaac to Dinah, and she knew her face had to be glowing with happiness. "We're all a family now."

"We are," she affirmed, feeling as if this were part of a wedding ceremony—the three of them declaring that they were a family, now and forever.

EPILOGUE

Weeks later Dinah carried Isaac, just awakened from his nap, out into the backyard, where he blinked at the afternoon sunlight. Then he seemed to be struck by all the activity. Jacob and Noah, Sarah's husband, were managing the apple press, where the golden mass poured out to be converted to apple butter. Daad supervised while the boys set up the heavy black apple butter kettle over the fire.

"Be sure you get all of it." Grossmammi had decided to check up on the pressing. "That's the last of the McIntosh apples, and they make the best apple butter."

"We will." Jacob grinned at her. "You might want to tell the twins to go easy on the apple juice. At the rate they're going, they'll drink it before we have a chance to stir the kettle."

Stirring the apple butter kettle was a coveted chore, and Noah's seven-year-old twins were clamoring to be allowed to stir this year. Lovina was waiting her turn and trying to keep them from getting too close to the fire.

"Lovina's getting wonderful grown up these days," Grossmammi commented, appearing at her elbow.

"Yah, she is." She bounced Isaac, who had seen Jacob and was making an effort to get down and crawl to him. "She knows how to do everything at the shop as well as I do."

Grossmammi nodded. "She'll be thinking of a partnership before you know it. Once you and Jacob are married, she can take over and give you more time off."

"Yah, she will." She watched Lovina, who was chattering to Jacob now. After their rocky start, they had become close, and she thought her solid husband was good for her flighty little sister.

Dinah's thoughts raced off to their wedding. Only another two weeks, and they'd be married. A quiet event, as befitting a woman who'd been married before, but that didn't matter to either of them. It was being married that mattered, not the wedding.

Smiling at the thought, she worked her way over toward where Sarah sat with her tiny daughter bundled up in her lap. Dorcas stood talking to her, as happy over her newly married state as Sarah was about her baby daughter.

Sarah's twin stepsons, Matthew and Mark, hurried over to tug at her apron. "Come and see our new baby. She's so pretty."

Will, who was supposed to be keeping an eye on the twins, gave them a lofty look as he tickled Isaac. "She might be pretty, but she doesn't do anything but sleep. Our baby can crawl, and pull himself up, and laugh when I tease him."

"They're both just right for their ages," Dinah said, making peace. "Now let me have a look." She bent close to see the perfect little face, pink-cheeked and rosy in sleep, with hands so tiny she couldn't imagine Isaac's ever being that small.

"She's beautiful," she told Sarah. "And your twins are so proud of her they're fit to burst."

"Give them time," Sarah said, a smile lighting her

serene face. "When she's mobile enough to get into their things, they won't be so thrilled."

They laughed, and she thought how happy Sarah was, to say nothing of Noah.

Warm hands closed on her shoulders from behind, and she leaned back against Jacob. Isaac, delighted to see him, immediately started to climb over Dinah's shoulder, so Jacob had to rescue him. He lifted him in the air, making him giggle, and then held him against his shoulder.

"What are you thinking about that makes you look so happy?" Jacob clasped her hand in his for a moment.

"About how things change in ways you don't expect," she said promptly. "Two years ago none of the three of us could have imagined where we'd be today. Sarah had been sure she would be an old maid, and look at her now, with the twins and a new baby, and Noah still looking at her as if she's the most beautiful thing in the world."

He squeezed her fingers. "I promise I'll always see you that way."

"And then there's Dorcas. She was always the reckless one, the one we all thought would jump the fence and be off to the outside world. And instead she was a wonderful gut teacher and now a new bride, just shining with happiness."

"And what about Dinah?" he said, teasing.

"Dinah is the happiest she's ever been." She looked from his face to Isaac's, her heart seeming to swell with joy. "We've all found our way to home and love. That's all."

"That's enough," Jacob said, giving her a look that melted her. "That's enough for anyone."

Glossary of Pennsylvania Dutch Words and Phrases

ach. oh; used as an exclamation

agasinish. stubborn; self-willed

ain't so? A phrase commonly used at the end of a sentence to invite agreement.

alter. old man

anymore. Used as a substitute for "nowadays."

Ausbund. Amish hymnal. Used in the worship services, it contains traditional hymns, words only, to be sung without accompaniment. Many of the hymns date from the sixteenth century.

befuddled. mixed up

blabbermaul. talkative one

blaid. bashful

boppli. baby

bruder. brother

bu. boy

buwe. boys

daadi. daddy

Da Herr sei mit du. The Lord be with you.

denke (or *danki*). thanks

Englischer. one who is not Plain

ferhoodled. upset; distracted

ferleicht. perhaps

frau. wife

fress. eat

gross. big

grossdaadi. grandfather

grossdaadi haus. An addition to the farmhouse, built for the grandparents to live in once they've "retired" from actively running the farm.

grossmammi. grandmother

gut. good

hatt. hard; difficult

haus. house

hinnersich. backward

ich. I

kapp. Prayer covering, worn in obedience to the biblical injunction that women should pray with their heads covered. Kapps are made of Swiss organdy and are white. (In some Amish communities, unmarried girls thirteen and older wear black kapps during worship service.)

kinder (or *kinner*). kids

komm. come

komm schnell. come quick

Leit. the people; the Amish

lippy. sassy

maidal. old maid; spinster

mamm. mother

middaagesse. lunch

mind. remember

onkel. uncle

Ordnung. The agreed-upon rules by which the Amish community lives. When new practices become an issue, they are discussed at length among the leadership. The decision for or against innovation is generally made on the basis of maintaining the home and family as separate from the world. For instance, a telephone might be necessary in a shop in order to conduct business but would be banned from the home because it would intrude on family time.

Pennsylvania Dutch. The language is actually German in origin and is primarily a spoken language. Most Amish write in English, which results in many variations in spelling when the dialect is put into writing! The language probably originated in the south of Germany but is common also among the Swiss Mennonite and French Huguenot immigrants to Pennsylvania. The language was brought to America prior to the Revolution and is still in use today. High German is used for Scripture and church documents, while English is the language of commerce.

rumspringa. Running-around time. The late teen years when Amish youth taste some aspects of the outside world before deciding to be baptized into the church.

schnickelfritz. mischievous child

ser gut. very good

tastes like more. delicious

Was ist letz? What's the matter?

Wie bist du heit? How are you?; said in greeting

wilkom. welcome

Wo bist du? Where are you?

yah. yes

RECIPES

Spinach Beef Casserole

8 ounces uncooked medium noodles
10-ounce package of frozen spinach
1 pound ground beef
1 quart spaghetti sauce
8 ounces cream cheese
½ cup sour cream
3 Tablespoons milk
2 Tablespoons chopped onion
½ cup shredded cheddar cheese
Bread crumbs (optional)

Preheat the oven to 350°F. Cook the noodles in boiling salted water for 10 minutes. Drain.

Steam lightly and drain the spinach.

Brown the ground beef and drain off the fat. Add the spaghetti sauce and simmer.

Mix together the cream cheese, sour cream, milk, and onion.

In a 2-quart casserole dish, layer half the beef-noodle mixture, half the cream cheese mixture, all of the spinach, and the rest of the beef-noodle mixture. Top with the rest of the cream cheese mixture and sprinkle with cheddar cheese. Add bread crumbs if a crusty topping is desired.

Bake for 40 minutes. Serves 6 to 8.

Pesto Ravioli Chicken

2 Tablespoons olive oil
1 pound chicken breast strips
¾ cup chicken broth
9-ounce package of refrigerated cheese ravioli
3 small zucchini, sliced
1 red bell pepper, sliced
¼ cup basil pesto
Parmesan cheese

Preheat the oven to 350°F. Cook the chicken strips in heated oil until browned. Add the broth and ravioli, cover, and cook for 10 minutes. Stir in the remaining ingredients, bring to a simmer, and pour into a greased 2-quart casserole dish. Sprinkle with Parmesan cheese.

Bake for 30 minutes. Serves 6.

Chicken and Broccoli Casserole

Cooking spray
1 head of broccoli cut into chunks
1 pound cooked and diced chicken
2 cans cream of chicken soup
1 cup mayonnaise
¼ cup lemon juice
1 teaspoon curry powder

Salt and pepper
1 cup shredded cheddar cheese
½ cup bread crumbs

Preheat the oven to 350°F. Spray a 9 x 13-inch casserole dish with cooking spray. Cook the broccoli in water only until steaming and bright green. Drain. Spread the broccoli in the bottom of the casserole dish. Top with the cooked chicken.

Whisk together the cream of chicken soup, mayonnaise, lemon juice, and curry powder. Sprinkle with salt and pepper. Pour the sauce over the chicken and broccoli. Top with shredded cheese and bread crumbs.

Bake until the casserole is bubbling and the cheese has melted, about 30 minutes. Serves 6 to 8.

Dear Reader,

I hope you'll let me know if you enjoyed my book. You can reach me at marta@martaperry.com, and I'd be happy to send you a bookmark and my brochure of Pennsylvania Dutch recipes. You'll also find me at martaperry.com and on Facebook at MartaPerryBooks.

Happy reading,
Marta

Don't miss

A CHRISTMAS HOME

A Promise Glen Novel

by Marta Perry

Available now
from Jove!

The buggy drew to a stop near the farmhouse porch, and Sarah Yoder climbed down slowly, her eyes on the scene before her. Here it was—the fulfillment of the dream she'd had for the past ten years. Home.

Her cousin, Eli Miller, paused in lifting her cases down from the buggy. "Everything all right?"

"Fine." *Wonderful.*

Sarah sucked in a breath and felt the tension that had ridden her for weeks ease. It hadn't been easy to break away from the life her father had mapped out for her, but she'd done it. The old frame farmhouse spread itself in the spot where it had stood since the first Amish settlers came over the mountains from Lancaster County and saw the place they considered their promised land. Promise Glen, that was what folks called it, this green valley tucked between sheltering ridges in central Pennsylvania. And that's what she hoped it would be for her.

The porch door thudded, and Grossmammi rushed out. Her hair was a little whiter than the last time Sarah had seen her, but her blue eyes were still bright and her skin as soft as a girl's. For an instant the thought of her mother pierced Sarah's heart. Mammi had looked like her own mother. If she'd lived . . . but she'd been gone ten years now. Sarah had been just eighteen when she'd taken charge of the family.

Before she could lose herself in regret, Grossmammi had reached her, and her grandmother's strong arms encircled her. The warmth of her hug chased every other thought away, and Sarah clung to her the way she had as a child, when Grossmammi had represented everything that was firm and secure in her life.

Her grandmother drew back finally, her blue eyes bright with tears. She took refuge in scolding, as she did when emotions threatened to overcome her.

"Ach, we've been waiting and waiting. I told Eli he should leave earlier. Did he keep you waiting there at the bus stop?"

Eli grinned, winking at Sarah. "Ask Cousin Sarah. I was there when she stepped off the bus."

And she'd seen him pull up just in time, but she wouldn't give him away. "That's right. I was wonderful surprised to see my little cousin—he grew, ain't so?"

"Taller than you now, Sarah, though that's not saying much." He indicated her five feet and a bit with a line in the air, his expression as impudent as it had been when he was a child.

"And you've not changed much, except in inches," she retorted, long since used to holding her own with younger siblings and cousins. "Same freckles, same smile, same sassiness."

"Ach, help!" He threw up his hands as if to protect himself. "Here's my sweet Ruthie coming. She'll save me from my cousin."

Ruthie, his wife of three years, came heavily down the back porch stairs, looking younger than her twenty-three years. She looked from him to Sarah, as if to make sure Sarah wasn't offended. "You are talking nonsense."

She swatted at him playfully. "Komm, carry those things to the grossdaadi haus for Sarah. Supper is almost ready."

"Sarah, this is Ruthie, you'll have figured out," Grossmammi said. "And here is their little Mary." The child who slipped out onto the porch looked about two, with huge blue eyes and soft wispy brown hair that curled, unruly, around her face.

And Ruthie couldn't have more than a month to go before the arrival of the new baby, Sarah could see, assessing her with a shrewd eye. When even the shapeless Amish dress didn't conceal the bump, a woman knew it wasn't far off.

Eli loaded himself up with Sarah's boxes, obviously intent on getting everything in one trip. "Surrounded by women, that's what I am," he said cheerfully. "And now there's another one."

He stopped long enough to give Sarah a one-armed hug, poking her in the side with one of her boxes as he did. "We're wonderful glad you're here at last, Cousin Sarah."

Sarah blinked back an errant tear. Eli hadn't lost his tender heart, that was certain sure. And Grossmammi looked as if she'd just been given the gift of a lifetime. As for Ruthie . . . well, she had a sense that Ruthie was withholding judgment for the moment. That was hardly surprising. She'd want to know what changes this strange cousin was going to make in their lives.

As little as possible, Sarah mentally assured her. All she wanted was a place to call home while she figured out what her new life was going to be.

Eli, finally laden with all her belongings, headed toward the grossdaadi haus, a wing built onto the main house and connected by a short hallway. Grossmammi had lived there since Grossdaadi's death, and when Sarah walked into the living room and saw the familiar rocking chairs and the framed family tree on the wall, she felt instantly at home.

"You're up here, Sarah." Eli bumped his way up the stairs until Sarah retrieved one of the boxes and carried it herself.

He flashed her that familiar grin. "What do you have in there? Rocks?"

"Books. I couldn't leave those behind. I just hope there's a bookcase I can use."

"If there isn't, we can pick one up at a sale. The auction house is still busy, even this late in the year. Almost December already."

"Grossdaadi used to say that any farmer worth the name had all his work done by the first of December."

"Ach, don't go comparing me to Grossdaadi," he said with mock fear. "Here we are. I hope you like it." He stacked everything at the foot of the old-fashioned sleigh bed. "Ruthie says supper is about ready, so komm eat. You can unpack later."

She'd rather have a few minutes to catch her breath and explore her new home, but Ruthie was her hostess. It wouldn't do to be late for their first supper together. With a pause in the hall bathroom to wash her hands, she hurried downstairs and joined Grossmammi to step the few feet across the hallway—the line that marked off their home from Eli and Ruthie's.

The hall led into the kitchen of the old farmhouse. Ruthie hurried them to their places at the table and began to dish up the food. Sarah glanced at her, opened her mouth to offer help, and caught Grossmammi's eye. Her grandmother shook her head, ever so slightly.

So something else lay behind the welcome she'd received. Best if she were quiet until she knew what it was.

This was a little disconcerting. She'd dreamed for so

long of being here, but those dreams hadn't included the possibility that someone might not want her.

Nonsense. Ruthie seemed shy, and probably she was anxious about this first meal she'd cooked for Sarah. The best course for Sarah was to keep quiet and blend in.

But once the silent prayer was over and everyone had been served pot roast with all the trimmings, it wasn't so easy to stay silent, since Eli seemed determined to hear everything about everything.

"So what was it like out in Idaho? I didn't even know there were any Amish there." Eli helped himself to a mound of mashed potatoes.

"Not many," she admitted. "It was a new settlement." She didn't bother to add that anything new was appealing to Daad—either they understood her father already, or they didn't need to know. "Ruthie, this pot roast is delicious. Denke." The beef was melt-in-your-mouth tender, the gravy rich and brown.

Ruthie's face relaxed in a smile, and she nodded in acknowledgment of the praise. "And your brothers and sister?" she modestly moved on. "How are they?"

"All married and settled now." They'd wisely given up finding a home with Daad and created homes of their own. "Nancy's husband is a farrier in Indiana, and the two boys are farming—Thomas in Ohio and David in Iowa."

"Far apart," Grossmammi murmured, and Sarah wondered what she was thinking. To say it was unusual to have an Amish family so widespread was putting it mildly.

"They all invited me to come to them," she said quickly, lest anyone think that the siblings she had raised were not grateful. "But I thought it was best for me to make a life of my own. I'm going to get a job."

Eli dropped his fork in surprise. "A job? You don't want to be working for strangers."

She had to smile at his offended expression. "Yah, a job. Some work I can do in order to pay my own way."

That wasn't all of it, of course. Her desire went deeper than that. She'd spent the past ten years raising her brothers and sister, and it had been a labor of love. What would have happened to all of them after Mammi died if she hadn't?

But that time had convinced her of what she didn't want. She didn't want to become the old maid that most large families had—the unmarried sister who hadn't anything of her own and spent her life helping to raise other people's children, tending to the elderly, and doing any other tasks that came along. She wanted a life of her own. That wasn't selfish, was it?

Even as she thought it, Eli was arguing. "You're family. You'll do lots of things to pay your own way. You can help Ruthie with looking after the kinder, and there's the garden, and the canning . . ."

He went on talking, but Sarah had stopped listening, because she'd caught an apprehensive expression on Ruthie's face. This, then, was what Ruthie was afraid of. She feared Sarah had come to take over—to run her house, to raise her babies . . .

Ruthie actually did have cause to be concerned, she supposed. She'd been in complete charge of the home for the past ten years, through almost as many moves and fresh starts. It wouldn't be easy to keep herself from jumping in—with the best will in the world, she might not be able to restrain herself unless she had something else to occupy her.

"I'll be happy to help Ruthie anytime she wants me," she said, using the firm voice that always made her younger siblings take notice. "But I need something else to keep me busy."

"And I know what," Grossmammi said, in a tone that suggested the discussion was over. "Noah Raber needs someone to keep the books and take care of the billing for his furniture business. I've already spoken to him about it." She turned to Sarah. "You can go over there tomorrow and set it up."

Sarah managed to keep her jaw from dropping, but barely. She'd intended to look for a job, but she hadn't expected to find herself being pushed into one as soon as she arrived.

"But . . . bookkeeping? I don't know if I can . . ."

"Nonsense," Grossmammi said briskly. "You took those bookkeeping classes a couple of years ago, didn't you?"

She nodded. She had done that, with the hope of finding something outside the home to do. But then Daad had gotten the idea of moving on again, and she had given it up. Did she really remember enough to take this on?

"Mostly Noah needs someone to handle the business side," Grossmammi went on. "The man loves to work with wood, but he has no idea how to send a bill. That's where you come in."

"But Noah Raber." Eli looked troubled. "Are you sure that's a gut idea? Noah's situation . . ."

"Noah's situation is that he needs to hire someone. Why shouldn't it be Sarah?" She got up quickly. "Now, I think we should do the supper cleanup so Sarah can go and unpack."

Grossmammi, as usual, had the last word. None of her children or grandchildren would dare to argue when she used that tone.

Carrying her dishes to the sink, Sarah tried to figure

out how she felt about this turn of events. She certain sure didn't want to continue being in a place where she was only valued because she could take care of children.

But this job . . . what if she tried it and failed? What if she'd forgotten everything she'd once known? Noah Raber might feel she'd been foisted on him.

And what was it about his situation that so troubled Eli? She tried to remember Noah, but her school years memories had slipped away with all the changes in her life since then. He was a couple of years older than she was, and she had a vague picture of someone reserved, someone who had pursued his own interests instead of joining with the usual rumspringa foolishness. Was he interested in offering her the job, or had Grossmammi pushed him into it?

But she'd already made her decision in coming here—coming home. She shivered a little as a cold breeze snaked its way around the window over the sink and touched her face. There was no turning back now.

"WHY DIDN'T YOU put your shoes together under the bed like you're supposed to?" Noah Raber looked in exasperation at six-year-old Mark, dressed for school except for one important thing—his right shoe.

"I did, Daadi." Mark looked on the verge of tears, and Noah was instantly sorry for his sharp tone. Mark was the sensitive one of the twins, unlike Matthew. Scoldings rolled off Matty like water off a duck's back.

"It's all right." He brushed a hand lightly over his son's hair, pale as corn silk in the winter sunlight pouring in the window. "You look in the bathroom while I check in here."

There weren't that many places where a small shoe could hide, but the neighbor kids were already coming down the drive, ready to walk to school with the twins. With a quick gesture he pulled the chest of drawers away from the wall. One sock, but no shoes.

From the kitchen below he heard Matty's voice, probably commenting on the fact that the King children were coming. But a woman's voice, speaking in answer, startled him out of that assumption. Who . . . ? Well, he had to find the shoe before anything.

When his mother had been here, this early-morning time had run smoothly—he hadn't realized how smoothly until he'd had to do it himself. Still, it had been high time Mamm had had a break from looking after his twins, and her longing to visit his sister Anna and her new baby was obvious. Naturally he'd encouraged her to go, insisting he and the boys would get along fine. If he'd known then . . .

"I found it!" Mark came running in, waving the shoe. "It was in the hamper."

He started to ask how it had gotten there and decided he didn't really need to know. The important thing was to get them out the door.

"Let's get it on." He picked up his son and plopped him on the bed, shoving the shoe on his foot and fastening it with quick movements. "There. Now scoot."

Mark darted out the door and clattered down the stairs, running for the kitchen. Noah followed in time to see Mark come to an abrupt halt in the kitchen doorway. He stopped, too, at the sight of a strange woman in his kitchen.

"Who—" He didn't get the question out before Matty broke in.

"This is Sarah. She's come to work for you, Daadi."

The woman put a hand lightly on Matthew's shoulder. "Only if your daadi hires me." She smiled. "Matthew and I were getting acquainted. This must be Mark."

Her eyes focused on Mark, hanging on to Noah's pant leg, but she didn't venture to approach him.

"I'm sorry. I don't . . ." His mind was empty of everything but the need to get the boys off to school. "Just a minute." He turned to his sons. "Coats on, right this minute. And hats and mittens. It's cold out. Hurry."

Apparently realizing this was not the time to delay, they both scrambled into their outer garments, and he shooed them toward the small mudroom that led to the back door. "Out you go."

"I think—" the woman began, following him.

"Just wait," he snapped. Couldn't she see he was busy? "Have a gut day, you two. Mind you listen to Teacher Dorcas."

He opened the door, letting in a brisk wind. A hand appeared in front of him, holding two small lunch boxes. The woman was standing right behind him.

"Aren't these meant to go?"

Instantly he felt like a fool. Or at least an inept father, chasing his sons out without their lunches. He grabbed them, handing them off to the boys, and saw to his relief that, by running, they reached the lane to the schoolhouse at the same time as the other children.

He gave one last wave, and then it was time to turn and apologize for his rudeness. The turn brought him within inches of the woman.

"Sorry," he muttered. "You must be Sarah, Etta's granddaughter. I didn't expect you so soon."

"No, I apologize. I shouldn't have come so early. My grandmother assumed you started work at eight, and I didn't want to interrupt."

Looking at her, Noah realized she wasn't quite so strange after all. Etta Miller had talked about her granddaughter coming, of course. He had said that he didn't remember her, but now it was coming back to him.

"You were a couple of years behind me in school, weren't you?"

She nodded, face crinkling in a quick smile. "That's right. By the time I was big enough to be noticed, you'd left school and started your apprenticeship, I guess."

"Sarah Yoder," he said, the last name coming to him.

Her mother had been Etta Miller's middle girl, her father a newcomer from down in Chester County. If he didn't remember anything else, he should have remembered hair the color of honey and eyes of a deep, clear green. She was short and slight, but something about the way she stood and the assurance when she spoke made her hard to overlook.

He realized he was staring and took an awkward step back. It seemed suddenly intimate to be standing here in the narrow mudroom with a woman he hardly knew.

"You're here about the job." He reached past her to grab his wool jacket from the hook. "Let's go to the shop and talk. No need to be hanging out in here."

She nodded, buttoning her black coat as she stepped outside, then waiting for him to lead the way to the shop.

"Didn't your great-onkel used to live here?" He heard her voice behind him as they crossed the yard through frost-whitened grass.

"Yah, that's so. We moved in about eight years ago." When he and Janie had married. When he'd still believed marriage meant forever. "My great-onkel used this building as a workshop, so I started my business here."

He found himself looking at the building he called the shop, seeing it through a stranger's eyes. It wouldn't look like much to her—hardly more than a shed with a small addition on one end.

But when he looked at it, he saw the future—the future that was left to him after what Janie had done. He saw a thriving furniture business where his handcrafted furniture was made and sold. He saw his sons growing, working alongside him in the business they'd build together.

"I understand from my grandmother that you need someone to handle the paperwork so you're free to spend your time on creating the furniture."

He nodded, liking the way she put that—*creating*. Each piece of furniture he made was his own creation, with his hard work and whatever gift he had pressed into the very grain of the wood.

"I'd best show you the paperwork, since that's what would concern you." *If I hire you,* he added mentally. But who was he kidding? He hadn't exactly been swamped with people longing to work for him, especially ones who knew anything at all about running a business.

He held the door open and ushered her into the shop, stopping to put up the shade on the window so that the winter sun poured in. Fortunately he'd started the stove earlier, so the shop was warming already, and the sunlight would help. He'd added windows all along one side of the shed, because he needed all the light he could get for working.

"Over here, in the far corner." He gestured toward the office area—a corner of the workroom with a desk, some shelves, and a chair. At the moment the desk was piled high with papers. "I haven't had time to get at it lately."

He wasn't sure why he was explaining to her. It was his business. But he guessed it was obvious he needed help. "You can take a look at it. See what you think."

Instead of commenting, Sarah walked, unhurried, to the desk. He followed her, not sure how to conduct this interview, if that's what it was. She began leafing through the papers, seeming to sort them as she went. After a moment she looked up.

"Where do you keep the receipted bills?"

"Um, there should be a box . . . yah, that. The shoebox."

Sarah looked at it, still not commenting. Her very silence began to make him nervous. "It's not always such a mess." Just most of the time. "My mother has been away on a trip for several weeks, so I've had the boys to manage as well as the business."

"I see. Sorry. That must be difficult. If you'd like me to see what I can do with this . . ." She hesitated. "I take it your wife doesn't help with the business?"

He froze, his stomach clenching. Didn't she know? Didn't she realize that was the worst thing she could possibly say to him?

SHE'D SAID SOMETHING wrong—very wrong. Noah looked as if she had hit him with a hammer. His strong-boned face was rigid, the firm jaw like a rock. His dark blue eyes had turned to ice. Remorse flooded her. If the poor man had lost his wife, why hadn't Grossmammi thought to tell her?

Standing here silent wasn't helping matters any. "Noah, I'm so sorry. I didn't know. I'd never have said that if . . . I suppose the family thought I knew your wife had passed away—"

"No." The word was a harsh bark. He swallowed, the strong muscles in his neck moving visibly. "Janie didn't die. She left us a few months after the twins were born. We haven't heard from her from that day to this."

Sarah struggled for words. "I . . ."

"There's no need for expressions of sympathy." His mouth clamped shut like a trap.

Whatever she did, she mustn't show pity. It wasn't easy, but she schooled her face to calm. "You are the fortunate one, then."

Noah gave a short nod, as if he understood her instantly. "Yah. I have the boys. They are worth anything."

He spun, turning away from her, and looked yearningly at his workbench. Clearly he didn't want to talk anymore. Did that mean he didn't want her around at all?

"What do you think?" he said, not looking at her. He gestured toward the desk with the papers on it.

Sarah touched the stack of papers in front of her, mentally measuring it. If Noah wanted to carry on as if nothing had happened, surely she could manage to go along with him.

"It might be best if I look through these and sort them. Then we'll have a better idea of where we are. If that's all right with you." She trod as carefully as if she were walking barefoot on broken glass.

"Yah, gut. Denke." He still didn't look her way. They were both being cautious and polite, trying to pretend nothing had happened. "However long it takes. I'll pay for the time it takes to decide if you want to do this or not."

"You don't need to—"

"The laborer is worthy of his hire." He flashed a smile. It was a feeble effort, but it was the first she'd seen from him. "That's what my daad always says."

She nodded, sitting down at the desk while Noah moved quickly to his workbench. Her family might have been better off if Daad had adopted that saying. His, unfortunately, had been more in the nature of *The grass is always greener on the other side of the fence.*

Somehow, no matter how often he had been proved wrong, Daad had clung to that belief. Still did, she supposed. But at least she wasn't going with him now, the way she'd had to for the sake of her brothers and sister.

They worked without talking, and the workshop was silent except for the gentle swish of fine sandpaper against wood. Sarah glanced around the room. It was well designed, she supposed, with that row of windows bringing in a lot of light so Noah didn't have to depend on gas lighting.

But there wasn't much space. The small addition, which she'd assumed was a showroom for his finished pieces, was instead filled with all the equipment he didn't have room for in here. She began mentally rearranging it, putting her desk and chair in the addition with a few display pieces and moving all the work into the larger space. It would still be crowded, but it would be a better use of the space.

Noah glanced up and caught her looking at him. "Did you want to ask me something? You can interrupt, you know. Unless I've got my fingers near a saw blade."

The attempt at humor encouraged her. He wouldn't bother, she thought, unless he wanted to make this work.

"I haven't run across any tax papers." Sarah said the first thing that popped in her head. "I suppose you do keep tax records."

"If you can call it that." He rubbed the back of his hand across his forehead. "If you can figure out the taxes, you're better than I am. The file is in the house. I'll get it when we stop for lunch."

Sarah nodded, but before she could go back to sorting, he spoke.

"So what do you think? You've probably never met such a mess in any of your other jobs."

The expectation revealed in the comment startled her. Clearly he thought she'd been working as a bookkeeper. What exactly had Grossmammi told him?

"It . . . it's just what I would expect if you haven't had time to do anything with it in the past month or so."

Noah grimaced. "Make that three. Or four." He looked a little shamefaced. "Even when my mother was here, I didn't spend enough time on that side of the business."

She nodded, unsurprised. "So I see." She hesitated. "Just so we're clear—I don't know exactly what my grandmother told you, but I haven't actually had a job in bookkeeping." Before he could react, she hurried on. "I took all the classes, and I'd accepted a job, but then we moved before I could start work."

"You moved a lot, did you?" His voice had grown cool quite suddenly.

So it did make a difference to him. Disappointment swept over her. She could do this job, she thought, but not if he didn't give her a chance.

"I kept house for my daad and took care of my brothers and sister. When Daad decided to move on, we went with him."

It wasn't as if she'd had a choice. So she ought to be used to disappointment by this time.

But she wasn't giving up on getting this job before she'd shown what she could do, so she continued.

"It looks as if it will take a week or so of full-time work just to get everything organized. Once a system is set up, you may only need to spend a few hours a day on it."

Sarah waited, giving him the opportunity to say that in that case, he wouldn't need her. Or to agree that he'd hire her. But he didn't say anything. He just nodded and turned back to his own work.

Well, she'd have to take silence as his permission to go on with the sorting, at least. Perhaps he was thinking that would buy him time to see how well it worked out, having her here.

Did her presence upset his work? She studied him covertly over a stack of receipts. His eyebrows, thick and straight, were drawn down a bit as if he were frowning at the curve he was sanding . . . the arm of a delicately turned rocking chair. The curves of the legs and the back were what many Amish would consider fancy, but the whole piece was so appealing that it seemed to urge one to sit and rock for a bit.

Maybe he wasn't disappointed in the work—that look might be one of deep concentration. His strong features could easily look stern, she supposed, even if that wasn't his feeling. The twins hadn't inherited that rock-solid jaw, or at least, it didn't show yet. Their faces were round and dimpled.

Did they look like their mother? She didn't even know if the woman was someone local or not. Obviously, Grossmammi had some explaining to do.

Thinking of the twins caused a pang in the area of her heart. She shouldn't let herself start feeling anything for those two motherless boys. She knew herself too well—she'd fall into mothering them too easily, and that wouldn't do.

Presumably Noah's mother would take over again when she returned from her trip. Noah had been fortunate to have her available when his world had fallen apart.

Grossmammi had offered to take Sarah and her siblings when her mamm died, but Daadi hadn't wanted it. And Sarah, at eighteen, had been fully capable of looking after the younger ones—not only that, but she'd felt it her duty. She couldn't regret the years she'd spent raising them, but she didn't want to do it again, not unless it was with her own babies.

She stole another glance at Noah, his closed face giv-

ing nothing away, his dark brown hair curling rebel-
liously as he worked. He hadn't offered her the care of
his children. He hadn't even offered her the bookkeeping job yet.

And if he did . . . well, given how difficult his situation was, she wasn't sure she should take it.

Ready to find
your next great read?

Let us help.

Visit prh.com/nextread

Penguin
Random
House